THE UNDERSEA SHELL GAME

Patrick,
I hope you enjoy
reading this.
Best Regards,
John

John L. Shea

This book is a work of fiction. Names, characters, places, and incidents are the product of the author's imagination or used fictitiously. Any resemblance to actual events, locales, or persons, living or dead, is purely coincidental.

ISBN-10: 0991528018
ISBN-13: 99780991528011
Library of Congress Control Number: 2014904668
John L. Shea, Milton, MA

Dedication

To Dolores, the love of my life.

Acknowledgments

I need to thank the many people who helped me turn a seed of an idea into my first novel. First, Norman Gauthier, who has always been a sounding board and a dream maker for me. The original idea of this book and the prologue were developed with Norm.

I am also blessed with the great fortune of meeting and engaging Michael Benson as my editor. Michael has a unique set of skills; in addition to being a great writer, he has deep knowledge of submarines from his experience coauthoring the The Complete Idiot's Guide to Submarines. Mike was great to work with (even though he is a New York City sports fan).

Thanks to my friends, supporters, and early readers that helped me see the forest through the trees as I was writing, especially Peter Noll and Russell Curtis. Lastly, I want to thank Jeff Beale for his support and encouragement—with this book, and in life.

I had the good fortune to have served in the U.S. Navy and gain the life experience to write a book like this. I am proud to have served in the "Silent Service" and as a member of the United States armed services. I commend all the people, all over the world, proudly serving their country.

I have to thank my mother, Mary Shea. She served in World War II as a WAVE in the Navy, and was the one that gave me my passion for reading. She read the second draft cover to cover at age 91 and told me it was OK to publish. My late father, James Shea, also a World War II veteran (of the Army Air Corps), would have loved to have been involved with this.

A special loving thanks to my children, Lynn, John, Eric and Mary, for their support while I was out in the sunroom writing. They proved to be a great sounding board for ideas—and excellent proofreaders as well.

Last but not least, thanks to my wife of over thirty years, Dolores, who has been through it all with me. She raised our kids while I was deployed. She has been extremely supportive of my dream of writing. She has listened to endless ideas over the years, proofread, selected editors and book covers, and helped with anything else that needed a creative eye. We have formed a great team and I am blessed to have her in my life.

Without Dolores and many others, there would be no book.

Prologue

JANUARY 7TH, 1978
LENINGRAD, SOVIET UNION

A tiny bell tinkled above the young man's head as he entered the shop carrying a guitar case. He was tall, angular—still green about the edges but made of the right stuff. There was a quarter-inch of snow on his broad shoulders.

"May I help you, young man?" asked the shopkeeper in clear English with a Russian accent. He was a few inches over six feet tall with a neatly trimmed salt-and-pepper beard and a matching, slightly overgrown, head of hair. His face had been lined by life. He looked about fifty, and stood very straight with shoulders back, projecting a proud and confident persona from behind the counter of his small music shop. Twenty-seven guitars hung on the walls of the small shop, and a battered and refurbished lot they were, too. "As you can see, we mostly sell guitars. Would you like to buy a guitar?"

"No, thank you, sir. I already have one," the young man said. His nose was red from the cold. He set down his guitar case, took off his navy blue wool cap, unzipped his goose down jacket and unwrapped his wool scarf from his neck. As he blew on his hands, there was an odd pause as the two men realized they resembled one another.

Father and son, perhaps.

The notion was ridiculous, the older man thought, unless the young man's mother had been a free spirit in Minsk during the late 1950s. But, no. Preposterous.

They had pitch-black hair. When their hair reflected any light at all, it looked deep blue. Their hair was even the same length, but the storekeeper had shaved more recently—and his hair color might've come from a bottle.

The young man's name was Jay, short for James R. Brown III. His actual father was James Junior and generally called James, grandfather was James Senior and went by Jim, so that made him Jay. He was nineteen years of age and looked even younger. Part of that was the downy excuse for whiskers he had on his strong jaw, dark but so thin that he rarely had to shave. When he did haul out the razor, it was just to avoid the abuse from his friends asking him if his mouse died.

"I would like to look at your guitars, though," he said, glancing around.

In addition to many guitars, there was a thumb-tacked poster of the Russian composer Mikhail Visotsky on the wall. Jay recognized the composer of "The Gypsies of Moscow," one of the great folk pieces ever written for classical guitar. Those who could play it well were the Eric Claptons of that world.

"Ahh, you are American," replied the shopkeeper. "Boston?"

Jay was impressed. The man could discern his Boston accent in just a sentence or two.

"Yes sir, I am," replied Jay. "Boston, Massachusetts."

"Go Pats!" the shopkeeper said, exhausting his knowledge of football. "And you are a 'military brat' as they say in Boston, Massachusetts?"

Jay was startled. He *was* a military brat, a navy brat to be specific. His father and grandfather were career navy. There were parts of his childhood that had been, to put it mildly, nomadic.

"Correct again, sir. You seem to be full of answers. I can understand you recognizing my accent, but military brat? Isn't that a tad specific?"

"I am sorry, young man, but we do not get many visitors in the shop. It entertains me to guess about people. Sometimes I am correct, but sometimes I am wrong. Today, I am—here's a good English word—astute. I assumed you were American not just from your accent, but also your dress. Levis and Converse All Star trainers are a sure give away. You dress like the Ramones, gabba gabba hey. The military brat guess came from your manners. You called me 'sir.' If there were a woman present, you would be saying 'ma'am'. I can tell from your unkempt hairstyle and fuzzy chin that you are not in the military. You are too young to be ex-military. That leaves military upbringing. You're too scruffy for military school. Of course, I am right more than wrong."

Jay smiled and let out a little laugh. "That is because you are astute."

"My name is Vlad, by the way. And your name?" He extended his hand to shake and Jay accepted.

"Jay. I'm surprised you didn't already know that. It is very nice to meet you, Mr. Vlad."

As a rule, Jay didn't engage in idle chitchat with strangers, particularly chatty strangers like Vlad. However, he would make an exception today. He was on an adventure, and his juices were flowing. He had ventured out alone in a country that he was discovering to be both foreign and familiar.

"Very nice to meet you, Jay. Please, just Vlad. So...what brings you to the beautiful but icy city of Leningrad?"

"Guess."

"All right. From the looks of your case, you must be a musician."

"Yes, sir. I am here on a college trip. We played today at the Leningrad Philharmonic. I play classical guitar."

"Today?"

"Yes."

"Just now?"

"A few hours ago."

"Congratulations. I'm guessing you were smashing."

"They seemed to enjoy—"

"And let me guess, you play a Russian guitar," Vlad replied, his dark brown eyes lighting up like a kid's on Christmas morning.

"*Katarina vyshla zdes,*" Vlad said loudly. Behind Vlad was a black curtain covering a doorway. From behind the curtain emerged an enchanting young woman close to Jay's age, maybe a little bit younger.

Katarina. Such a musical name. Jay caught a whiff of her powdery perfume and was slightly embarrassed by his visceral response. She had a slow, delicate and graceful manner—so feline. For a moment, before Jay recalled his own manners, he couldn't look away. Her eyes were large, almond-shaped and green. Her hair was long, wavy, brownish red and impossibly smooth. She wore no makeup, stood about five-six and was dressed in unflattering clothes—a plaid flannel shirt with loose jeans held up by a thick leather belt. On her feet were natural leather work boots.

"*Chto vy khotite ottsa?*" said Katarina.

"Please speak in English, Katarina, for our American guest," said Vlad.

"Certainly, Father," Katarina replied. She boldly looked up and down, up and down, the flustered American boy. She had a slight grin as she locked onto Jay's eyes. His eyes were hazel and his lashes long for a guy, which only was a factor when they sometimes rubbed the inner lenses of an ill-fitting pair of sunglasses.

Jay returned her gaze. Her emerald eyes were riveting, unmoving and calm. He wondered if they glowed in the dark.

Jay, hopelessly monolingual, felt inadequate. He wished he could speak to this woman in Russian, although the way she spoke English was damned cute.

Jay spoke just a little too loud: "Katarina, hello, my name is Jay." Then, somewhat robotically, he extended his hand for a handshake.

Katarina looked at his hand, and leaped forward. She kissed his cheek quickly three times, on alternate cheeks. The perfume was intoxicating at that range, and he was aware of his urgent gender. His cheeks, where they had been kissed, turned instantly hot, burning hot. The shopkeeper and his daughter laughed at the redness of Jay's blush.

"Hello, Jay, you can call me Kat." She pretended to scratch him with her right hand formed as a paw. Now, Jay was completely off guard. He was befuddled and discombobulated. His fight-or-flee instinct flared. Part of him wanted to flee. Part of him wanted to stay forever.

Vlad allowed the uncomfortable flirtation to linger, one, two, three, then spoke, "So, Jay, am I right? Is it a Russian guitar?"

"Uh, wha—? Yes, yes, it is. A Russian guitar, but made in the United States. Made by a man in the United States."

"A Russian man?"

"No, sir. But a man expert at making Russian guitars. Would you like to see?" Jay replied.

Vlad directed Kat and Jay to sit on the bench seat in the middle of the store. "Set the guitar case on the table in front of the seat," Vlad said.

Jay opened the guitar case. It was a well-kept, expensive but common-looking seven-string Russian guitar. Vlad reacted as if the fat man had just pulled out the Maltese Falcon.

"Vlad, why are you so excited to see this? It is common enough... Uninteresting..."

"Father, what is it?" Kat said.

"Uninteresting?" Then louder, "Uninteresting! Ha! Jay, that is where you are wrong. This Russian guitar is *very* interesting."

Vlad cleared his throat.

Kat said, "Uh oh, he does that when he will soon donate a lecture."

"I'll settle in," Jay said, and the "youngsters" exchanged knowing smiles.

Vlad continued, ignoring them, "As you know, when someone walks into my shop, I enjoy guessing who they are and where they have been, and why, of all places, they have just entered my shop. Well, this seven-string American Russian guitar is the same thing. It has a story! First, some context." Vlad gestured up at his wall. "In our country, these sad guitars you see on display here were the only guitars available to our people—until recently. They were built as seven-strings, but many people altered their guitars to six strings with traditional Western six-string tuning. Some were modified even further, with four bass strings."

"So, you could have the Beatles," Jay said.

"Precisely. We loved them but kept our love hidden in soundproofed cellars because Western music was forbidden. So practically none of these seven-stringers played the music for which they were originally intended, Russian classical folk music. Now, this instrument,

I can tell that it has never been altered. Oh, look at the lovely wear patterns on the neck and bridge. Oh me oh my."

Kat laughed. "I don't think Americans say 'oh me oh my.'"

"I've heard it, not recently," Jay said to be nice.

"I got it from an Aretha Franklin song," Vlad said. "My point is, this guitar is perfect, unlike any of the Russian-made guitars that you will find on my walls. I rarely do not see a guitar this good."

"You rarely see," Kat corrected.

"Yes, I rarely see? I am really excited," Vlad said. "I rarely see such quality. Every once in a long time. You in America would not bother to alter a seven-string guitar because you have alternatives available to you. You would just go out and buy a six-string, or a bass," Vlad said. He slowed his speech now, letting Jay know he was about to dispense wisdom: "Here, sometimes we alter the way something is supposed to be because we have no other choice."

"May I play it?" Kat asked.

Jay nodded yes vigorously. Kat gracefully picked up the guitar. She stroked the varnished wood for a moment, loving it, and that gave Jay an excuse to focus for a moment on her hands. Her fingers were long and smooth and finely tapered, with perfect nails, just the correct length for plucking at a seven-string. Jay wanted to hold one of those hands and never let go. She plucked at the strings tentatively for a moment and made a sour expression.

"Do you mind if I tune it?" she asked.

"Since I had my concert earlier today, tune away. I thought it was in tune."

"There are actually many ways to tune these. I will tune it in a way you might like."

"Thank you, I came here actually to learn more about the guitar and see if you had additional music for the seven-string. Maybe something more folk, less classical. I know Beethoven often embedded Russian folk music in his string quartets."

"I believe that was at the demand of his patron. Beethoven, of course, inserted the Russian music flawlessly, but the jury is still out on if he was happy about it. Russia, Germany. There has always been a history," Vlad said. "It is still too soon to discuss German composers to any large extent inside these walls. But if you want Russian folk music, you came to the right place."

Kat finished tuning the guitar and started to play. She looked so natural, Jay thought. The guitar became an organic extension of her body. Her hands were singing as they floated over Jay's guitar. Jay wondered what it could possibly be like to be touched by hands like that.

The music grew in intensity. Vlad clapped loudly and banged his foot. When Kat perfectly executed the music's frenzied finish, Jay and Vlad applauded.

"What was that?" Jay asked Kat.

"*Tetris Son.*"

"Very rhythmic."

"It is, as you Americans say, a classic, a Golden Oldie," Vlad said, and reached on the wall and grabbed one of the guitars. He handed it to Jay. It was a Russian seven-string that had been converted to six-string, then back to seven.

"You two play together," Vlad said.

"Would you like to play *Tetris Son*?"

"Yes."

"The chords are..."

"I can figure out the chords. I was watching your fingers," Jay said.

Jay strummed away while Kat played, but they got off to a poor start because Jay's guitar wasn't tuned in a familiar way.

Vlad motioned to Jay with a twisting motion to tune away. "Tune to your heart's delight," he said, eyes twinkling. "Here in Leningrad, we tune because we love!"

Jay efficiently tuned the guitar to his liking and again played along with Kat. Vlad watched happily as the youngsters shifted back and forth between playing lead and rhythm. Kat looked so natural while Jay frowned with concentration, focused and attentive, trying to keep up. Still, although he found Jay's playing to be mechanical, Vlad was impressed by Jay's mental prowess, taking a piece he had heard once and approximating it expertly, even with the occasional variation, in a converted scale. The music came to a fiery, fast-and-furious climax then ended. Jay wondered if Katarina might light a cigarette.

As Jay put the guitar down and shook his hands and fingers, Kat did not light up. Instead, she continued to strum quietly.

"Bravo, bravo," said Vlad.

"Thank you," Jay said, taking a small bow, a somewhat dopey smile on his face.

Kat remained in her own world, staring at the guitar and softly playing it. Jay's father bought it for him a year before, in a shop in Louisiana run by a man named Jimmy Foster. (Who knew that Louisiana was the place to go for a hand-made Russian guitar?) The occasion was Jay's acceptance to the Berkeley Conservatory of Music on a jazz and classical-guitar scholarship. The guitar cost 5,000 dollars, quite a sacrifice for the Browns, even though Jay's dad was a U.S. naval commander.

"So what can we do for you, Jay, now that you have entertained us? Can I interest you in some sheet music or strings?" said Vlad.

"I am interested in as many Russian chords as I can learn," Jay said. "They say there are more than a thousand chords for the Russian guitar," stated Jay.

"I believe to play some of those chords correctly, you need exceedingly long fingers," Vlad said, his eyes twinkling as he got up. "Well, let's take a look in the back."

Kat contentedly played Jay's guitar in her own little world. Was she in a trance? Vlad motioned for Jay to stand up and walk with him.

Following Vlad, Jay passed though the black curtain to the back room, where he noticed a one-foot square shadow box backed with red cloth and built into the back wall. In the middle of the box, mounted on the red cloth, were Russian submarine service insignia. All around the box were other military decorations and insignia.

The submarine insignia were different from those that Jay had seen on both his father's and grandfather's uniforms. The American insignia depicted two dolphins facing a World War II submarine bow. The insignia on this box showed a submarine with a red star in the middle. Along with the insignia there was a uniform shoulder board with three gold stars and two gold stripes, plus a number of other medals and ribbons.

Jay looked at framed photos on either side of the box. One showed a submarine tied up to the dock in port with about 100 sailors on the deck. The other was of an unbelievably young Vlad in uniform shaking hands with Leonid Brezhnev, the long-time General Secretary of the Central Committee of the Communist Party of the Soviet Union.

Jay was mesmerized by the mementos of Vlad's military career. Vlad was unconcerned with Jay's attention toward his military memorabilia, and was distractedly rummaging through an old metal file cabinet.

"*Nashel yego*," shouted Vlad. "I found it." He held up a thin music book. "It is all in Russian, but you can understand the illustrations—hundreds of chords depicted in this book for the seven-string guitar."

"Great, thank you," Jay said. Vlad handed him the book. Jay's eyes drifted from the book back to the shadow box in the wall.

"You seem very interested in the old memories of my military service," said Vlad.

"Well yes, you served in submarines, maybe commanded a submarine, certainly a very successful career. My father and grandfather both served in the submarine service," said Jay.

"Very observant, Grasshopper," said Vlad.

Jay felt for a second as if his mind would explode.

"How could you—? Hold it. Wait. How—? You, you watch *Kung Fu*?"

"Yes. I watch *Kung Fu*. It is on now in Russia. Snatch the pebble. How do you think my English has gotten so fabulous? I listen regularly to American television. *Kung Fu* is one of the few American shows the Russian government allows to be broadcast here."

"Why that one?"

"Probably because it makes Americans look so bad." Vlad laughed.

"What kind of submarine did you command, if you don't mind me asking?"

"When you go home, tell your dad and grandpa that you met, alive and in person, the commanding officer of a Victor class submarine. I actually commanded the first one made. There are many of them in the Russian fleet, the equivalent of the American Sturgeon. And that is about all I can say, I'm afraid," said Vlad. He held his palms up in a "what-can-you-do?" gesture.

"Amazing," replied Jay.

"Not as amazing as hosting the son and grandson of navy men with whom I might have shared the undersea world. What does your father think of you pursuing a music career as opposed to becoming a submariner?"

"My father is very proud of me taking a different path. He felt forced into a naval career and is happy that I have made my own choices." When Jay heard himself say it, he thought it sounded tinny.

"Was it your choice?" Pause. "Or was it your father's choice?" asked Vlad.

Vlad seemed like a friendly guy and all, and his daughter was a doll, but Jay was starting to dislike the questioning.

"I believe it was my choice, *sir*," said Jay.

"Do you mind if we play a little game?" asked Vlad.

Jay sighed. It was all part of the adventure, he told himself. "Sure, I love games," he said.

"Humor me anyway. What is your first memory of the navy?"

"I remember as a little boy, waiting on the dock for my dad's submarine to return from being away for a long time."

"Yes, tell me about that."

"I was in Groton, Connecticut. My mother had us standing in our Sunday best out at Eastern Point Beach, waiting for the submarine to appear, and we watched it pass. Then we packed up the car and drove to the pier to watch and wait and wonder where this underwater boat had been and what they had done and what it was like to be under the sea. I felt wonderment and awe," said Jay.

"OK. Now tell me about your first memory of hearing a guitar."

Jay thought for a second. "It was probably at my first lesson. That was around the same time."

"As?"

"As seeing my dad's submarine return. The teacher played a few chords and then asked me to try a few things."

"That's it?"
"Yes, that's it."

But that wasn't it. Jay's mind was flooded with memories. He recalled how his father had nurtured his fascination with submarines. He couldn't have been older than eight when Dad gave him two presents, a two-by-three-foot poster showing a cutaway illustration of the *Turtle*, the first submarine, and a book, a thick and lushly illustrated book about the history of underwater vessels. The poster was his favorite when he was very little. The *Turtle* only held one guy who rode in a standing position, his hands and feet working the controls. He was breathing through a brass tube, which was attached to a scuba tube that stuck up above the surface of the water. There were float valves so that the guy wouldn't drown if the scuba tube inadvertently went underwater. The handles were attached to paddles on the outside of the sub that moved and propelled the sub in the desired direction. The foot controls operated valves that added or subtracted water from inside the hulls to alter the buoyancy of the craft. The guy in the drawing—who was, Jay presumed, Sergeant Ezra Lee, the world's first submarine warrior—had George Washington hair, which made sense because the *Turtle* was used in the American Revolutionary War. The Americans used the *Turtle* to attack British ships that were docked in New York Harbor. There was a cock-eyed plan to paddle the submarine up to a ship, use a drill to attach a bomb to the enemy ship then paddle away before it blew up. Lee didn't even come close. The drill wouldn't go into the enemy hull. He made a racket trying to get the drill to work and eventually had to flee prematurely, jettisoning his bomb as he evaded the pursuing boat. The bomb blew up later and caused a huge geyser to fly up from the harbor, but no damage was done.

Jay would never forget his dad's precise words: "Son, that's the first practical submarine ever built. It didn't just submerge, but it could do things while it was down there as well. That was new. It was built for war," Jay's dad said, with a note of solemnity.

As Jay grew older he spent more time reading the large book than looking at his poster. He learned about the CSS *Hunley*, used during the American Civil War, a Confederate submarine and the first sub ever to sink an enemy vessel.

Jay, again, heard his dad quizzing him.

"Where did the *Hunley* make its attack?"

"In the waters off Charleston Harbor, sir."

"And what was the purpose of its mission?" It was to attack Union ships that had formed a blockade. The blockade was preventing supplies from getting to the Confederate troops."

"Very good, Jay. What was the *Hunley*'s nickname?"

That was a tough one, as Jay had read the word but never heard it out loud.

"It was the peri-, the peripa-, the…"

"Peripatetic," his father said, patiently.

"The Peripatetic Coffin."

"And how did it earn its name?"

"Because it killed many more of its own men than it did the enemy, sir."

"How is a submarine like a bat?

"It navigates and detects everything by sound."

Dad suddenly changed course: "If you are the captain of a ship and a broken meter suggests danger, what do you do?"

"I believe the broken meter to be on the safe side. I believe my indications, sir."

"Very good, Grasshopper."

Jay remembered his father patting him on the head, a tender gesture of approval that he could still (almost) feel when he thought about it.

"What is a submariner?"

"A submariner is a one-trick pony. He figures out what works and applies it."

"Does it have to be sexy?" Dad asked. Jay understood this to mean fancy and attractive. Did it need to look appealing?

"No, sir. It just needs to work."

Jay heard a voice and snapped out of his daydream.

"Katarina, can you please join us back here," shouted Vlad.

"Yes, sir." Kat was like jazz, like freestyle poetry read to a bongo beat, smooth as silk as she entered the back room through the black curtain.

"Kat," Vlad said, "tell us about the first time you heard a guitar play."

Kat sat down and closed her eyes. The tip of her tongue flickered outward and moistened her full lips.

Jay noticed the voluptuous way she filled her flannel shirt. Jay, to his chagrin, could not distinguish the details, but he could tell there was a lot happening in that shirt.

"Ahh," she said. "Here is an early memory. My mother and I were walking in Leningrad and a man was playing the guitar in the street for money. I was fascinated by how much music was coming from that thin instrument. I stopped and stared and my mother wanted me to move along because she felt like she should give money to the man if we listened for too long. I could not walk away. The man did not seem to care that we were not going to put money in his guitar case. He simply seemed happy to be playing. My mind escaped my surroundings and traveled with the music."

Vlad turned to Jay and said, "Sometimes our true destiny is not our choice. I know I have just met you, but please allow me to state what seems obvious: Jay, you have saltwater running through your veins, just as Katarina has music playing in her soul."

The burning in Jay's cheeks returned. He felt flush and lightheaded. An emptiness within him was filling up with something magical, like high-octane fuel in a long-empty tank. With the music book in his hand he pushed through the black curtain to re-enter the shop. Jay picked up the cheap guitar that he was playing with Kat and put it in his guitar case with the book and closed the case.

Jay said, "I think that is a fair trade."

Vlad replied, "Don't be crazy. Your guitar is worth ten, twenty, thirty times that battered guitar. I will not allow this."

Jay bundled up for the cold, wrapping his scarf around his neck, zipping up his jacket and tugging his wool cap over his black hair. He walked over to Vlad and hugged him. Then he moved toward Kat, who was looking shell-shocked by Jay's generosity. He kissed her three times on alternating cheeks.

"Vlad and Kat, you have no choice. This is our destiny. I don't need that guitar anymore. You have provided me a gift that money cannot buy. Thank you," Jay said. He turned and walked out of the guitar shop with his guitar case in his hand.

The little bell above the door tinkled as the door closed behind him.

I

August 23rd, 1992 Underwater Operating Area, Connecticut, Usa

"*All stations, this is the XO. I have the deck and the conn,*" announced Lieutenant Commander (LCDR) Jay Brown as he assumed control of the USS *Quincy*, a first flight 688 class also known as a Los Angeles class fast attack submarine.

The Los Angeles class submarine had a beautiful shape. Jay thought it the sexiest of the subs, looked great even when tied up to the pier. The hull was long and cylindrical and black, with only a few feet sticking up above the dark water of the slip. (Jay understood that it did not need to be sexy, it merely needed to work, but he was glad it was sexy nonetheless.)

The conn controlled the driving of the submarine; the deck had control of everything else.

The *Quincy* was hull number SSN 693. It was a first flight 688, the sixth submarine of its kind after the lead submarine of the class, the SSN 688, USS *Los Angeles*. The *Quincy* was part of the first thirty-one submarines of the Los Angeles class, a class that ended with the USS *Honolulu* SSN 718. It had four torpedo tubes, but no vertical launch capability.

When a submarine was on the surface of the water, the sail was the prominent structure that stuck up. Old-time submariners called the sail the conning tower.

On first flight 688 submarines, there were fins called planes on the sail. One twenty-foot-tall plane housed the masts, antennae, and periscopes. The sailplanes helped to control the submarine's depth when it was submerged—but served no purpose on the surface.

On second flight 688 submarines, the planes were in the bow of the submarine and underwater even when the submarine was on the surface. Bow planes were more efficient and practical on submarines built after 1985.

Jay just took over control of the *Quincy* from Lieutenant Junior Grade (LT jg) John Little, who went into the radio room to learn what radio operators do when the submarine goes to periscope depth. The submarine's youngest officer, in his second year onboard, he recently took over responsibilities as the communications division officer. Little had completed his nuclear engineering qualifications and was now learning the operations on the forward end of the ship to earn his gold dolphins.

When Jay announced to all stations that he had the conn, he spoke from the control room through an open microphone. When an officer assumed control of a submarine or "took the conn" they were also said to have "assumed the duties of officer of the deck (OOD)."

Those driving the *Quincy* included the senior enlisted man in charge of maintaining the boat's depth (called the diving officer or just "dive"), the chief of the watch (in charge of maintaining the submarine's required buoyancy), and the helmsman (who usually controlled the sail or fairwater planes). The helmsman took rudder orders from the OOD and trim orders from the dive.

Other groups and individuals controlled by the OOD included the quartermaster (who maintained the submarine's track on the chart), sonar supervisor (in charge of a group of sailors that listened to the water), fire control supervisor, as well as radio and electronics control. Radar and radio didn't work while submerged. Radio signals travel poorly underwater but have an important roll when the sub is at periscope depth.

Only a commissioned officer could stand watch as OOD on a submarine, and even then only after the commanding officer or submarine captain was comfortable with that individual's experience and judgment. This process of gaining trust was called "qualifying."

Once an officer of the deck assumed the conn, all of the groups were expected to acknowledge the change of control. (The same individual, who was known as "officer of the deck" to the watch standers that controlled the operation of the submarine, was known as "conn" to all other watch standers.) It sounded almost like a roll call. The speaker that broadcasted everything that was said in the control room to the various stations also broadcasted to the commanding officer's stateroom, adjacent to the control room. The captain didn't acknowledge the change of OOD, but he certainly listened to make sure everyone else did.

Following Jay's announcement, the captain heard:

"The XO has the conn, Officer of the Deck. Helm, aye, sir."

"The XO has the conn, Officer of the Deck. Dive, aye, sir," said Master Chief Eduardo Haskell, who was standing the diving officer watch. Haskell, as the senior-most enlisted man aboard, was also the chief of the boat (COB).

"The XO has the conn, Officer of the Deck. Chief of the Watch, aye," Senior Chief Lionel Ledbetter replied. Ledbetter was also the Chief Yeoman of the *Quincy*. The yeoman department was the only department that reported in to the XO. All other departments reported in to the captain. When the chief was not on watch, he was in charge of payroll, keeping track of leave, transfers, and the paperwork of promotions. (After the captain, the chief yeoman is the one person you never want to piss off. He could accidentally-on-purpose screw up your pay for eternity and have you accidentally transferred to a trash barge in Panama.) Ledbetter was also an excellent chief of the watch and diving officer.

"The XO has the conn, Officer of the Deck. Quartermaster, aye," First Class Petty Officer Rusty Dunn replied.

Reports were heard from other stations not directly in the control room.

"Conn, fire control, aye."

"Conn, radio, aye."

"Conn, ESM, aye."

Jay awaited a report from sonar. Silence. He stared at the overhead speaker. More silence.

"Sonar, conn. Are you awake?"

The control room giggled.

There was a curtain in the forward starboard side of the control room that entered into the sonar space. The curtain usually remained shut to keep the sonar control room as dark as possible, to best see the sonar displays. Jay walked through the curtain, and yelled: "Hey, sonar! Stop listening to whale farts and start listening to me."

Sonar supervisor Ferris Wright said, "Hey, XO. No shit, I think we got a Russian submarine in our local operating area. It sounds like a Victor class."

The *Quincy* was steering a course due west—or 270—and Wright had noticed on his sonar display a contact bearing 300, moving slowly across, toward the bow of the *Quincy*.

"Nice work, Ferris. What do you need me to do to keep contact?"

"Keep steady course speed and depth and we will try to lock in a few frequencies for tracking," replied Ferris Wright.

The XO returned to the control room.

"All right, boys and girls, it's show time. We have a possible Russian submarine bearing 300. We are going to maintain course, speed and depth, until we can get a lock on him. Fire control, commence tracking the contact bearing 300. We will refer to the contact as Victor Three. Chief of the Watch, pass the word to rig the submarine for ultra quiet."

"Pass the word to rig ship for ultra quiet. Chief of the watch, aye, sir."

Captain Joe Davis heard what was going on and returned to the control room. No rest for the weary. Joe was not a nickname. That was his name as it was written on his birth certificate. Joe. No middle name. No middle initial. Joe Davis. Good solid name, his dad said. Joe grew up along the Gulf Coast in Louisiana, the son of a shrimp-boat captain. He was the first member of his family to graduate from college. He often joked that the Naval Academy, or "Boat School," might not really count as going to a "real college." The members of his family were homebodies. Not a traveler in the bunch. He also joked he was the first Davis to set foot outside Louisiana.

The captain was a large man, six-three, with a thick frame—built for power rather than speed. He was a fair and strong leader, well loved and respected by his crew, including his second in command, his executive officer, his XO, Jay Brown.

The captain could be an earthy man who perhaps shared more than he should about his bathroom habits and loved to tell ribald stories. For example, he claimed his earliest memory of being on his dad's shrimp boat involved pulling out of his pants a live shrimp that was trying to swim up his ass.

Jay announced, "Captain in the control room."

"At ease, men. What do we have, XO?"

"You can see it on the sonar display, Captain."

Wright reported, "Conn, sonar, we have a frequency lock on Victor Three. Request your maneuver right for target motion analysis."

The XO looked toward the captain, nodded yes, and said, "Conn, sonar, aye. Maneuvering to the right for TMA. Helm, right fifteen degrees, rudder steady, on course 330."

"Right fifteen degrees rudder, steady on course 330. Helm, aye, sir. My rudder is right fifteen," said the helmsman.

"Very well, helm," Jay replied.

"XO, let's figure out how far away this guy is. Then we'll decide what to do next."

The helm said, "Sir, I am steady on course 330."

"Very well, helm," replied the XO. "Fire control and sonar, we are steady on course. Let's get a solution for what this guy is doing. Quartermaster, keep us safe while we chase the bad guys."

"Working on a solution," said fire control.

"Working on a solution," sonar echoed.

Quartermaster Rusty Dunn reported, "I'll keep us safe."

The captain looked at the quartermaster's chart to make sure he understood where the *Quincy* was relative to other navigational hazards. He gave the XO a thumbs-up, and the quartermaster a mild slap of approval on the back.

Fire control: "I have a solution."

Jay and the captain ran to the fire control station to see what it looked like. He had his opinions but waited to see what the captain had to say, a largely political technique called "recognizing the right answer when told."

"This son of a bitch is heading toward the continental shelf," the captain said. "He could be escorting a Delta class ballistic submarine. More likely he is doing independent operations, sniffing around to see what's coming out of Groton and the Electric Boat shipyard."

Jay found himself thinking about his encounter many years before in icy Leningrad with the retired Russian submarine captain, Vlad, and his spellbinding daughter, Katarina. He always thought of Vlad when he heard American servicemen de-humanizing Russians with Cold War blather. If there was one thing the XO knew, it was that Russian and American sailors were all peas out of the same pod, they were just like us, out there to do the job they'd been told to do. Jay hoped they didn't end up having to shoot anyone with a torpedo.

The captain said, "What do you think, Jay? Do we move in on him and spook him—or, do we go up to periscope depth and report him to the Submarine Forces Atlantic?"

Jay replied, "If we go up to periscope depth and report him, we could lose him—and there is no telling where he would go from there. We could track him for a while and see what he is up to. Once we have a better idea of his plans we can report him to Sublant."

"All right, Jay, I trust your instincts. You've been chasing the Russians on fast attacks for your entire career. I have spent most of my career hiding from them on boomers," said the captain with a flicker of a smile. "Hang back about 3,000 yards."

A boomer was a ballistic missile sub such as the Ohio class SSBN-726. Unlike the Los Angeles class fast attack submarine, designed to find and chase enemy submarines, the boomer was a floating nuclear missile silo designed to avoid detection. Boomer submarines were so important to the navy and national defense that they were assigned two crews to maximize their time at sea. The two crews were called the blue and gold crews. Each had a separate captain, XO, and every other officer and sailor required to operate the submarine.

Jay said, "All right, Captain, I am going to stay deep in Victor Three's baffles and remain about 3,000 yards behind."

A baffle was the "acoustic blind spot" directly behind the submarine, a "cone of silence" astern where sonar reception was hindered by engines, turbines, screws and other mechanical equipment located in the aft. The *Quincy* tracked directly behind the Soviet submarine, watching with its best sensors and hiding in the Soviets' baffle.

"Very well, XO," replied the captain formally, trusting Jay to track without being detected.

Sometimes an XO had to wait years for a smidgen of underwater intrigue. Some never encountered anything more interesting than a school of fish, or a previously unknown crevasse at the bottom of the ocean. But Jay had precisely eight weeks experience as the *Quincy*'s XO, the youngest XO in the fleet, with a little more than nine years on active duty.

For day-to-day business, the commanding officer was in charge of the operation of the submarine while the XO was responsible for all things administrative. In this case, the XO was operating the submarine as the most senior and experienced submarine driver on the ship behind the captain. There was an important distinction, however, between control and responsibility. The captain was relinquishing the former but never the latter. As he had earlier specified, the captain thought the XO to be best suited to handle this situation.

Jay kept the various watch stations informed of the plan and provided a series of rudder-command and engine-speed orders. His object: to ensure the *Quincy* stayed in Victor Three's baffles. Victor Three was still bearing 270, and the *Quincy* was steering course 270.

The captain was impressed with his XO. Jay commanded the men that controlled the submarine with precision and grace. Jay felt it, too. At that moment, the men and the submarine's controls were extensions of him, just as the guitar had been to Kat in Leningrad. He might as well have been inside the *Turtle*, with his four limbs controlling all of the ship's functions. Vlad had been so right. Submarines were in his blood. He couldn't feel this way, feel this control, if he hadn't been born for undersea adventure.

The captain remained in the control room to support the XO, who clearly didn't need that much support. While Jay's skills were particular to submarines, the captain would have been an effective leader of men even if he'd been assigned to a cargo ship supplying Guam. Some guys had it like that. Four years of back and forth to Guam. The captain didn't need to be on a submarine to conjure up his own greatness, but it was different for his XO, who seemed to grow two inches taller and 50 IQ points smarter when given control of the submarine. Of course, some of that was an illusion. Part of Jay, as it turned out, was caught up a little bit too much in the "look-at-me-I'm-driving-a-submarine" moment.

The captain knew how to play people's strengths. He himself was a flawed sailor, not a man of exceptional nautical skills, but with a keen eye for men who were, and he surrounded himself with personnel that made up for his own shortcomings. If his men realized this, it probably was only on a subconscious level. His men just knew that Captain Davis put together machines that were well oiled. That didn't mean he wasn't keeping an eagle eye on everything his XO did. Jay Brown was gifted, but was he mature? Did he have wisdom? Jay needed to be watched because he could be impulsive, too aggressive.

After an hour of tracking Victor Three at relatively high speed, the captain said, "Hey Jay, let's take a look at the chart and see where we are and where Victor Three is."

"Aye aye, Captain."

They examined the plotting chart.

"How far behind Victor Three are we, XO?"

"Captain, I am keeping at least 3,000 yards behind just as you ordered."

"I see that, XO. Nice job. Where are you relative to Victor Three's stern?"

"We are at the edge of the port baffles, Captain."

"Let's say Victor Three turns left, how long before we would be out of his baffles and counter detected?"

Jay felt the color drain from his face and a quick mist of nervous sweat form across his forehead. Before even replying to the captain, Jay yelled out, "Helm, right five degrees rudder, steady on course 270."

The helmsman repeated the order and announced, "Officer of the Deck, we are steady on course 270."

"Sorry, Captain. I lost track of the big picture and was just focused on staying 3,000 feet behind."

"Don't worry about it, XO. That is what I am here for. Remember, Jay: Don't think about just driving the ship. Always think about the tactical picture. What are we out here for?"

"Yes, sir. Captain, we have been cruising pretty fast for a while now. I wonder what our trim looks like."

"That's another reason I wanted you to drive deeper into his baffles, so we can speed up and close to about 2,000 yards. Then we slow to sort out trim."

"Aye aye, Captain."

Jay sped up the submarine until they were about a mile behind the Russians.

"Helm, all ahead two thirds."

"All ahead two thirds. Helmsman, aye. Officer of the Deck, the engine room acknowledges all ahead two thirds."

The XO, standing with his feet shoulder-width and his hands folded at the small of his back, responded, "Very well, helm."

The *Quincy* had only one propeller, yet it was customary to preface engine orders with "all".

As the submarine slowed, Jay said, "Diving Officer, neutral your planes. Chief of the Watch, check your trim." They slowly sank deeper than the 400 feet they'd been operating at. The depth gauge rose.

"XO, what would you have done if the depth had started increasing or decreasing rapidly?" the captain asked.

"The officer of the deck would have ordered the submarine to speed up and ordered the diving officer to take control of the depth."

The oral exam was interrupted by real life.

The chief of the watch reported out, "Officer of the Deck, we are slightly negative. Request to start the main ballast pump, and recommend the diving officer takes control of depth."

Jay said, "Very well, Chief of the Watch, start the main ballast pump. Dive, take control of depth. Maintain 400 feet."

The chief of the watch said, "Officer of the Deck, starting the main ballast pumps." He was the gatekeeper on behalf of the officer of the deck for all things noisy. Starting a main ballast pump was *very* noisy. If the *Quincy* hadn't remained in the cone of silence behind the Russian submarine, the pump's racket would have resulted in instant detection.

The *Quincy* had sunk to 500 feet.

"Three degree up bubble," said the diving officer to the two young planesmen in front of him.

The diving officer wanted to get the submarine back to its desired depth without too much of an upward angle, which might cause loose items to fall and create more unwanted noise. The "bubble" was the up or down angle of the submarine, so-called because the original inclinometer on a submarine was a bubble level, like a common carpenter's bubble level, mounted in the control room and oriented to detect the forward and aft incline or decline of the submarine. Although the traditional bubble inclinometer still existed, the diving officer in 1992 looked at an electronic inclinometer on the ship's control panel in front of him. The term *bubble* was still used, as in "losing the bubble," meaning losing control of depth. It was also used by submariners as a synonym for sanity. You never wanted to lose the bubble on the ship—or in your head.

The *Quincy* was only slightly negative because both the diving officer and the chief of the watch were experienced, well chosen by the captain.

Jay went over a checklist in his head. The submarine had been operating for the last couple of hours under a number of conditions that could affect buoyancy. Every time a sailor used the head, some seawater from outside the submarine was used to drain the toilet into the sanitary tank. Toilets on submarines didn't flush. Too noisy. They simply drained.

Water was also being introduced inside to be distilled into fresh water to drink and operate the nuclear power plant. Fresh water was required in the oxygen generator that broke up H_2O into oxygen and hydrogen components. There were also things the submarine did that made it lighter underwater, but not while the submarine was rigged for ultra quiet.

The chief of the watch and the diving officers worked together to get the submarine as close to neutral as possible. The chief of the watch used the main ballast pump to empty the tanks located up and down the *Quincy*'s length. He wanted to make the submarine neutral without becoming heavier in the aft end than the forward end. To compensate for such an imbalance, the planes would have to maintain a down angle to keep a "zero bubble." Operating the planes that way at full speed could cause water bubbles to form in the seawater that the submarine was driving through, an affect, called cavitation, that was also on the noisy side.

The chief of the watch announced, "Officer of the deck, I have a good trim. I recommend speeding up."

"Very well, Chief of the Watch," said Jay, and looked to the captain for guidance.

The captain said, "Why don't you speed back up, close back in to 2,000 yards, and follow him like we were? I am anticipating a maneuver by Victor Three. Once he turns we will have a better idea of what he is up to."

"Aye aye, Captain," replied Jay. "All ahead full, helm."

The submarine returned to full speed and continued to track.

It was rare to spend three tours on the same class of submarine, but both the XO and the captain had done so, Jay on Los Angeles class, the captain on Ohio class.

"Captain, what's this guy doing? Have you seen this type of thing before?"

"You bet. The Russians come in sniffing around to check out the new subs out of New London. This is pretty typical unless they cross inside the TML," that is, the twelve-mile limit, the internationally recognized demarcation of international waters. Beyond that line, pal, and you were in U.S. territorial waters in violation of numerous treaties and possibly in commission of a hostile act. "Once he maneuvers we will pop up to periscope depth and send a situation report so we can get some assistance keeping an eye on him."

Ferris Wright said, "We are hearing cavitation from Victor Three. Sounds like he is maneuvering."

Jay said, "Conn, sonar, aye. How's that for timing, Captain?"

The captain's eyes were fixed on the sonar display in the control room. With a note of concern, he added, "Looks like we have more maneuvering than we anticipated."

"Yes, it does," replied Jay.

"You gonna call it?"

"Yes, sir," replied Jay. "All stations, all stations, Crazy Ivan, I repeat, Crazy Ivan. Engage Crazy Ivan procedures. This is not a drill."

II

August 23rd, 1992
Approaching New London, Connecticut

"*This is the captain. I have the conn.*"

The Russians were pulling a "Crazy Ivan" and it was time Captain Davis took control.

The "Crazy Ivan" was a common enough maneuver, but always an adrenaline-pumper, usually initiated by Russian submarines when leaving their own waters, designed to determine if another submarine was following them, and often conducted in concert with a second Russian submarine waiting quietly and listening at a predetermined location. Once found, the object was to detect then shake the other submarine.

"Crazy Ivan" was so-named because it was crazy dangerous, essentially a U-turn at high speed. Once completed, the submarine continued speeding in the opposite direction for a time then slowed and listened. (Nature has determined that speeding and listening cannot be done simultaneously as sonar sensors are deafened by the flow of water.) When a trailing non-Russian submarine was detected at close proximity, what ensued was an aquatic game of chicken, a submariner joust that could result in a head-on collision without survivors.

Captain Davis took control not to better protect the submarine—he trusted Jay's ability—but rather to take responsibility in case of an incident. It was part of being captain. Like going down with the ship.

The crew had been trained to react to a Crazy Ivan. While the safety of the ship was the primary concern, the object was still to remain undetected.

The chief of the watch put his hands on the emergency blow valves that would surface the submarine in seconds if the captain gave the order. Hopefully, not. The emergency blow filled the main ballast tanks to increase buoyancy, but it also resulted in immediate detection.

"Conn, sonar, Victor Three appears to be 200-plus feet deeper than us."

"Very well, sonar. Quartermaster, power down the Fathometer," said the captain. The Fathometer stopped pinging rhythmically out the bottom to determine the depth of water under the submarine. The Russians could hear those pings if they were directly below.

With the Fathometer powered down, the *Quincy* waited silently. The Russian submarine approached nose-to-nose but at a water depth below. The *Quincy* slowed to a crawl, hiding.

"Captain, we are slowly rising. Our depth is 300 feet," said the dive.

Seconds felt like forever as they ticked past. The *Quincy* had less than three minutes before it would bob to the surface where hiding was impossible. Speeding up or increasing ballast would result in instant counter-detection. Captain Davis decided to sweat it out. Perhaps the Russians would pass by, at which time the *Quincy* could again increase speed. Perhaps the Russians would listen, hear nothing, and proceed with their mission.

Ferris Wright entered the control room and flicked off the switch that controlled all public address speakers. He said, almost whispering, "Victor Three has slowed and is directly beneath us."

The captain replied, "*Are you shitting me?*"

Wright replied in a tense whisper, "I shit you not!"

These are the kind of strictly-by-the-book communications that are reserved for situations like these.

The captain said, "XO, tiptoe around the ship and kill anyone that is making noise. But kill them quietly."

"Tiptoeing and killing quietly, aye, sir."

As Jay walked on little cat feet, some of the less mature control room watch standers were quietly giggling. Jay pretended to shoot them with his finger then put that finger to his lips.

"Shhh."

Dive said, "Captain, we are starting to sink. Must be hitting warm water. We are at 300 feet and dropping slowly."

"Very well, Dive." The captain turned to the sonar supervisor and said, "Where did I go wrong as a child?"

Wright replied, "I think it worked out just fine for you, sir. All that clean living is paying off for us all. Victor Three is continuing eastbound and speeding up."

There was a collective sigh of relief. Captain Davis turned control of the submarine back to his XO and went back to his stateroom. Jay tracked Victor Three.

"Looks like he's heading back to the mother land," Jay said. "Prepare to go to periscope depth."

They needed to make a SITREP (Situation Report), as well as take care of some housekeeping. The SITREP would provide enough information to allow other U.S. submarines to help track the Russian sub.

Jay said, "All stations, conn, making preparations to go to periscope depth. Dive, make your depth 200 feet. Helm, all ahead two thirds."

Jay took the submarine just above the underwater thermal layer to listen for any ships above before proceeding to periscope depth. A submerged vessel lacked the benefit of visuals or radar because electromagnetic waves travel sluggishly underwater. So it listened. A modern submarine rarely transmitted "active"—that is, made pings to figure out what was around it—for the simple reason that those pings would give the submarine's location away. A submarine typically listened "passively". Sub duty was called the silent service for a reason.

Jay said, "All stations, we are on steady course 090 at 200 feet. Radios, prepare to transmit all of the messages that the captain has approved. SITREP is to be sent first. At periscope depth, download all of the ship's traffic."

"Conn, radio, transmit SITREP first, then all other messages, and download all ship's traffic, aye."

"Sonar, conn, report all contacts."

"Conn, sonar, reporting contacts. Continue to hold Victor Three bearing 270 and opening. Also hear a distant trawler bearing 280 and a likely merchant ship bearing 300."

"Very well, sonar. All stations, clearing baffles to the right. Helm, right fifteen degrees rudder, steady on course 045." Jay was turning the ship to the right in order to see if there was anyone behind him. Plus, by maneuvering, sonar and fire control would get a notion of the trawler and merchant ship's course, speed and distance.

Victor Three had cleared baffles by making a 180-degree course change. The U.S. Navy almost always had a more subtle—and safe—approach to the maneuver, slowly clearing baffles with a large course change to the left or right at slow speed.

"Officer of the Deck, we are steady on course 045," said the helmsman to Jay.

"Very well, helm," replied Jay.

Going to periscope depth was a dangerous undertaking. The submarine was driven to a keel depth of about seventy feet. If there was a ship directly above the submarine, the underwater vessel could crash into it.

The commanding officer granted permission to go to periscope depth and to transmit radio messages to special military satellites from antennae that protruded out of the water at periscope depth. The same satellite that securely received the message would, in turn, relay the message from the submarine to the proper recipient. Those satellites also transmitted message traffic to the *Quincy* from military shore facilities. The messages, also called "message traffic," were received electronically then printed out.

When requesting permission from the captain to go to periscope depth, a phone in the control room was used to call and brief him.

Jay picked up that phone and pushed a button. "Captain, this is the officer of the deck. My depth is 200 feet. I have cleared baffles and we hold two surface contacts outside of two miles from the ship, our SITREP is ready to transmit, and I have instructed radio to get the ship's radio traffic."

"Very well, Officer of the Deck, proceed to periscope depth," replied the captain. "If you can't get all of the radio traffic in ten minutes, assuming the SITREP is transmitted, go deep without it and we will get it next time we're at periscope depth. I don't want to let Victor Three get too far away."

"Aye, sir, proceed to periscope depth, no longer than ten minutes, get the broadcast after the SITREP is sent, then go deep and continue to track Victor Three," said Jay. "All stations, conn, proceeding to periscope depth. Raising number two periscope. Dive, make your depth seventy feet."

The diving officer acknowledged the order and all stations acknowledged the move to periscope depth. Now there was complete silence in the control room except for the diving officer calling out the depth as they rose from 200 feet to seventy feet below the surface.

Once the periscope broke the surface of the water, the officer of the deck did a number of quick 360s and announced, "No close contacts." If the officer of the deck had seen a close contact, he would have announced "*emergency deep*," and the scope would have been quickly lowered.

After the initial arrival to periscope depth, contacts further away would be identified. The officer of the deck, or a qualified delegate, would continue to scan visually as long as the submarine remained at periscope depth. Now that it had been affirmed that the *Quincy* was safe from collision, Jay ordered, "Chief of the Watch, raise the number one radio antenna. Radio, transmit and receive."

Five minutes later, radio reported, "Officer of the Deck, all traffic transmitted and received."

"Very well, radio. Chief of the Watch, lower number one antenna. All stations, conn, going deep. Dive, make your depth 400 feet. Lowering number two periscope."

Jay lowered the periscope, and the *Quincy* again tracked Victor Three.

After a while, Jay got on the open mic, "Lieutenant Little, three hours after I relieved you for a quick trip to PD, I am still out here, tracking your Victor Three. I gotta hit the head. How about you come back out here and relieve me?"

True, Jay had only been on the *Quincy* for eight weeks, but he'd grown fond of Little, a young guy who was in his third year on the *Quincy* and knew the ship as well as his mother's face. Little was what some might call a *schlemiel*. He never seemed to catch a break. He was a guy *plagued* by Murphy's Law. If it could go wrong with him, it did. He'd twice been on a plane that crash landed (which in another sense was extremely lucky), lost his girlfriend to his best friend back home only three weeks after he enlisted (and maybe that was a blessing, too, one never knew), and had some nasty scar tissue on one shoulder from being hit on his bicycle as a kid by a hit-and-run driver. There was no positive spin for that one, although he did meet some nice people in the hospital. Despite what seemed like an eternity of bad luck, he never let it bring him down.

Jay sometimes wondered about the wisdom of serving only a few feet away from Little, a guy who had a perpetual black cloud over his head. On this day, he found himself on the ass of a daring Russian sub that pulled a Crazy Ivan, so it only seemed reasonable that Little was only a few feet away.

Little reported back, "I'll be right out, XO. The captain got a personal."

It is not uncommon when at sea for the commanding officer to receive personal messages. Sometimes it was operational orders, sometimes info regarding a crew member. It could have been anything.

"Lieutenant Little, the radioman can bring that to the captain. Need for relief becoming urgent. I need some reading material, did you get news and sports?"

Little delivered the personal to the captain, and brought Jay the news. Jay hurriedly passed along the instructions regarding the tracking of Victor Three and the safe operation of the *Quincy*. Jay went to his stateroom, which was next to the captain's quarters, with a head in between.

Jay stuck his head in on the captain and said, "Captain, I turned back over to Little. He has his instructions for tracking Victor Three. You might want to turn up your open microphone speaker. There is also a personal for you that you should see in the next few minutes. We also have news and sports. I hope you don't need to use the head in the next few minutes."

"All right, XO. I may shift to the control room if you are going to wreck the head. I need to keep an eye on Little. Nice job today, XO."

"Thank you, sir."

Jay retreated to the head, went about his business efficiently, and returned to the control room, where the captain asked him, "Anything interesting in the news? I haven't looked at it yet."

"Actually, yes, from the Associated Press. A senior naval officer in the Pentagon committed suicide. The name is being withheld pending family notification."

"I wonder if your dad knew him."

"I was thinking the same thing. He knows just about every senior officer in that building."

"Maybe not, though. The press gets it wrong sometimes..." the captain said, with a shrug.

Jay's dad was a vice admiral. Heavy, heavy stuff. Head of naval intelligence, a regular at White House dinners. He advised the Joint Chiefs of Staff.

Jay's mom could have been one of those fancy Beltway ladies who hosted all the right parties, and raised funds for all the right charities. But Mom was content to do her charity work in relative anonymity, and circling nose-to-butt among a pack of women who were trying to impress each other was not her idea of a good time. She was happier pushing scrumptious dishes of food at the people she loved.

The captain and crew, of course, knew all about Jay's exceptional heritage. In fact, before he reported for duty there had been much conjecture about the quality of Jay's character. Admirals' kids were oft times assholes. Once Jay came onboard, however, he quickly earned respect on his own merits. He was a regular guy who's dad could have just as easily been a truck driver.

"XO, watch Little while I read my message traffic." The captain retired to his stateroom while Jay stayed in the control room with Little.

"Little, do you know what you're doing?" Jay was only half joking. The situation had eased somewhat, but it was still tense. What if Victor Three pulled another Crazy Ivan?

Little replied, "Yes, sir. I am staying at least 2,000 yards behind. I am mindful of our trim, and I am staying deep in his baffles."

It was the correct answer and Little knew it. Jay would have complimented him, but he didn't want success to go to Little's head.

"You having fun, Little?"

"Absolutely, sir."

The captain then walked into the control room from his stateroom with a distressed expression on his face.

"XO, I need you to supervise Little bringing the submarine back up to periscope depth. I need to find out if one of the other submarines in our squadron is picking up the trail of Victor Three, and I also need radio to set up a secure communication between me and the commodore."

"Aye aye, sir."

It was uncommon to set up direct communications between an operational submarine and shore side unless it had been set up in advance. Jay could only assume this had something to do with the personal message the captain had received—perhaps regarding Victor Three.

As Jay supervised Little bringing the submarine back to periscope depth, the captain had a communication with his boss, the commodore, privately from his stateroom.

Once the submarine returned to normal submerged operations, the captain emerged from his stateroom and ordered, "Officer of the Deck, break trail of Victor Three and reverse course. We are heading back to port."

Little repeated the order. Jay was perplexed, not an uncommon state when working on a submarine. If you needed to know, you were told. If you didn't need to know, you followed orders.

The captain remained in the control room until the *Quincy* was on a safe return course.

"XO, can you join me in my stateroom?"

"Yes, sir."

In the stateroom, the captain closed the door and motioned for Jay to sit in the chair next to the captain's small steel Formica-covered desk. The captain looked very serious—grim even. It was scaring Jay.

"Jay, I don't know how to tell you this any other way than just directly. Your father shot himself in the chest and was found dead in his office in the Pentagon this morning."

Jay felt simultaneously flush and nauseous.

"It can't be true," Jay said. It was a mistake. A joke. A trick. It was, was, anything but the truth.

"Jay, I just talked to the commodore. That is the report he got. This is a hell of a way to find something out like this, but I felt I had to tell you. We are heading back to port so you can get home and work out the details. I am very sorry. Please, when you get the opportunity, offer my deepest condolences to your mother."

Jay's thoughts continued in denial. It couldn't be true. It didn't make sense. There was no reason. His father had three stars, was in the prime of his career.

Denial wore off and grief struck—a combination of grief and something akin to morbid curiosity. What in the world could have caused his father to do such a thing? He wasn't going to rest until he had the facts.

III
AUGUST 29TH, 1992
THE NATIONAL CATHEDRAL, WASHINGTON, D.C.

Jay sat in full dress whites between his grandfather—retired Rear Admiral James Brown, Sr., also in his full dress whites—and his mother, Jane Fitzpatrick Brown. Next to Mom sat Jay's older sister, Janet Brown O'Brien, and her husband, Michael O'Brien. Huddled together for comfort, they stared blankly at the flag-draped casket. They were numb, and that was OK with them. All of the feeling they were doing was bad. Numb was good.

Admiral Frank Conner, the chief of naval operations (CNO), delivered the first eulogy. A career submariner, Admiral Conner struggled to speak without his voice quivering and cracking. A consummate gentleman from Tennessee, he had a reputation for being extremely articulate, and supportive of his men—even when they made mistakes.

Jay felt dazed, almost in a dream state with grief, as he listened to Admiral Conner's words: "President and Mrs. Bush, Mrs. Brown and the Brown family, Secretary Howard, members of the Joint Chiefs of Staff, Unified commanders-in-chief, the leadership and members of Congress who are here, to our great navy sailors and all of America's armed forces—one of our great leaders has lost his way. As we say in the submarine force, he lost the bubble." The admiral discussed James

Brown's career, his pleasant demeanor and his dedication to duty. In closing, Admiral Conner said, "James will be missed—as a friend, a leader and family member. I now introduce retired Rear Admiral Jim Brown, Sr."

Jay's grandfather walked up to the altar slowly, but stood tall and proud, appearing younger than his seventy-three years. Jim Brown saluted Admiral Conner, who saluted him back. The men shook hands and then pulled each other in for a quick embrace.

Jim Brown took his place behind the lectern and spoke without notes: "Thank you, Frank. To the president and Mrs. Bush and all the dignitaries mentioned by Admiral Conner, to my family, and my extended navy and armed forces family." He paused for a moment to gather his composure then continued, "I am not sure if I want to mourn the death of my son, or revive him from the dead so I can slap some sense into him. As a parent, I have always selfishly prayed that my wife and my only son would outlive me. I lost my best friend and wife Betty of more than fifty years to cancer almost two years ago. Betty and I were…"

He paused and briefly pressed a fist to his mouth.

"…so proud of our only child that rose to the rank of three star admiral. He had to beat me by that one star."

The audience laughed a little.

"Betty and I are even more proud of our lovely daughter-in-law, Jane, and my beautiful and loving grandchildren, Janet and Jay. There is no greater gift in life than family."

Admiral Brown paused again.

"It not easy, is it?" he asked. There was a murmur of affirmation from the pews.

Jim spoke as if talking to a dear friend, while actually he was addressing hundreds: "We have all been there—either at sea, or waiting for a loved one at sea. Taking on more than our share, luck not going in our direction."

You could hear a pin drop. The only sound was an occasional cough in the back.

"But we endure, and sustain, and endure some more. We endure!" His words came out slower, but louder.

He looked down at the star-spangled casket and shook his head wearily. He stooped a little as if suddenly all of the weight of the moment had fallen onto his shoulders.

"I am sorry, Son. But I cannot celebrate your life right now. I am angry that you left me. Your job was to stand up here and bury me! Heck, I don't know what God thinks. Maybe this was God's will. But it certainly was not my will. I will miss you, Son."

He pulled his eyes from the casket and again looked out at the gathering.

"Remember this day, people. And don't any of you, in a moment of despair, make this ultimate indiscretion. Don't do it. Don't do it. That's all I have to say."

The admiral returned to his seat in the front pew and Father Hartman finished the mass.

The casket was walked at dirge-speed into the hearse by the deceased admiral's staff. The immediate family followed the casket out. Jay's mom went weak in the knees a couple of times and needed to be supported by her son and son-in-law. After helping Mom get in first, the rest piled into a black limousine. A lengthy funeral procession followed the hearse to Arlington National Cemetery.

The Brown family sat in the same order at the cemetery. Five riflemen rendered the fifteen-gun salute toward the sky. The initial five-gun report caused the entire Brown clan to just about jump out of their skin. The noisy salute seemed to the Browns inappropriate considering the manner in which Admiral James Brown met his demise. The second volley seemed way too loud. By the third and last round, well, it seemed like way too many shots were being fired.

"Taps" was played by a bugler, Sam Kuhls, that had, so they said, attended Annapolis with the admiral, but Jane had never heard James mention him. The six-member honor guard meticulously collected the flag from the coffin and folded it twelve times. The head of the honor guard tried to hand the flag to the widow, but Jane starred blankly into the honor guard's eyes with her hands folded on her lap. Jay watched his mother with consternation on his face. The guard was uncertain how to proceed. Jane would not reach out and accept the flag, so he looked to the admiral for guidance. Jay's grandfather nodded and the guard placed the folded flag gently upon the widow's lap. She put one hand tentatively on the flag, as if to admit defeat. By accepting the flag she was accepting the fact that James, who had been her boyfriend since she was a girl, her one and only, was gone for good. Jay and Janet wrapped their arms around their grieving mother. The grandfather and son-in-law quickly followed. Enveloped now in a familial cocoon, Jay's mom sobbed.

Jay stayed with his mother for a few days after the burial. Janet, Mike and the grandfather visited frequently. Except for Jay, who lived in Connecticut, they all lived nearby and travel was not a problem.

Time was a blur. There were so many things to take care of. To everyone's dread, that included cleaning out the Pentagon office where Jay's dad shot himself.

That day, they knew, when it finally came, would be one seriously bad day, a day that laid heavy on the shoulders and made the knees ache. It would be a day that tightened the skull, now full to the brim with emotional trauma, morbid curiosity and a smack of intrigue. Not surprisingly, Jay pulled the clean-out-the-office duty, so he filled his lungs with a deep breath and took on the assignment with a gloomy tenacity. Jay had to battle an irrational notion that, the instant he entered that office, a part of him was going to die too, the part of him that was a son, perpetually learning from his dad, his *life teacher*.

On the dreaded day, Jay wore his khaki uniform and one row of three ribbons above his left pocket representing his highest decorations. For an LCDR, Jay was highly and exceptionally decorated. His highest award was a Distinguished Service Medal ribbon (DSM). Next was a Meritorious Service Medal with three stars, indicating that he received this award four times. The final ribbon, closest to his shoulder, was a Presidential Unit Citation (PUC), a distinctive ribbon with horizontal blue, yellow and red stripes. Above his ribbons were his Gold Dolphins; below was a silver scuba diver pin.

He drove his own car, parked and approached the five-sided building on foot. The sign read, "Staff Entrance." Jay pulled out his ID. There was a marine on duty.

"Good morning."

"Morning, sir."

Jay saw it in the marine's face as he read the ID. He recognized the name. The marine looked like he was working on something to say but remained mute. Instead, he snapped off an especially proud salute, which Jay returned with gooseflesh running down his back.

Now the marine spoke, but—in an unfamiliar social situation—struggled with proper etiquette, not to mention English: "I have instructions to call your father's, I mean, the ex-admiral, I mean…"

The guard's nameplate identified him as Staff Sergeant Kenneth Crafton.

"Relax, Staff Sergeant. I understand you have to call my father's staff to come down and get me. This is certainly not a routine you are used to."

"Yes sir, thank you, sir. It's just that I knew Vice Admiral Brown. I was always part of his special security details. He treated me and the other marines well. He followed marine officer tradition and made sure the men ate first. That's a silly example, sir, but I am sad that he is no longer with us."

"Knock it off, Staff Sergeant Crafton. You are going to get me all choked up before I even start this process."

"I apologize, sir. Can I call in some marines to help you?" asked Crafton.

"No. The big stuff I am just going to label and have the navy ship to my mother's house."

"Sir, are you certain you trust government movers? I can call on the standby security detail. I can secure a truck, a large roll of bubble wrap and some tape in less than thirty minutes. It would be my pleasure, and the U.S. Marine Corps' pleasure."

"Good point. Government movers could fuck up a wet dream. I don't want anyone to break regulations—but I might take you up on this."

"Sir, I will get the wheels in motion after I call the vice admiral's staff." Crafton returned in just under a minute. "Staff Analyst Lieutenant Commander Voxer is coming to get you."

Jay thought, Voxer? Voxer? He'd had a classmate named Joe Voxer. Last Jay heard, the guy had gone navy air—but maybe he shifted to intelligence. Truth was, Jay hoped this Voxer was a different guy. He hadn't been particularly fond of Voxer in school. He was kind of arrogant—perfect personality for a navy aviator. Ha! The trouble with pilots during warfare? They had too much damned fun!

But it was probably Joe Voxer. That would figure. That would be just his luck, emptying out Dad's office with that ass wipe watching. He thought about his grandfather's eulogy and felt anger toward his father. And that was what he was thinking when he looked up.

And saw *her*.

Walking out of the Pentagon staff entrance with the grace of a thoroughbred race horse's gait came the lovely Cassie Jones, another classmate of Jay's, now an LCDR. Cassie looked just fine in her dress blues with no name tag. Cassie had light-brown hair, cute little haircut, short, just above her collar. She was petite but with a voluptuous yet athletic build—voluptuous but athletic in the hottest possible way. Looking at her now as she approached, Jay felt a somewhat intense wakening. Spotting her, Crafton also snapped to attention and saluted. Cassie returned the salute.

Jay and Cassie hugged each other. Cassie felt something during their embrace that made her think about it way too much later.

Jay said, "Cassie, how the hell are you? What a pleasant surprise. I haven't seen you in nine years."

"I saw you at the funeral. But you didn't see me."

"I was totally numb that day. I shook hands with the president and I barely remember. I am still pretty numb actually."

"I completely understand."

"So where is Voxer?"

"I am Voxer."

"Really, you didn't marry our classmate Voxer, did you?" Jay's distaste was evident.

"As a matter of fact I did!"

Ug, Jay thought. Open mouth, insert foot.

"I am sorry, Cassie. I didn't mean to say it that way. I hope you are very happily married to our former classmate. Is he flying?"

"Don't worry about it, Jay. Yes, Joe is flying. He is an F-18 pilot, currently deployed. Well..." Cassie clasped her hands together and squeezed rather tightly. "OK then, I know you have a lot to do, so let's get up to the office. Maybe we can catch up tonight over dinner."

Cassie turned to lead Jay into the Pentagon. He'd been there before, of course, but at that moment he was aware of how enormous the complex was, headquarters for a military that served as the world's police force. If only it all wasn't so goddamn necessary.

Jay paused and looked back toward the guard. "Staff Sergeant, I will call you in a bit. Thank you for your help."

"Sir, you are very welcome. And one other thing: dream on...sir."

Jay gave the marine a smirk and jogged in the wake of LCDR Voxer's remarkable kinetics.

Dad's suite had four work stations in an outer space that provided the entry way into his private office. He'd been a deputy chief of naval operations, a guy who—as his position implied—reported directly to the CNO, a guy who was director of naval intelligence, and all that that implied. Dad was one spooky dude.

The work station against the window and closest to the admiral's office was occupied by Captain Robert Royce, the chief of staff, a pudgy man with soft fat fingers and the thick lips of a spoiled child. You looked at him, and—no matter how hard you tried—you couldn't imagine this guy making it through basic.

The other window station belonged to Cassie. Across from Cassie sat Silvia Boyle. Jay had met her before. It was rumored that she had been sitting at that same desk on D-Day.

The final desk was manned by the flag lieutenant, or *aide de camp*, Lieutenant Jeff Cody.

Royce was the acting director until the admiral's replacement. During normal operations, the porcine Royce was the gatekeeper, managing the admiral's schedule. He also screened all correspondence: messages, email and letters.

Cody, the flag looie, drew the crappy jobs that the chief of staff didn't want to do. He arranged transportation and coordinated events. His entire week was dedicated to the funeral and burial of Jay's father.

Silvia Boyle handled all correspondence in and out of the office, and maintained the files. She knew how to keep her mouth shut. Dad had been her fifth director of naval intelligence. The job was spy versus spy, she knew, and it could chew a man up.

Jay learned that Cassie was Dad's staff analyst. She did real operational navy work on a daily basis: reviewed messages and daily briefs, and digested the info down to the items that would interest him. She arrived at 0600, briefed the admiral at 0730.

All members of the staff held top secret clearances with polygraph. As Jay entered the office, they stood to greet Jay in the proper pecking order, starting with Captain Royce.

"I am very sorry for your loss, Lieutenant Commander Brown. We all miss the admiral. We are also very sad how…" Captain Royce faded. "I mean…"

"It is quite all right, Captain Royce. This is an awkward situation for all of us. Thank you for your kind regards, sir."

Captain Royce continued: "Lieutenant Cody will be assisting you with the gathering of the personal effects. We will arrange to have it shipped."

"Captain, if it's OK with you, I have transportation arranged with the marine transportation division of the Pentagon to haul the stuff away today."

"No, that is really not appropriate."

"Captain, if you are concerned with the approval, I think Admiral Conner is right down that passageway. I would be happy to get his approval if needed. He told me at the funeral to call him if I needed anything. It will be easier on my mother if she has some help putting his personal belongings away, and I am heading back to my boat this weekend."

"We can have it delivered as early as tomorrow."

Jay didn't like the fact that the captain was being adamant. It made Jay feel stubborn, so he stretched the truth like silly putty.

"Captain, I am sorry to be difficult, but my mother, grandfather and sister are all lined up to help me put this away tonight. Let's talk to Admiral Conner. He asked me to check in with him today anyway," said Jay.

The captain was clearly outmanned.

"That's fine, Jay," said Captain Royce.

"Thank you, sir."

Lieutenant Jeff Cody and Silvia Boyle were next to offer condolences. Jeff came off as submissive in an unhealthy way, like a beaten dog. Jay wondered if maybe Jeff had an abusive father. Jay chided himself for psycho-analyzing the poor guy based on slumped shoulders and a fluctuating ability to maintain eye contact.

Jeff Cody wasn't quick enough with his condolences, apparently, as Captain Royce called out, "Cody, we have to get this party started. I don't want to keep the admiral's family waiting."

Jeff nearly jumped out of his skin when the captain spoke. Clearly the dog beater was Royce.

"Aye aye, sir," said Cody. "I'll get my things together to inventory the personal belongings." He gathered his papers onto a clipboard and stood at the ready.

Jay greeted Silvia, who looked like a cookie-baking grandmother. She spoke softly and was very complimentary of the deceased admiral.

Silvia said, "God bless you—and your family, Jay." As she shook his hand, she slipped him a note that had been neatly folded and palmed. She whispered, "Call me if you ever want to talk. That is my home phone." She leaned forward even more and said softly, "That Royce son of a bitch is one of the biggest douche bags I have ever worked with. You heard me correctly: a major D.B."

Cody heard "D.B.," knew instantly what Silvia was talking about, and spontaneously burst forth with a gloriously broad and toothy grin.

Cassie Voxer sat at her desk and worked her computer. Something about the way her fingers danced over the keyboard made him think of the Russian cat-woman, the way she smelled, the feel of her lips on his cheeks, and her supernatural guitar capabilities.

Jay told himself to get a grip. It was just an old friend hard at work. But, oh me oh my. Cassie worked feverishly, yet maintained a perfect posture. You could have balanced a slender volume on her fine head. Her fingers were curled and her typing was quick and precise, just the way she'd learned it in a military typing class. Seriously, Jay admired that. He still had to hunt and peck, and made three, four typos per line. He also admired the cut of her jib which, he had to admit, made him feel a little funny. Cassie appeared to be on a deadline, and ignored all around her.

Captain Royce took a phone call. Jay didn't absorb the meaning of Royce's words, just their tone, which dripped with a nasty over-sized sense of personal domain. This was a man that felt it was his right to abuse others—verbally, at least—and who knew what else?

"Cody," Royce said. "List everything that is to be taken out of the office. Make certain that every item removed from the Pentagon receives a property tag and is noted on a property transportation list."

Jay said, "As per Admiral Conner's instructions, I can take anything from the office that is not a permanent fixture. He specifically mentioned that this included the desk and chair." Jay originally had not intended to take the furniture, but with Royce's snotty attitude he reconsidered.

"All right, I'm going in," Jay said, and took a deep breath.

Cody turned the doorknob and opened the door, and Jay bravely strode through the threshold.

Jay's first thought: Bigger than he figured. At least as large or larger than the entry office occupied by his staff.

His second thought: The desk was large and oak and fantastic. Jay knew his dad had carved his initials in it somewhere, but who knew where? He remembered talking to his brother-in-law Michael O'Brien about it. The admiral had been carving his initials in his furniture since he was seven, and the locations of the carvings had grown more elusive with time. The initials carved into the desk were probably not in an easy-to-find spot.

With his third thought, Jay swallowed back panic:

Dad shot himself in this room. With a dreadful expression, he searched for signs of gore. He sniffed for the wafting scent of death. But all surfaces were shiny and clean. All he could smell was Lemon Pledge.

Jay had to combat the horrible images that invaded his brain just then. Dad. With a gun. Not just any gun. His service pistol. Turning it on himself. The barrel to his chest.

With two shaky steps, and then three more that were self-assured, Jay circled around the desk to look at the wall behind it. His eyes scanned up and down, and then from side to side. He examined the chair.

"There was no exit," Cody said.

"Tell me about the night," Jay replied crisply, almost startling Cody.

"Do you really want to hear this, sir?"

"Please tell me."

"Captain Royce found the body at around 2200 hours. There'd been a reception. After, they both came back to the office, just to pick up some things before going home. The admiral said he had some things to take care of and stayed behind while Royce headed home. Royce got all the way to the parking garage and had forgotten his car keys in his coat. When he came back, he found the admiral."

"When did you find out?"

"Lieutenant Commander Voxer, Silvia and I were all called at home and notified. We were to report into the office for questioning at 0700 hours."

"Did you personally see the body?"

"No, by the time we got there in the morning the admiral was no longer there."

"What about the note?"

"We all received the same email from the admiral. I've had it printed." Cody reached in his top pocket, unfolded a piece of paper and handed it to Jay. Jay had heard about the note but had not seen it. The note read as follows:

From: Vice Admiral James R. Brown, Jr. USN
To: Dist
Subj: Farewell My Friends
To my sailors, loved ones, Pa, Jay, Janet, Mike and my beloved Jane.

I never intended to take the coward's way out, but at this point there is more honor in death than in living.
I hope you all find it in your hearts to forgive me someday.

V/R
James

Jay read the note and could feel the words hurting him, ripping open internal wounds. *Don't lose it, don't lose it,* he repeated to himself. Instead of losing it, he took a few deep breaths and handed the note back to Cody.

"Could I get a copy of that?"

"Of course, sir. You know I am not supposed to even have this copy. I will make you a copy. Just don't tell anyone where you got it."

"Who said you can't make a copy?"

"Captain Royce."

"This Royce seems like a real beauty."

"That's one term for it."

Cody and Jay systematically and efficiently tagged everything for removal. Jay started with the desk, and moved on to the office chair, a coffee table, a wooden submarine model and a model of an old wooden ship with square rigged sails. Jay scanned an inventory in his mind.

"Hey, where is my dad's pistol?"

Pause.

"Well?"

"It's in the captain's safe."

"Well, I want it. Do you want to talk with the captain, or should I?"

Cody replied, "I'll talk to him. If I need you, I'll come get you."

Cody departed, perhaps a little relieved to be getting away from the grieving son, and Jay was in his father's office alone for the first time. He scanned the walls and ceiling, the beautiful rug, just like the ones they always had at home. The admiral chose them because they simulated the pace of a real green when he practiced his putting.

Jay imagined if things were different, if his dad were still alive. The daydream was short-lived as Jay heard voices rising in the other office.

Surprisingly, the voice he heard was Cody's: "The marines are transporting everything. Of course, they can transport a firearm. He will just pull the CNO card, sir. Do you want to appear to be unsupportive of a three-star's family, sir?"

"Fuck it," said Captain Royce. It sounded even dirtier when it came out of that despicable mouth.

Royce went over to a painting of a submarine at dock in New London that was hanging on the office wall. Behind that painting was the artillery safe/locker. Royce's fingers were nimble as he spun the dial, causing the tumblers to fall into place. Three turns of his wrist and a tug, and the safe was open. Cody positioned himself to look into the safe and saw there were five boxes in there. Royce reached in with both hands and pulled one box out, a wooden box that housed a Colt 1911 .45 pistol.

Cody returned to the admiral's office with the box. Jay called the marines, using the phone number that Staff Sergeant Crafton had given him.

Captain Royce poked his head in the admiral's office and said, "I am securing for the evening. You are in good hands with Cody. Here is my card with my contact information if you ever need anything. I am sorry to meet under such sad circumstances. Your dad is—was—a great man." Royce extended his hand to Jay, they shook hands, and Royce departed.

The instant Royce was gone, Silvia came in and gave Jay a hug.

"You have my number. Feel free to call me even if you just want to talk. It's going to take some time to get over what we have all experienced. I have seen many, many directors of naval intelligence over the past, well, several decades. Your dad was the most hardworking and dedicated of all of them. God bless you and your family."

Silvia was still looking deeply, almost searchingly, into Jay's eyes when Staff Sergeant Crafton arrived. Cody immediately started verbally listing the items that were going. It was a long list, yet one that Cody had apparently memorized.

"No problem, sir," Crafton said, unfazed by the size of the task.

Crafton's communication device looked futuristic.

"What is that thing?" Jay asked.

"Nextel radio. Like a walkie-talkie, only it involves satellites!" Crafton said. What Crafton didn't say was that it was cellular technology, like the phones people had, but shielded from the listening ears of foreign enemies.

Jay said good-bye to Silvia.

To Cassie, he said, "You still up for dinner? I should be free in a couple of hours."

"Oh, I don't want to take you away from your family this evening," said Cassie.

"To tell the truth, there is no one home. I said that to mess with Royce. I just have to put all this stuff in my mom's garage, lock up the pistol, and it's either a TV dinner or out with my classmate."

"But, I thought..." Cassie stopped and re-started: "Never mind, of course. Let's meet at Union Street in Old Town at 2000.

"It's a date, er, a deal, I mean."

"Shut up, Jay. I know what you mean. See you at eight, and don't be late. We have a lot to catch up on." She was collecting her things to go home.

There could be no doubt about it: The marines were the world's greatest movers. In a flurry of activity, shouted instructions—lean it to the right to get it through the door, let's put a blanket over it so it won't scratch—the admiral's office was stripped bare.

All that remained was the wooden box. Cody, Jay and Crafton stood together in the outer office.

Crafton said, "Sir, I need to look at the weapon to make sure the serial number matches what's on the controlled equipage list."

"Sure, Staff Sergeant, here you go."

Crafton opened the box, checked the serial number against that on the controlled equipage list. He appeared perplexed.

"Don't tell me the numbers are wrong?" said Jay.

"I checked the numbers three times. I know they are right."

Crafton's brow was deeply furrowed. He ran through a checklist in his mind and didn't like the answers he was giving himself.

"The numbers are right, I just do not know why you are taking this pistol instead of the one that was your father's." Crafton said.

"What do you mean?" said Jay.

"Yeah, what do you mean?" echoed Cody.

"Your dad shot himself with an ivory handle service 1911. I know because I checked the piece out. It was a classic Colt 1911 Commander with pearl grips. This is definitely not your father's firearm."

IV

AUGUST 31ST, 1992, WASHINGTON, D.C./ ALEXANDRIA, VA

Good God, Jay thought, feeling fatigue blend with frustration, confusion, and grief. *Could life get anymore complicated?* He didn't really *want* the gun. He'd read an article somewhere along the line that said it was psychologically harmful to keep souvenirs of bad happenings. Bad-vibe memorabilia tended to reinforce rather than alleviate trauma. Still, he felt it was important for him to have it. There was something about the events of the day, the attitude of Royce in particular, that made him feel it was important. The gun could be a link to something—somewhere, somehow—to help explain why his father shot himself.

"You have to be shitting me, Staff Sergeant Crafton."

Cody mouthed the words "douche bag" toward Jay.

"Sirs, clearly there has been an error, but not one difficult to rectify," Crafton said. "For it just so happens, as the on-duty NCO for the Pentagon security detachment, I have access to every artillery locker in the Pentagon." Crafton pulled a ring of keys from under his shirt where they hung on a lanyard around his neck. He quickly chose a key, put the key in the safe, spun the combination and opened the safe.

"Uncanny, Staff Sergeant Crafton," Jay said, "I am very lucky to have crossed your path."

"Sir, I am just doing what I am supposed to be doing. Let's take a look at the fine pieces in this safe."

Crafton's admiration for the firearms in the safe disconcerted Jay. It was hardly the time or place for fun, yet there was a note of mischief in Crafton's voice. Jay thought maybe he was being too heavy. He kept thinking of the gun as a symbol of his father's death, when in reality, when you stripped the emotions away and looked at the raw reality, the gun was just a tool, like a hammer or a wrench. This line of thought sent Jay spiraling down a swirling maelstrom of ugly images as his fatigued mind tormented him. He saw other ways his father might have chosen to commit suicide and many of them weren't pretty. Hell, all of them weren't pretty, but some of them were downright gruesome, and he shook his head to jerk himself back into reality.

Crafton flipped happily through the wooden boxes and found the ivory-handled piece.

"Here it is, sir."

"May I take a look, Staff Sergeant?" said Jay.

"Of course, sir"

Jay stared at the pistol.

"You can handle it; it has been cleaned. Only one shot was fired out of it."

"It must have been a mess," Jay said.

"Actually not at all, sir. Do you really want to hear this?"

"Yes, please."

"Roger that, sir. The suicide was conducted with a single low-power lead semi-wadcutter bullet, the kind you use for bull's-eye pistol shooting. Interestingly enough, this is one of your dad's target pistols, but one out of which its user would typically shoot full load, full metal jacket bullets. The semi-wadcutter bullet punched a neat hole in his chest and bounced around his chest cavity, never to exit."

"Where did he get the ammo?"

"He must have brought the one bullet from home. We only have full metal jacket ammo in the lockers. There was a partial fingerprint on the bullet that matched the vice admiral's."

Jay, Dad and Grandpa were lifelong bull's-eye pistol shooters. The .45 caliber Colt 1911 and the .22 caliber Smith and Wesson Model 42 were their target pistols of choice. Grandpa loaded his own ammunition for target shooting and had reloading equipment in his basement.

Jay thought, *Goddamn it, Dad. Tainted forever. A hobby we all enjoyed together. Now, just a reminder of this nightmare you've left us.*

Jay heard himself speak. "OK, Staff Sergeant, thank you very much. Let's get the paperwork in order and this stuff out of here. I will meet the truck at my mom's in Alexandria."

"Roger that, sir," said Crafton.

"You should leave."

"Captain Royce insisted I stay until the office was empty and locked up."

"Do you anticipate any trouble with the pistol swap?"

"What pistol swap?" Crafton asked, and left to join the rest of the moving crew at the truck.

When the office was secured, Cody stood in the hallway looking lost.

"Cody, would you like to join Cassie and me for dinner?"

Jay thought: Cassie wouldn't mind, right? Heck, she was a married woman. Right?

"Thank you, sir. I would like that," Cody said. "I do not have appropriate civvies, sir."

"We're about the same size. You can wear some of my duds."

"Aye aye, sir." Cody reminded Jay of a puppy going on a road trip, so excited to jump in the car. Jay felt like he was leading a convoy to Alexandria—he in his dad's '86 ragtop Corvette, and the white marine moving truck just behind, carrying Crafton and his burly colleagues.

Jay learned Cody's life history during the drive. Jay asked one question and listened most of the way to his mom's. Cody was Annapolis, class of 1988, math major. Entering the service, Cody became an NSA cryptographer. Cody was only recently assigned as flag lieutenant for

Vice Admiral Brown. It was highly unusual for an admiral to choose an *aide de camp* that didn't match his warfare specialty—in this case, submarines.

"It was a coveted position with many worthwhile candidates," Cody said.

"Why did my old man pick you, Cody?"

"He said he liked my mind. His words, not mine. And he trusted me. What sucks is, now a new admiral will be assigned and will bring his own guy and I will be crunching Bessel functions in the NSA next month." Cody paused for a second then said, "I am so sorry. My problems are so small compared to yours."

"What did my dad have you doing?"

"Actually, the admiral had me working on a project that he termed his own puzzle project, seeking patterns and ciphers out of some musical scores. They were Russian classical guitar pieces. Nice music, but I could never get a bead on anything."

"Funny, I used to play classical guitar—but if you tell anyone I will have to kill you."

"Wow, why is it such a secret? Did you transmit codes via your music?"

"I am just kidding, but I really don't want to be labeled as a musician."

"Ahh, joke."

"Mail me the music you were analyzing when you get a chance. Just send it to the *Quincy*," said Jay.

"Will do, sir. I tried everything, even tried to capture code from the fretting of the guitar."

"Any idea where the music came from?"

"I shouldn't know this, but it was music Captain Douche Bag used as background music for a PR video we put out."

"Public relations?"

"Yeah. Soliciting our services to the Soviets, er, former Soviets."

"How did Captain D.B. wind up on the staff?"

"He was the chief of staff for now-retired Vice Admiral Hicks, your dad's predecessor. Vice Admiral Brown kept him on for some project that was started by *his* predecessor, a project for which I lacked authorized access."

"Very interesting," replied Jay, reprising the old *Laugh-In* running gag.

They continued to drive south on route 395 with modest traffic and got off at the King Street exit. Jay's parents' home was on a quiet cul-de-sac in lovely Rosemont. As they approached, streets grew narrower. At one point, when they were only houses away from their destination, the government truck smacked hard on some low-hanging tree branches.

"What's that noise?" Jay asked.

Cody craned his neck. "The truck is having trouble getting under those trees back there."

Jay stopped and looked back.

Crafton yelled out the window, "We're good to go, Commander. Onward and upward. Uh rah!"

Without further incident, the two-vehicle convoy arrived at its destination. Jay jogged up the driveway and opened both doors to the two-car garage. Jay drove the Corvette into the right bay. The truck backed down the driveway and faced the bay to the left. The marines opened the truck and unloaded everything into the garage. The desk, coffee table, ship model and art would eventually be moved into the house, but for now the garage was good enough. There were five cardboard totes of personal effects, including some clothing, photos and files.

While the marines were unloading, Jay grabbed two six-packs of Budweiser beer from the kitchen refrigerator and offered them to the men.

The staff sergeant saw the beer and said, "Commander, we could not think of taking your beer."

"Please, Staff Sergeant, I am heading back to the fleet at the end of the week, and my mother doesn't drink beer." That mustered no reaction, so Jay continued, "It will go to waste, and might serve as a painful reminder for my mom."

Crafton replied, "In that case, we will be happy to be of service."

The beer lasted seventeen minutes.

When it was time for the marines to pack up and go, Staff Sergeant Crafton saluted Jay, then turned and walked away in tears. Alone now, Jay and Cody sat in the garage.

Jay said, "Cody, when we go out tonight with Cassie, let's stay off the topic of my dad. I need a fucking break. I just want to talk about the navy and our careers and how we are going to solve all the world's problems. I'll say the same thing to Cassie, but if you can help, I would appreciate it."

"I understand. Speaking of Cassie, we had better get going."

"I promised you civvies," Jay said, slapping the tops of his thighs as he stood.

The men shifted into standard liberty attire, jeans, and tee shirts with logos representing a naval operation.

"I'm in intelligence, not submarines. Is it bad form to wear a shirt commemorating an operation of which you weren't a part?" Cody asked.

"I don't think it's a big deal."

"What other shirts do you have?"

"Come on, it's not like you are pretending to be a SEAL. The worst thing that can happen is some bubble head will hit you with his slide rule. Pick a damn shirt."

Jay donned a USS *Groton* West Pac 89 tee shirt. Cody finally settled on a Rim Pac tee shirt that had no submarine dolphins on it but did sport a drawing of a submarine. The shirts were designed by members of a submarine crew during a major exercise. They were sold to raise funds for the ship's "recreation and fun fund" a.k.a. the beer money.

Jay and Cody got back in the convertible, top down, and headed down King Street to Old Town, just minutes from Rosemont. Finding parking was an unexpected hassle and they ended up five minutes late entering the Union Street Public House. Sitting at the middle of the bar was Cassie—shining, Jay thought, as if illuminated from inside—in jeans and a light blue mock turtleneck shirt. As she turned and saw him, her face lit up with a big smile. Jay was grinning ear to ear. She was so much prettier than he remembered.

No words were exchanged as Jay approached her, then Cassie noticed Cody and her face fell.

"You're late," she said.

"Uhhh, traffic was…"

"Never mind, Jay, it doesn't matter."

She stood and gave Jay a hug. She smelled and felt great to him. Like heaven. He told himself to snap out of it. But that was going to have to wait until the end of the hug, which didn't come as fast as one might think. This ran three Mississippis past being a casual hug. When the old friends finally separated, Cassie looked at Cody.

"Hey, Cody."

"Hi, Cassie."

He approached her for a hug and she stiff-armed him with a thump to his chest.

"Ow," Cody said, and used his fingertips to gently massage his sternum.

"Don't worry, Cody. I'm a trained professional. It won't leave a mark. Let's get a booth," said Cassie.

Cassie chose one in the back right corner. She sat, and Jay sat across from her. Cody was indecisive. Which side to sit on? He decided to sit next to Jay.

The waitress stopped by, chewing gum and trying not to look bored. Tips suffered when she looked bored.

"Drinks?"

They all wanted a mug of draft beer.

"Coming right up," the waitress said and sashayed away. Tips improved when she sashayed away.

Jay raised his glass, "Cheers, old and new friends. I regret we were not meeting under better circumstances."

Cassie and Cody replied, "Hear, hear." Everyone took an especially large swallow. After a day of emotional upheaval, a draft beer was the perfect prescription.

"So Jay, how do you become an XO just nine years out of school?" Cassie inquired. "Some of our classmates are just going into their department head tours."

"I have no life," Jay said with a small laugh. "So, I spend all my time drilling holes in the ocean."

"You make it sound sad," Cassie said.

"Not sad. Maybe one-dimensional. I have had little to no shore duty with the exception of nuke and submarine schools. I have become sort of an expert on the first flight 688. I'm like the guy who has the only key to the men's room. Operational necessity keeps bringing me back to the fleet, after back-to-back sea tours. I have almost seven years of sea time. It's fucked up."

"And they say the operational tempo has ramped down after the Cold War," said Cassie.

Jay didn't want to talk about operational tempo. "What about you, Cassie?"

"Well, I am about to get deployed for the first time—just as my husband rolls off being deployed for most of our marriage. He is getting back from a six-month Mediterranean deployment and I am being assigned to a forward deployed asset continuing some work I started for your father."

"About which you can't tell me or you would have to kill me."

"Exactly," replied Cassie.

The three discussed their jobs, and their dysfunctional work relationships. The conversation didn't get too personal, although Cassie had made it clear that she'd spent most of her marriage bunking alone, a factor that Jay suspected meant she was restless and lonesome. Not that he was an expert on women. What he knew about women was a thimble-full of knowledge in an ocean of mystery. Nobody talked about the recent tragedy, which suited Jay just fine.

They drank more beer and ate pizza. As things wound down, Jay paid the check.

Cassie said, "Can you give me a lift home, Jay? I took a cab over, but at this hour I would rather a ride with my two charming escorts."

Cody replied, "No room, Commander. We are in a two-seat Corvette. Sweet ride. Convertible."

Jay smiled at Cassie. "Too bad, Cody," Jay said. "We are either going to have to strap you to the back, or you are going to have to cab home. Lady and rank first."

Cody was a little hurt by the unexpected turn of events, but he adjusted well. "Ahh. OK, sure, I can take a cab."

Cassie said, "Of course you can."

On the street, it was a mild and calm summer night. There was a slight breeze coming in off the ocean. They worked together to flag down a cab. Mission accomplished, Jay and Cassie strolled lazily down the street to the Corvette.

Jay's mind was cooking now. Elongate the moment, he told himself. "Do you want to take a walk over by the marina before we head home?"

"Sure," she said and moved a little closer to him, almost ready to settle in under his arm, but not quite.

They walked a couple of blocks to the marina and looked at the boats. Jay stood close enough now to feel the warmth of Cassie's body. She raised her arms and leaned back into Jay. He wrapped his arms around her from behind and her hands came down upon Jay's head and hair. They remained this way for almost a minute then Cassie pushed Jay away.

"Oh my, this is so wrong. I am sorry. I am a married woman. I am so sorry."

"Relax, Cassie. We didn't do anything."

Cassie was clearly shaken and disturbed. She held her head in her hands for a moment.

"Why didn't you call me after we graduated? Why didn't you? That thing that just happened just now, that thing felt good to me, way too good. Clearly, you don't feel that same way."

"Cassie, you are married."

"You didn't even know I was married until today, you *putz*. What about the last nine years?"

Cassie thumped Jay on the chest. It was apparently her assault point of choice. Painful—but, of course, it could have been worse.

"I didn't think you liked me. I was such a geek in school," he said, but he didn't like the sound of it when he said it.

"Why didn't you ask? I wrote you letters. Of course you were a geek! You're still a geek. I love geeks!"

"I answered every letter you wrote me."

"You answered the letters like they were letters to your mother or sister or something. I hate your guts, Jay Brown. I hate yours and your dad's. You both abandoned me."

As the great Jim Croce would have put it, had he been there, Jay looked a little like a jigsaw puzzle with a couple of pieces gone.

Cassie looked up at Jay through her tears. She hurled herself forward into his arms and hugged him tightly.

"I am so sorry. That was so selfish and uncalled for. I am so sorry."

"And I'm so sick of people telling me they are sorry. I don't want this kind of attention. I don't want to be the guy whose dad shot himself in the Pentagon. You think you hate Vice Fucking Admiral James Brown Junior? Well, I hate his guts."

Jay burst into tears on Cassie's shoulder. Some people coming and going from their boats passed them, ogled a bit out of curiosity, but kept walking.

So, Jay and Cassie cried together for a few minutes, then composed themselves. They found a park bench overlooking the water to sit on.

Cassie said, "I know you didn't want to talk about this tonight, but, hell, we are already both such a mess. Do you mind if I go there?"

"No Cassie, go as you please!"

"I just don't understand it. Your dad was, like, on top of the world. The consummate professional, clean living, loved by everyone. He seemed to genuinely enjoy people. He even got along with that creep Royce. It makes no sense."

"There is an investigation going on by the CNO's office," Jay replied. "Maybe it will shed some light on the situation. I am surprised by what you just said, Cassie. I have spent so much time at sea, very little contact with my family over the past nine years. I thought, maybe, he unraveled under all the pressure of Washington and the Pentagon, intelligence and counter-intelligence. Everyone thinks I'm the youngest executive officer in the fleet because my daddy is a vice admiral. Was. But I hardly ever spoke to him. I remember every fucking conversation I ever had with the man. Mostly he asked me questions and I answered. And I hadn't spoken to him at all in a long time. What was he working on?"

"I can't talk about it. But I will tell you that even if I blabbed everything I knew, you wouldn't be any closer to figuring out why your dad did what he did. I only know my pieces and parts. He was definitely working on something tied to the Russian government's nuclear material cleanup program, which happy taxpayers will be pleased to learn was sponsored by the U.S. government to the tune of billions of dollars. The program is completely unclassified, but there are aspects of the program that naval intelligence is deeply involved in."

"I am not familiar even with the unclassified aspects of this program. Can you give me the flag summary?" said Jay. That is, "in a nutshell."

"Sure. Post Cold War, U.S. is helping the Russians and other former Soviet nations to inventory, catalogue, and safely store all of the non-installed nuclear material associated with nuclear power and nuclear propulsion. Nothing to do with weapons-grade nuclear material. Only power- and propulsion-related nuclear material. In the old Soviet Union, there were many facilities that supported nuclear power and propulsion plants. We—the U.S. of A.—want to help our new allies to control this material for the benefit of all of the world's inhabitants. Of course, when you are talking about a multi-billion dollar spend—and some of the very corrupt governments that remain in former Soviet nations—you get all kinds of possible trouble."

"Very interesting. Who are the benefactors of the money?"

"U.S., international and former Soviet nations are all collecting on this one. A few humongous U.S. defense contractors are getting most of the money. The usual suspects. War Profiteers, Inc. Now they are making the big bucks off of peace, but you have to wonder."

"What was the last thing my dad was involved in?"

"A reception in the Pentagon with a group of former Soviets, the defense contractors and a bunch of brass from all services. Naval intelligence was basically doing a public relations campaign to offer their services to watch-dog the massive cleanup process."

"What was the entertainment for the reception? Was there any?" asked Jay.

"Kind of a strange question."

"Uh huh."

"Well, there were classical Russian guitarists."

"No kidding, any chance you could get me a recording of the music?"

"Sure, the whole event was taped from multiple angles—audio and video. I should tell you, Jay, we have already reviewed the tapes. There was nothing but the typical sniffing-each-other's-butt dialogue that goes on at those events. Diplomatic drivel and its ilk."

"I just want the background music. All of it, please."

"I don't think that is a problem. I can make an audio copy of the tape. I'll put it on a cassette. I don't think we can separate the music from other ambient noises in the big room, at least not without some complicated audio forensics."

"I think background noise will be OK. As long as I can hear the notes that are being played."

"You know something..."

"Can't tell you."

"Have to kill me?"

"Seriously, though, Cassie, if you could, please send me the cassettes. Send them to me on the *Quincy*, and please keep it to yourself."

"This will be another one of our growing number of little secrets?"

"Yes, Cassie. Before little secrets turn into big ones, let's get you home," said Jay.

Jay dropped Cassie off at her apartment—a rather tender and slightly moist kiss on the cheek followed by some soulful eye contact—then drove back to Rosemont and slept in the spare bedroom of his parents' house.

V

SEPTEMBER 1ST, 1992
WASHINGTON, D.C.

Jay awoke the next morning, a beautiful Tuesday morning, to the barking of the family dog that had just arrived home with his mother and sister.

"Jay?"

"I'm in the guest room, Mom."

The dog found Jay first.

"Hey, Lucky," Jay said happily to the black Lab.

Jay's mom had stayed overnight at his sister's house. Mom didn't want to be home when her husband's effects arrived from the Pentagon. She'd been expecting some file cabinets and was a little surprised to see the desk furniture in the garage.

Like her son, she gave everything a careful eyeballing, afraid that there might be bloodstains or other gore.

Mom and Janet entered the kitchen with noisy overlapping dialogue. The mother and daughter, Jay realized, had mastered the technique of talking and listening at the same time. The dog started barking again and a mute and slightly somnambulant Jay felt truly outnumbered.

Jay shuffled down the stairs in sweatpants, tube socks and the same tee shirt he was wearing the night before. It still smelled a little like Cassie.

The women in the kitchen now directed their simultaneous speech at Jay in the form of urgent questions.

"Did you leave anything in the office?"

"How will Mom park her car in the garage?"

"Where is all of that stuff going to go?"

"We didn't expect Daddy's whole office to be in the garage!"

Jay held out a hand of surrender.

"Wait, wait, wait. Mom, Janet, I just woke up, still pre-coffee. Give me..." He yawned. "...a chance to explain."

"I am sorry, honey," Mom said. She grabbed Jay by the back of his neck to make him stoop. Jay lowered his head and she kissed the top of it. "Let me make you some coffee. Would you like eggs?"

"He's not a baby, Mom. Let him take care of himself," Janet said.

"Whoa, who asked you?" he said to his sister, and turned to his mother: "I would love coffee, and two over easy on white toast would be great."

"You are such a spoiled brat," said Janet.

Jay stuck his tongue out at Janet while his mother turned away to make coffee.

"Would you like something, Janet?" Mom embraced the normal domesticity. Cooking breakfast was so much more fun than grieving.

"Sure, I'll have a cup of coffee too, please," Janet said. As she sat down, she mouthed, "Brat," to her brother.

Coffee was served. Jay and his sister—who really were grown-ups—stopped with the sibling rivalry shtick. Coffee was the glue that held the Brown family together. They all drank a lot of it, every day, at all hours.

Janet started, "So what's the scoop with the office in the garage?"

"I went overboard," Jay replied. "I swear, when I first went in there I planned to grab Dad's personal effects and get out. But there was this jerk, a creepy guy who'd been Dad's chief of staff, a Captain Royce. He acted so strange."

"Strange how?" Janet asked.

"He didn't want me to take things, and he didn't want me to arrange my own transport. He wanted to maintain control of that stuff.

It wasn't overt. But I sensed it. So, well, I couldn't let him have it and took it all. When he squawked, I mentioned Admiral Conner's name a couple of times and that did the trick."

"I've met Captain Royce," Mom said. "He seems like an odd one. Funny you should mention, Admiral Conner's office called me last night at Janet's and informed me the investigation is complete and he wants you and me in the Pentagon this afternoon for a debriefing."

"How did he know you were there?"

"I didn't ask. He must've...I don't know."

"What about Janet? Is she invited?" said Jay.

"I'll take a post-meeting summary, thank you very much," Jay's sister piped in. "I have no desire to set foot in the Pentagon. So, what do we do with all of this stuff?"

"Let's just put it in storage," Jay suggested. "It's really not that much stuff. It's a big desk, a big chair, coffee table, ship model and a few large portraits."

Mom said, "I just want to be able to park my car in the garage. Is that too much for a mother to ask?"

"You know what, Mom, Mike and I can just put the stuff in our basement for now," said Janet.

"Thank you, Janet. I really think all or some of that stuff is going to be important some day," said Jay.

"Even though you are a little brat, I trust your instincts," said his sister.

They ate, and sat around the kitchen table for about an hour. Janet washed, Jay dried. The conversation stayed unemotional and comfortable. Janet made arrangements for the furniture to be picked up while the others were being debriefed.

Jay uniformed up.

Mom went business casual: grey slacks, a blouse and a navy blue blazer.

She joked, "Admiral's wife uniform of the day."

"You look great, Mom. Let's get this over with," Jay said. For that she gave him another kiss on top of the head.

Jay and Jane Brown arrived at Admiral Conner's Pentagon office. The painted letters on the glass portion of the outer office read: Chief of Naval Operations. When they entered the outer office, a young man at a desk surreptitiously pressed a button, and in a heartbeat Admiral Conner himself was there greeting the widow and her son.

"Please, come into my day room," Admiral Conner said, and they followed. The day room was like a big living room with a couple of couches and, Jay counted, seven big cushioned brown leather chairs. Captain Royce was already there, and stood to greet them. Jay noticed that two of the easy chairs had been turned to face the couch and correctly assumed that this was where they'd settle. The admiral and the douche bag took the easy chairs. Jay and his mother took the couch. Between the couch and the chairs was a coffee table, and on it were four red folders. Two thin red folders were positioned in front of the couch for Jay and his mom. A slightly thicker folder was in front of the admiral, and in front of Royce sat a cassette tape recorder/player, a small moleskin black binder and an almost one-inch thick red folder.

Admiral Conner started: "I am very sorry to be meeting you just nine days after the death of your beloved husband and father."

Mom's response was uncharacteristically snippy: "Frank, spare us the horse shit and tell us what you know. This is so confusing for me and our family. If you could get to the point, it would be very beneficial."

The admiral did as he was told. "Jane, it looks like James got himself into a situation in which he felt his only alternative was to kill himself."

Jane reacted, "Frank, you're killing me here, no shit."

Jay had known since he was a little boy that, if the situation called for it, his mother could curse like a sailor, but he didn't expect that side of her to come out with the admiral. It meant she wasn't just sad; she was mad, burning white hot with anger.

"I am sorry, Jane, but our investigation produced evidence that James got himself involved in illegal deals with leaders of the former Soviet Union," said Admiral Conner.

Jane grew flush and her mouth fell open.

"That's crazy. James never gave a shit about money. I do all the bills and finances."

It was Jay's turn to snarl: "And I suppose Captain Royce here led the investigation," said Jay. He looked with disgust upon Royce.

"Careful, son," said Admiral Conner.

"Yes, sir." But he shot Royce one last hateful glare before turning his eyes downward to his lap.

"I know this is shocking news. That is why I want to go through all of the findings with you both. Keep in mind, this is a top secret briefing that I am disclosing to you as courtesy to our fallen leader. Neither of you may discuss this with anyone other than the people in this room. Is that understood?"

Jay and his mother remained mute, eyes down.

Admiral Conner insisted, "I need you to acknowledge that you will not discuss this, and I will need you sign something to that effect before we get started."

Captain Royce handed Jay and his mother what appeared at first glance to be boilerplate confidentiality agreements. Mom signed hers without reading it. Jay started to read his but felt the acute impatience in the room, all eyes on him, and he signed the release half-read.

Jay said, as he handed the release over to Royce, "Sir, could I get a copy of this before I leave?"

"Of course," said Royce.

For the next hour, the admiral and Royce—mostly Royce, after some preliminary remarks—systemically presented the evidence against Vice Admiral Brown, as if they were prosecutors at trial. Royce produced evidence of a Swiss bank account in James Brown's name. There were also incriminating memos, documents and emails. The investigation had followed the money, and the money always ended up in Dad's account. Royce flashed hand-written notes from Dad's moleskin notebook.

Jay and his mother simultaneously reached for the little notebook, but Royce pulled it away, motioning that it was not to be touched. Royce turned on the tape player and played recorded phone conversations between Admiral Brown and the Swiss bank. Royce stopped the machine at about the halfway mark, and presented forensic audio evidence that the voice on the tape actually belonged to Brown and not to an impersonator. Jay and his mother didn't need the forensics. They heard the tape. Pure Boston charm. It was Dad, all right. It was painful to hear. Royce then turned the tape back on so the family could hear the rest. Dad talked about millions of dollars and his patrons were all Russian. There was much talk of Chancellor Vladimir and the Saint Petersburg customs office.

Jay's mom didn't make it to the end of the tape. "Enough! Enough already. OK, my husband of almost forty years was not who we thought he was. I get it!"

The admiral spoke soothingly: "Jane, I know it's hard. You need to know. On the day of the reception, a Russian official turned informant notified our office of James's inappropriate dealings. I pulled James aside and told him of the allegations."

Jay's mom asked: "What did he say when you spoke to him?"

"He didn't even act surprised. He said, 'Of course, I am being accused.' He even smirked and laughed almost in a bitter way that surprised me. Thirty minutes later he shot himself in his office. Jane, we are considering James's death from circumstances in the line of duty. You will receive his pension for the rest of your life, and—although we cannot pay out on his life insurance—we will be paying you the coverage amount from other sources. It is important that these arrangements are kept private."

"Of course," said Jane.

Royce smacked his thick lips wetly. "Mrs. Brown and Lieutenant Commander Brown, the briefing you just heard is highly sensitive. The government compensation is contingent upon you keeping this to yourself and also never investigating further into the circumstances surrounding Vice Admiral James Brown's death, since these actions could harm national security and create an embarrassment for our nation. You have both signed a release that you agree to what was just said."

Jay looked at his mother, a powder keg ready to blow. Suddenly bitter, teeth-clenched words came out of her mouth: "It's unfortunate that you never really know someone. Not even after almost forty years of marriage. James turned out to be the person that made me the happiest and saddest person in the world. I will never forgive him for his cowardly act. Thank you, gentlemen." Jane extended her hand to shake both Captain Royce and Admiral Conner's hand, then looked to Jay and said, "Let's go."

As they left, Jay whispered: "I'm already regretting signing those forms."

"I need the money."

"I know, but that was bullshit, that presentation. That tape—that was Dad undercover. I know it. He was working an op, not committing a crime, and somehow his cover was blown."

"What did your father always say about friends and enemies?"

The Pentagon hallway was the longest Jane Brown had ever seen, like a hallway to infinity, you couldn't see the end. Luckily there was a red exit sign no more than thirty yards ahead. Even though the space was huge, its vibe gave her a twinge of something akin to claustrophobia.

"Keep your friends close but your enemies closer," replied Jay.

"He got that expression from me, Jay," she said.

Jay put his arm around her and said, "I know, Mom, I know. I love you, Mom."

On the highway, on the way home, Jane took out a notepad and started writing. She said, "Jay, tell me everything you remember from the briefing."

"Mom, you're creating a top secret notepad."

"I'll keep it in my underwear drawer. It'll sure to be safe there. Start talking."

The brainstorming began and Jane wrote down all of the details they could remember: names, partial account numbers, banks, dates and times. They kept it up until Jay pulled into his mother's driveway.

Jane's car was still in the driveway. Janet and Mike had already moved the furniture, at least the furniture they could lift, but the desk was a problem. It weighed a ton.

"Looks like your father's desk has found a new home," Jane said. But she didn't dwell. She wasn't done brainstorming. "Before you move, let's just list all the things that make *no sense.*"

"Mom, what are you going to do with this info?"

"Why did you take all the furniture from Dad's office?"

"I don't know. I thought it might come in handy someday."

"Well, that's the same answer I have for you."

"Fair enough. So what makes no sense? That slime ball Royce makes no sense."

"That's the truth. And not being able to look at the notebook. That was odd."

"The suicide note was very strange. A suicide email? Are you kidding me?"

Jane wrote it all down diligently. She said, "I think Frank is completely on the level. He believes the horseshit Royce has been feeding him. He can definitely be trusted someday if we need him."

"I agree. The bullet Dad was shot with makes no sense. It was a low-power target round. Very, very strange."

"Really strange, no blood spatter with an exit wound. Seems too perfect."

Jay was impressed: "Wow, Mom. You know your stuff."

"You bet. I watch a lot of crime shows on TV."

"Dad was doing some analysis with music. Something that I have a hunch might be tied to the background music at the reception. What was it Cody said? They were seeking patterns and ciphers out of some musical scores. Cody was doing a little side project for Dad."

Mom said, "That is very, very interesting. How often was music mentioned during our visit to the Pentagon today?"

"I believe that number is zero. I have Cody sending me the sheet music to my ship. I also have Cassie sending me background recordings from the reception. I plan to analyze them on the *Quincy*."

"What are you thinking, Jay? What do you think is going on?"

"I think we're in the neighborhood, close but no cigar. We know where to look, but we still don't know what we're looking for."

"I'm so glad you took those guitar lessons when you were a boy. You could've been one of the greats."

"Thanks, Mom, but I'm tons better at being a submariner than I was as a musician. But you're right; all of those lessons are going to come in handy right now. Thank you for that. I'm not sure where to begin, thinking about music as a bed for a cipher. I may not be able to decipher anything—but I think I am smart enough to provide the raw materials to someone that could. I also need my guitar. I am going to bring it back to the ship with me. Do you have any idea where it is?"

"In the attic. Buried, but I know exactly where it is. That would be wonderful if you started playing again."

"Any musical instrument on a submarine is not the most popular choice of pastimes, but I may start practicing in port." Jay's tone became serious again. "So, Mom, what are you going to do with that notebook? Be very, very careful with it. You could lose your pension."

"I told you where I was going to put it."

"Yes, Mom, I remember. Never mind."

"Jay, honey, this is going to be old news soon enough for our friends in the Pentagon. No one is going to care about what I do while mourning the loss of my husband."

"Well if anyone does take interest, won't that tell a story?"

"Yes, Son, it will."

In the attic, they dug out Jay's guitar. It was buried, under boxes marked "Christmas Decorations." Jay took the dusty case into the spare bedroom and opened it up. He felt pangs of guilt as he gazed upon the scratched up guitar, the cheap Russian guitar he'd traded for. He never told his parents about the exchange. When he came home from Russia he left the part about the guitar out and skipped directly to "I'm applying to the Naval Academy." As Jay looked at the guitar his mind rolled back in time, to January 1978. Just back from Leningrad, Jay transferred from prestigious Berkeley to the not quite as prestigious and now defunct Boston State College, where he loaded up on math and physics courses. Jay received an appointment to the Naval Academy Prep School in Newport, Rhode Island, for the fall 1978 term. NAPS was a program usually better suited for student athletes who needed a little extra academic development. Jay graduated from NAPS spring 1979, had a month off and commenced his four years in Annapolis. Since Jay had accrued so many credits at NAPS, Berkeley and Boston State, he was able to complete two majors at the Naval Academy, a bachelor's in both marine engineering and oceanography.

Jay thought dual majors would help him get into submarines, but later learned that the nuke people cared only about his math and physics grades.

Jay ran his fingers lightly over the guitar. He felt a transient ache of sadness for the road not taken, a bit of fluffy nostalgia that he tried to thrust to the back of his mind. The music that Vlad gave him was still in the case. Jay had not played the guitar since that day in the guitar shop. Then he thought of Kat and Kat's hands, and the ache returned. Jay shut his eyes, sighed, and closed the guitar case.

Mom walked in, opened the guitar case, and looked at the instrument.

"Wow, that looks pretty banged up for something your father spent thousands of dollars for. At least you got a lot of use out of it."

Jay considered coming clean, then thought better of if. "You bet, Mom," Jay said as he closed the case.

Jay spent a couple of days living in his mom's guest room and hanging out with the family. Significantly, Cassie visited him both days, and on the second day stayed for dinner.

On Saturday morning Jay's plans were simple: grab Amtrak to New London; get a good night sleep in his apartment; meet with the captain and other *Quincy* officers on Sunday afternoon to prepare for the three-month deployment that began Monday morning.

Jay sat shotgun as his mom drove him to Union Station in her white Ford Tempo. Janet and Cassie sat in the back. Her third visit in three days, Cassie had become an honorary Brown. Jay packed light. All he had was a leather shoulder satchel and a guitar case.

Mom pulled up in front of Union Station and parked at the curb for unloading. Jay and the three ladies got out of the car simultaneously, almost synchronized. Jay felt stress. Cassie. How should he say good-bye? It turned out that he had no choice. Jay extended his hand to Cassie, who pushed it away and gave Jay a big hug and a kiss on the check. It was only a little awkward, but enough to make Janet laugh. Jay pulled away and kissed his mother and sister good-bye."

"Stay safe, dear."

"Don't spring a leak, brat!"

Mom pulled Jay up onto the sidewalk and spoke closely: "I know your father did not kill himself."

"I know, Mom."

Cassie, whose focus had been almost exclusively on Jay since she first saw him talking to the marine outside the Pentagon, was a bit of a lip-reader, a good skill when you worked intelligence.

VI

September 6th, 1992
USS *Quincy* Wardroom

Jay lived three blocks from the New London train station and walked home. His apartment was a two-bedroom in the Crocker House, an 1873 hotel. The place had history. It had been visited by multiple presidents, authors and—most notably in Jay's mind—the great bare-knuckle fighter, John L. Sullivan.

Jay was not a guy who memorized a lot of things. He knew a lot of stuff, but not necessarily by rote. But one of the few things he could recite from memory was the lineage of the world's heavyweight boxing champions from the great John L., all the way to Lennox Lewis.

The first part of Jay's agenda went smoothly. He did, indeed, get a good night's sleep in his apartment. He woke refreshed, and with a bit of the heaviness of grief relieved, as if solid slumber had repaired some of his frazzled nerve endings. He readied himself for the *Quincy*.

He hoped his own bed would allow him to sleep well, even though Jay historically tossed and turned as new assignments were about to begin. And he didn't even know what his assignment was yet, which allowed his worries to be open-ended.

Instead of counting sheep, he tried to lull himself with memories of his father quizzing him relentlessly.

"What type of submarine did the Japanese use during the attack on Pearl Harbor?"

"Midget submarines, sir."

"Were they effective?"

"No, sir."

"How did they get to Hawaii?"

"They were towed by a larger submarine and released off the waters of Hawaii."

"Do you know the name of the U.S. ship that sunk one of the midget subs?"

"Yes, sir, the USS *Monaghan.*"

"With the failure to be effective at Pearl Harbor, Jay, did the Japanese give up on the tactic?"

"No, they did not. Midgets were used in, oh, the spring sometime of 1942 in Sydney harbor. The midget fired a torpedo at the USS *Chicago,* missed and killed twenty-one sailors aboard an Australian barracks ship. Another midget blew up—hit a depth charge."

"What was the initial defense against U-boat attacks on merchant ships during the early days of World War II?"

"Sir, the ships began to cross the Atlantic in well-guarded convoys."

"At what point of the war were U-boats most effective?"

"Soon after the U.S. entered the war. The Germans filled the waters off North America with submarines and sunk 102 ships during the first three months of 1942."

The tactic worked and Jay drifted off, not waking until 0800. He bounced out of bed, up and ready to swill coffee, pack, and get to the *Quincy* across the Thames River. Jay didn't know which was named first, the city or the river, but the names clearly went together. He filled a green duffle bag with all of his underwear, three sets of navy blue coveralls, and clothing he did not care about getting wrinkled. Most of the time underway on a submarine, you wore blue coveralls, maybe with insignia. (Maybe not, depending upon the captain.) The officers and chief petty officers wore khaki belts, while the crew wore navy blue belts, each with the man's buckle of choice. Footwear: sneakers or boat shoes, anything with soft soles that didn't clunk when you walked.

Jay set aside some uniforms, a set of wash khakis for working on the ship when the ship is in port and a set of dress khakis for going ashore. He also set aside his dress blues and his white combination hat.

Jay secured his apartment. He didn't pack quite so light this time. He still had the guitar but now was burdened with a huge stuffed-to-capacity green duffle bag, which he slung across his shoulder. He wore jeans and a tee shirt. Captain Davis didn't expect his officers to show up for weekend briefings in uniform. Jay had worked under other captains who expected officers to be in uniform all the time. It was a matter of personalities.

Tomorrow Jay would put his car in the long-term parking lot. Long-term was a ways from the ship, and he didn't want to make that hike with the duffle bag. Today, he would park in his spot right on the dock next to the ship. That's right: his spot. The captain, XO and chief of the boat had named parking spots on the dock. It was pretty doggone civilized.

While in Washington, Jay left his Mazda RX7 in a parking garage affiliated with the Crocker House. Jay hoofed it to his car, slightly hunchbacked from his load. He threw his stuff into the front passenger seat and drove to Groton Submarine base. He passed through base security, and then lower-base security.

On the dock, Jay encountered yet another armed security guard, this time a sailor from the USS *Quincy*'s crew on guard duty. He was Rusty Dunn, the quartermaster.

Dunn saluted and said, "Welcome back, XO. I am very sorry for your loss."

"Thank you, Petty Officer Dunn. It's good to be back. I can't wait to get under way."

"Me too, sir."

Jay turned to enter his parking spot, and was miffed to find it occupied. In Jay's spot was another RX7—one owned by Joe Silio, the chief engineer, who when onboard a nuke was always called the Eng, with a soft g. Jay parked directly behind the Eng's car, almost touching his rear bumper, to highlight Joe's error in judgment.

The spot to the left of Jay's was vacant, the captain's. Jay liked to always show up just before the captain and leave just after. Old school courtesy, and Captain Davis kept reasonable hours.

The XO started to unload his car, duffle bag on his shoulder, guitar case in his hand. Jay gladly handed off the items to the eager men. Being number-two on a ship had its perks.

One sailor said, "I didn't know you played the guitar, XO."

Jay replied, "I used to play a long time ago and recently decided to take it back up."

So much for keeping a lid on that. In minutes the entire crew would know. The XO had a guitar onboard. The potential for that to become annoying was sky high.

Jay and his helpers entered the submarine via the weapons shipping hatch, forward of the sail. There were two other hatches aft of the sail that were not used for access while in port for security and safety reasons. The hatch just forward of the reactor compartment and aft of the crew's mess was open but occupied by a huge shore power cable carrying 440 volts to the submarine. When plugged in, that cable provided power to the entire submarine while tied to the pier with its reactor shut down. That hatch was also called the forward escape trunk, and had two watertight hatches to allow entry and exit from the submarine while submerged. There was a similar hatch that went directly into the engine room called the aft escape trunk. "Forward" on a submarine usually indicated the compartments forward of the reactor compartment. "Aft" indicated the reactor compartment and engine room, not to be confused with the auxiliary machinery room, which was in the forward compartment.

The XO went to his stateroom and unpacked his belongings. The guitar fit perfectly in the hang up locker in his stateroom. Jay did not want to leave the guitar out in the open because he wanted to first tell the captain of his intentions. Even though the captain would probably find out about the guitar from the informal communications chain, he was usually the last to find out gossip. Jay wanted to make sure the captain didn't think he planned any underway serenading and to assure him that the guitar was for in port use only. Jay had not decided how much he wanted to tell the captain about the little investigation he was conducting. Jay figured his investigation would present no problem. Some guys read or watched movies in their free time underway. Some exercised. Jay planned to do some investigating.

The XO stateroom had a bunk bed that was normally folded down to make the bunk look like a couch. The bunk was exactly 6 feet long, which was about 3 inches too short for Jay's 6 foot 3 inch long body to sleep with his legs extended. If VIPs like an admiral were traveling on the sub, they took the top bunk and shared the XO's stateroom. Unusually, the top bunk was just folded down like a couch and the XO slept on the bottom part where visitors sat. Currently a tan Naugahyde cover was on the bottom bunk and the folded down top bunk, to give the appearance of a leather couch. Pillows were in the drawer under the bottom bunk. Underway, depending upon the sleep schedule and instructions provided by the XO to the chief steward, the mess specialists (MSs) uncovered the bunk and turned down the sheets before bedtime. When the XO was up for the day or the evening—depending upon which shift he was on—the MS on duty would make the bunk and cover it with Naugahyde again. The MSs also changed the sheets for all officers weekly.

Jay looked up at the ship's clock in his stateroom. Almost 1100. Jay didn't need to wear a watch while underway. There were clocks everywhere on the *Quincy*. The quartermasters were in charge of winding and making sure all the ship's clocks were synchronized.

Jay went down to the wardroom via the ladder forward of the control room. Stairways and ladders were all called ladders on a submarine. In this case, it was actually a steep stairway. The ladders in the weapons shipping hatch and the forward and after escape trucks were vertical ladders. All officers and crew, except for the captain, and the XO when the captain was not onboard, knocked before entering the wardroom, which was where the officers ate and had meetings.

Jay walked into the wardroom without knocking and found his chair, to the right of the captain's, occupied by the Eng. Sitting across from him was young Lieutenant Little. They were both wearing cotton khakis with their rank insignia on their collar. Little had single silver bars on his collar that were actually hard to differentiate from gold ensign bars. The gold plating on ensign bars wore off after a while, exposing the silver below. Silio was a newly promoted Lieutenant Commander with gold oak leaves on his collar. Silio also had gold dolphins pinned above his left pocket while Little had nothing above his. No name tags. With only 120 men, everyone knew who was onboard.

The seat Silio had chosen was reserved for the senior man on the submarine. The Eng had been the senior man while the XO was on emergency leave, and so he was appropriately sitting in that seat in the XO's absence. No one sat in the captain's seat except for the captain—unless the captain offered it to an admiral or the squadron commander when visiting.

The Eng muttered an obscenity and stood up.

Jay said, "First you take my parking space, now you take my seat."

Silio replied, "XO, I wasn't supposed to have duty but..."

"Give it a rest, Eng—and sit down. I am just messing with you."

Jay walked over to the coffee pot and poured himself a coffee from the industrial strength Bunt coffee maker on the aft end of the wardroom.

Silio went to sit back down in the XO's seat and Jay said, "Sit back down—but not there."

The Eng said to Little, "How about you change the channel on the TV to the weather. It's time for Meteorologist Valerie Voss to come on."

The TV remote was mounted in the wall of the wardroom, but officers without dolphins, "non-quals" like Little, were used as human remotes. This was one of many little incentives to help keep non-quals motivated to get qualed. The gold dolphin signified an officer was qualified to drive the submarine. The more qualified drivers onboard, the better it was for all of the officers. As the saying went, "Many hands make light work." The silver dolphins on enlisted men signified a certain level of knowledge and watch standing capability. Only commissioned officers could earn gold dolphins.

Little got up and changed the channel, slightly put out by the mild hazing, then sat back down.

"What's for lunch?" Jay asked.

"Sliders," replied Little, meaning greasy hamburgers that slid down your throat.

"Gee, I wish I drank more last night. Sliders are always good for a hangover," said the Eng as he grabbed a cup of coffee, and sat down next to Jay. "How are things going, XO? I am very sorry for your loss. The past week had to suck."

"It really did suck."

Eng said to Little, "John, can you turn that down?"

Little turned the TV down and said, "I am going to make my engine room rounds before lunch."

"Good idea, John. Why don't you do my duty officer rounds for me as the under instruction duty officer," said Silio.

"Aye aye, Eng," John Little said, half in jest.

The Eng was the duty officer acting on behalf of the captain as the officer in charge of the *Quincy* and the enlisted watch standers in port. Little was the engineering duty officer (EDO) in charge of the engineering spaces and enlisted engineering watch standers.

"XO, you didn't take much time off. Are you sure you want to come back this soon? I mean you could meet us when we arrive in the Med," said the Eng.

"You just want my seat and my parking space, Eng."

"I really don't, XO. I don't like dealing with the old man all day. I have my day job running the nuclear plant."

"Just kidding, Eng. I am so glad to be back. I would rather be drilling holes in the ocean than dealing with a bunch of people telling me they're sorry for my loss."

"Well, you got me out of the way. Only 119 more to go on the *Quincy*."

Jay changed the subject: "So, you think we are heading to the Med?"

"Where else would we be going?" asked the Eng.

A speaker squawked: "*Quincy* arriving." The captain was coming aboard.

"I guess we will find out from the horse's mouth momentarily," said Jay.

The captain entered the wardroom from the aft end through the pantry. As he opened the door, Jay called out, "Attention on deck."

The Eng and XO came to their feet. This was a courtesy offered the captain the first time he entered the wardroom after being ashore.

"Relax, XO and Eng. Welcome back, XO. I am sorry for your loss."

The Eng mouthed to Jay: "One-hundred eighteen to go."

Jay smiled wearily. "Thank you, Captain."

"And what asshole took your parking spot?"

"I would be that asshole, Captain," said the Eng.

"I know, Eng. I just wanted to hear you say it."

"I came in this morning and forgot I had the duty. For some reason I thought it was Saturday," said the Eng.

"Don't really give a shit, Eng. Oooh, I smell sliders. How does the pre-underway check look, XO?"

"Captain, I just got here a little while ago. I figured you'd let us know what's going on, and I'd do my checks this afternoon."

"Sounds good, XO. I am going to go home after our briefing so just give me a call regarding the status at home, once you know."

"Aye aye, Captain."

The rest of the officers of the *Quincy* filtered in. The TV was turned off and was closed into the wall by metal doors that were covered with wood-like contact paper. The mess specialists served the sliders.

"Man, that's good eatin'!" the captain said. No one enjoyed a slider more.

In theory, a nuclear submarine could have remained underway forever, if it weren't for its food supply. Everything else was near-limitless. The water to cool the reactor, spin the turbines and quench the thirst was made from boiling saltwater onboard. Oxygen was created from fresh water that had been broken down to its oxygen and hydrogen components. The oxygen was collected and emitted into the submarine for the crew to breathe. The hydrogen was discharged overboard. The reactor had enough nuclear material to travel to the moon and back two-and-a-half times at standard speed. If the captain routinely hotrodded, he might only be able to make one round trip.

Lunch ended at 1300. The captain said, "I want everyone back here at 1330 for the pre-deployment brief."

Jay thought it was somewhat odd for a pre-deployment briefing to take place *before* getting underway. Usually, the captain waited as a security consideration. There could be unwanted "ears" when ashore.

All the officers dispersed to brush their teeth, stow their gear and scout out their respective areas, checking for problems of cleanliness and maintenance.

The captain and XO went up a level to stow their gear in their staterooms. The doors to the head were open. They could see each other.

"Hey, XO, did you really bring a *guitar* onboard?"

There it was. Proof. The only thing that traveled faster than the speed of light was a rumor on a submarine. The captain said the word *guitar* as if it were beyond bizarre, like a polka-dotted unicorn or a two-headed monkey.

"Yes, sir," Jay responded quickly, "but I have no intention of playing underway."

"That's too bad, XO. I was thinking of having a talent show during our transit. You could be Simon and I'll be Garfunkel."

"If that's the case, Captain, of course I'll play," said the XO. He hoped that the captain was joking. He couldn't be sure. Captain Davis was a bit of a stone-faced comedian. As they walked together to the briefing, neither spoke.

The captain called the briefing to order at 1329.

"Let's go, XO. Let's get this over with. Rig the wardroom for top secret."

"Aye aye, sir."

Jay counted heads, locked the pantry door and closed the viewing window. He locked the small door used to pass food into the wardroom from the pantry. Little was at the forward end of the wardroom and locked the forward door.

The *Quincy*'s twelve officers sat around the wardroom table, some with coffee cups in front of them. Others drank soda. Jay had a huge blue coffee cup with a dolphin on it that held three cups, leaving room for milk and sugar. There had been gripes about Jay's massive coffee consumption. Every time he went for a refill, the complaint went, you had to brew a new pot. Jay always responded the same way. "I come from a coffee family." Jay usually tried not to bring up his family. It felt to others like pulling rank. In this case it was OK. The Browns didn't drink coffee because of the navy. They drank coffee because they were Browns.

The captain began, "All right, gentlemen, underway time is 0900 tomorrow. We are transiting across the Atlantic and will be spending some time in the north Atlantic. Bring your long johns because we could be going to some cold places. We will be on a diplomatic mission, docking in former Soviet Union ports to show the United States' support for some of the new independent nations that were formerly part of the USSR. The Pentagon is issuing a press release that will be in all the papers telling the world of this unprecedented port call. When asked by your friends and lovers, feel free to say you are part of this diplomatic mission, but you do not know where you will be docking. I don't even know where we are pulling in yet."

Little whispered loudly to the junior officer sitting next to him, "Very cool. Soviet Union. I can't believe we are friends with those guys now."

The captain, after too many years of Cold War shenanigans, was rankled. "Friend is a strong word, John. Of course, we are not going to send a submarine up there without *some* intelligence gathering objectives."

The officers chattered among themselves, speculating. Little said he wanted to see Red Square—preferably not while wearing handcuffs.

Others found the mention of intelligence intriguing. Special operations! Oh, man. SpecOps were what a fast-attack submarine officer lived for. Maybe they were going to deploy SEALs. Maybe they would be spying on a new Russian ship or submarine, one for which we still didn't know its specifications and capabilities. Maybe they were going to the North Pole to look for Soviet ballistic missile submarines that were ice picking—that is, tucked up under the ice pack. The captain remained silent as his officers tossed off theory after theory, each sounding more like a potboiler thriller than the one before. The captain's stone face moved easily into a coy grin as he watched the excited officers' faces.

He continued, "This past week, the tops of the two BRA-34s have been equipped with radiation and contamination detection devices. In concert with the nuclear clean up treaty that the U.S. government has invested billions of dollars in, we have been asked to check for radioactive contamination and background radiation levels where we dock and some other places that we will be told of later."

Jay understood that BRA-34 was short for AN/BRA-34, which was in turn short for Army Navy Broadband Radio Antenna model 34. The BRA-34s were a multifunction, multi-radio frequency antennae. The transmit and receive antennae telescoped out of the sail. There were two identical units side by side, but they raised and lowered independently. A BRA-34 didn't look like your standard set of antennae, more like a skinny telephone pole painted black. The sturdy hollow telescopic pole was necessary so that the antennae could be out of the water while the submarine was submerged. Regular antennae would bend or break with the flow of water. The tops of the BRA-34s had a cap to make the antennae flush with the top of the sail when retracted. The *Quincy's* cap had been modified to house this special radiation detection equipment.

The officers were deflated. They wanted intrigue. Instead, they got to wave Geiger counters.

The Eng, not intimidated by the brittle silence, shattered it by saying, "So, Captain, we have one sensor that is measuring background radiation, and another measuring contamination?"

"That's right, Eng. The radiation levels are being measured in a recording device that captures the time and location for the reading. The contamination detector is pretty clever. It has a roll of thin cloth that filters radioactive contaminants for a set time, then the radiation levels are measured to determine how much bad radioactive stuff is in the air or water. You control these devices from a control box by the number-two periscope. The Weps is going to walk you guys through the operation. The contamination detector has a finite number of samples it can take. Then the sample unit is replaced on top of the sail. I want to make sure at least three JOs know how to make the swap after we break."

The Weps was in charge of all of the weapons systems. His title had been changed for some time to Combat Systems Officer (CSO) since all the systems are computerized now. But the new name didn't stick and everyone still called him the Weps. His real name was Lieutenant Commander Eric Armstrong. This was his second tour as a *Quincy* department head. He'd spent two years as Eng, then—after a couple of months of school—returned as Weps. Armstrong was senior department head. That put him in charge of the in-port and at-sea watch rotation.

Jay figured the Eng must've done something to piss the Weps off recently. Just before the briefing, the Weps gave the Eng unexpected watch immediately—the day before a three-month deployment. Ouch. Jay assumed the matter was trivial, and found Eric Armstrong to be a bit of an enigma.

Armstrong was a computer and mechanical genius—but was also a varsity wrestler for Iowa State under Dan Gable. He never won any national championships, three times getting as far as the regional semi-finals. Still, twelve years since his last wrestling meet, he did not look like someone with whom you would want to mess. Being a star college wrestler sounded like a great gig, but it brought out the stupidity in people, who were always asking him if he knew Hulk Hogan or Randy "Macho Man" Savage.

But that wasn't it for this eclectic and exceptional man, Jay thought. Armstrong's other passions included coin collecting and strip joints. Strippers were his expertise. Just as Jay could recite submarine facts by rote because of the big book he memorized as a child, Armstrong knew the history of exotic dancing, and even as he was slipping a dollar bill into a lacy garter belt he might simultaneously lecture to a friend about the glory days of burlesque. He knew the best gentleman's clubs in ports all over the world, and the names and perfumes of the most attractive, flexible and imaginative dancers.

There was still more. Armstrong knew the history of the currency for every port as well. He was already talking coins of Europe. Eric could talk with equal passion about his favorite ladies and international coinage.

If you took the fact pattern as shown so far, you might think Armstrong was a party guy. Quite the opposite. He did not drink alcohol. He said cornball things like, "I'm high on life."

Jay learned to avoid computer topics with Eric Armstrong. There was no point. Within thirty seconds he had no idea what Armstrong was talking about. Cyber-*what*?

Jay watched with interest as the Weps grabbed a nine-by-fourteen-inch green metal box from one of several cabinets behind the captain. Armstrong placed the box precisely at the center of the wardroom table.

Armstrong began, "First of all, this is the last time this box will ever be outside of the radio room. Even though it seems boring, these sensors are top secret. No one is to talk about this equipment even with the crew. This is why we have the controls by the periscope, not in the radio room. We are going to have to come up with some kind of code words for when we're doing the radiation monitoring. The control room will be recorded at all times."

The captain stood and interjected, "Be careful what you say, boys. We don't know where these tapes will be going, so keep the language clean. We are picking up riders somewhere on the other side of the ocean."

Jay asked, "Riders, really? Interesting, no?"

"This mission could wind up being *a lot* more interesting than advertised. This riders business smacks of adventure, gentlemen," the captain said, trying to rekindle some of the spirit he'd felt earlier. "Any ship could be used to measure radiation. There's more to the story. We'll find out."

Armstrong opened the box. Inside were two doors. One door was blue. The other had on it the magenta-and-yellow radiation emblem. He opened the blue door and underneath were nine black cartridges arranged three-by-three.

"Little mini laser ink cartridges?" the Eng asked.

The Weps took one out. "This is a fully contained contamination detection cartridge. Each is good for ten samples unless in the unlikely event we get a real contaminated sample, in which case the cartridge needs to be replaced before sampling again. There are special gloves and a carry case for the cartridge. Used cartridges go in the dirty side." Weps opened the yellow and magenta door revealing nine empty slots.

"I need three volunteers to train how to do the swap out on the sail," Weps said.

The captain pointed to three junior officers, one of whom was Little. The three volunteers stood up.

Little said, "Touch and sniff." Nobody paid any attention to him, so he said it again, almost urgently: "Touch and sniff!"

Jay said, "Little, what the hell are you talking about? It's *scratch and sniff,* you knucklehead."

Little continued, "I am not sure what you are talking about, sir, but I was thinking that those could be our code words. You know, when we are monitoring we are *touching,* and when we are measuring for contamination we are *sniffing.*"

The captain said, "Good call, Little. I like it, let's use it. We are going on a touch and sniff operation."

Weps led the junior officers to the sail. The captain brought the rest of the officers to the control room to learn how to operate the equipment. It was now clear to Jay why this briefing needed to be conducted today. Once they were overseas, they would want to be able to quickly change out the sensors on the top of the sail without drawing attention, a ritual that required rehearsal.

The walk-throughs were completed without incident, and everyone was free to go home except for the Eng and Little, who had duty officer and engineering duty officer responsibilities. Others lingered as well. Jay reviewed the status of the pre-underway checklist, for which the duty officer was responsible. Pre-underway checks included making sure all the food and provisions were loaded, all in-port work was completed, and all on the submarine was normal.

Jay reviewed the checklist, called the captain at home to let him know the status of the pre-underway checks, and got in his car to go home.

At 0600 on the morning of the underway, the engineering crew arrived in order to start up the reactor. The Eng supervised the EDO in directing the highly trained enlisted engineering watch standers. Using a remote switch, the reactor was taken critical by slowly removing the control rods. Once the reactor was critical, the turbine generators were put into service, shore power was removed and the propulsion turbines were warmed up.

At 0700, the rest of the crew arrived. The forward compartment was prepared to get underway. The "Rig for Dive" check was run, during which every hull opening and penetration to the sea was checked and double-checked by an officer to make sure the ocean stayed on the outside. The checks were not completed until after the submarine was underway and everyone was down from the sail.

By 0800, family and friends of the crew had gathered on the dock with signs and tears, wishing their loved ones a fond farewell.

Getting a submarine underway for a long deployment involved serious showmanship. Oh, the pageantry! This was especially true of Captain Davis, a vain but compassionate man who'd never encountered a ceremony he didn't like. The captain arrived at the dock with his family at 0830. Rear Admiral Bennett, the two-star admiral in charge of submarines assigned to Groton submarine base, was on the dock to say good-bye. Admiral Bennett was the Submarine Group Two commander.

When the *Quincy* was ready to get underway, a tug boat was tied adjacent to the sail—in a reverse power moor, snugly facing aft and perpendicular to the forward starboard quarter of the submarine—to help pull the *Quincy*'s bow off the dock. The submarine was equipped with a stern thruster to push the stern. The control room was abuzz, everyone at their stations, both periscopes up. Men took turns ogling a woman with finely turned legs on the dock, while simultaneously tracking the progress of the captain who was saying good-bye—with surprising gusto—to his wife.

At exactly 0850, the captain kissed his children good-bye, saluted the admiral and stepped lively up the gangway onto the ship. He stopped halfway across the gangway to salute the U.S. flag at the stern. The announcement was made: "USS *Quincy* arriving." The instant the captain stepped onto the ship, the gangway was removed.

The captain grabbed his orange floatation jacket, attached his walkie-talkie to his belt, and clipped his mic onto his collar. At 0850 he was standing on top of the sail with the Weps, who was the officer of the deck for getting the submarine underway. Temporary metal fencing had been installed on top of the sail rigging, often called "the playpen" because it looked like a large black playpen. The fence allowed a man to stand up there without fear of tumbling off into the salty abyss.

Captain Davis called out from the playpen, "Single all lines."

The officer on deck below repeated, "Single all lines, aye, sir."

The captain sang out the thoroughly predictable orders with a pizzazz, a sense of showmanship that other submarine captains lacked. Getting underway was wonderful, Captain Davis thought, and he called the orders like a priest saying the mass in Latin. He was good and loud, and in touch with the rhythms of his orders, until there was a chanting quality.

"Cast off the spring lines!"

The officer on deck repeated, "Cast off all spring lines, aye, sir."

The criss-crossed spring lines where untied from the dock bollards, pulled aboard and brought below.

"Cast off the stern line, slack the bow line!"

The officer on deck repeated, "Cast off the stern line, slack the bow line, aye, sir."

The actions were again completed smartly. The captain looked at his watch. 0859. Tick, tick, tick, tick. All eyes on deck were on him.

"Cast off the bow!"

The officer on deck repeated, "Cast off the bow."

The bowline was cut loose from the pier. The captain counted down in his head: three, two, one.

"Chief of the Boat, blow the whistle."

After the whistle, the chief of the boat placed a bullhorn to his mouth and squawked, “Underway, shift colors.”

The crew dropped the Ensign (a U.S. flag) and the Union Jack (blue with fifty white stars). Up in the sail behind the captain, the underway colors were raised, the stars and stripes. Captain Davis felt like taking a bow. Another perfect underway!

VII

Morning, September 7th, 1992
USS *Quincy* Transiting
The Atlantic

The *Quincy* navigated off the dock with the help of tugs, and drove on the surface for a few hours due east in order to get beyond the continental shelf. Two men were up in the sail: the officer of the deck and the lookout. The officer of the deck was now Lieutenant Frank Wright, who wore a dolphin.

Frank was another fine, three-dimensional example of the steadfast rule: Nukes were an odd lot. Frank grew up a beach bum, surfing with long blond hair. Right after high school he even lived for a few months at the beach, in what amounted to a shack, but it was on a beach that wasn't too crowded and the waves were optimal. Frank was the only person Jay knew who could use the word "gnarly" without sounding like a complete douche. Although Frank eventually earned a B.S. in physics at U.C. Berkeley, he originally went to Stanford where, after two undisciplined years, he was asked to leave, "to prevent further embarrassment to Stanford and the Wright family name." No one knew precisely what Frank did to get the boot. Rumors were that it had involved nihilism and wretched excess. Frank picked physics because he found it easy, and was much more comfortable with saying "Cool, man" than "Yes, sir." Frank transferred to Berkeley on a scholarship from NUPOC, the Navy Nuclear Power Officer Candidate Program. Frank was committed to five years in the navy, which he had planned to do in an uncomplicated fashion, and get out. Things had not worked out that way. As the *Quincy* got underway, Frank was, as usual, ambivalent toward the navy. It was either his savior or his prison, and after all these years, he still couldn't tell which.

The other person in the sail was the lookout, Seaman Billi Snipes from West Virginia. Blame his illiterate parents for that i instead of a y. Billi was the first member of his family to correctly spell Ox—and he had to be spotted the first letter. Billi was one of a handful of sailors that reported aboard a submarine without any training or specialty. He went to basic training, completed basic submarine training and reported to the *Quincy*. He was part of a program in which a sailor selected a specialty and tried to learn it, a process called "striking". Billi, assigned to the *Quincy* for less than a month, was a mess specialist striker. He worked hard, but discipline was difficult for him because of his sloppy upbringing. For Seaman Billi Snipes, the sun shining down on him on this fine September day, life had never been so good.

As the *Quincy* cleared the continental shelf, Frank quizzed Billi, partially to keep the lad on the ball, and partially to keep his own head focused.

"How far away is that contact off the port bow now, Seaman Snipes?"

"What, sir?"

"That ship off our port bow."

Earlier Frank had told Billi a rough thumb rule used to calculate distance to the horizon in nautical miles. The answer is the square root in feet of the height of your eye from sea level. Frank found this a ridiculously simple concept. Billi, not so much.

Frank began to lecture. Billi's eyes glazed over.

"So, a six-foot man standing on the top of the sail that is twenty-seven feet from the water line is the square root of 1.5 times thirty-three feet, which is seven nautical miles. Or, you can just remember that the horizon is about seven nautical miles when standing on the sail."

Billi frowned and squinted at the ship, which appeared to be right on the horizon.

"Use your binoculars."

Billi put the heavy black binoculars to his eyes.

"Sir, contact is approximately seven nautical miles away from the USS *Quincy*."

It was a minor victory, but Frank liked it, and gave Billi a hearty "Well done." And he continued: "By knowing the approximate height for the ship and figuring out how many range ticks the ship takes vertically, one can calculate with similar math the range of a ship. I calculate mentally, both from the height of eye and using readings from the range-finding binoculars, the approximate range to the contact to be 6.6 nautical miles away."

Billi's eyes glazed over again.

Frank got on the horn: "Conn, radar, report distance to contact off our port bow."

Frank and Billi heard the squawking response: "Report distance to contact off our port bow, radar, conn, aye. Contact range is 6.6 nautical miles from the USS *Quincy*."

Frank smiled and, celebrating his own cleverness, gave Billi another firm clasp on the shoulder.

As Frank found a teaching moment for Billi in the playpen, the captain, XO and other officers kept a constant watch using one of the periscopes in the control room. Of course, they were looking around to make sure the submarine was safe, but they also wanted to get their last good look at the surface and the sky before they submerged for a week. The view from the periscope while the submarine was on the surface was majestic. The scope poked a good thirty feet over the water. When submerged, the view from the periscope was sometimes obstructed by choppy waters, and always reminded Frank Wright of the view he got when he paddled his surfboard out to sea.

The captain spoke into the mic: "Officer of the Deck, this is the captain. Shift control from the bridge to the control room, break down the playpen then rig for dive. Your relief is Mr. Armstrong."

Frank acknowledged the orders then transferred control of driving the submarine to the Weps in the control room, who was Frank's immediate boss. The sonar, torpedo and fire control divisions all reported into the Weps.

With the Weps in control, Frank and Billi donned safety harnesses and broke down the sail's temporary fencing. With the playpen removed and bundled up, Billi headed below.

First Class Petty Officer Mawa "Pete Pal" Paloli came up to the sail with a rope in one hand and a small ditty bag holding tools in the other. Paloli was Hawaiian. Fourteen years in the navy, the *Quincy* was his first submarine. He needed experience outside of Hawaii to make chief petty officer, so here he was—another laid-back surfer, a veteran of the big waves on the island of Hawaii's north shore. Pete Paloli and Frank Wright had something in common, so when they encountered each other just then, they pumped up the surfer attitude a couple of notches.

"How's it, Lieutenant Wright, sir?"

"Goes good, brother."

"Solid."

Paloli, with his rope and ditty of tools, went to the bridge to remove the electronic communications box in the sail and protect the electrical contacts before submerging. Paloli removed the box. He sealed and covered the special receptacle the box plugged into, and used his rope to lower his tool bag and the communication box into the control room.

Paloli had been qualified in submarines for many years and worked in tandem with Frank Wright to rig the sail for dive. He shut every valve and hatch, until the sail was watertight, and made sure there was nothing in the sail to rattle around and make noise. Frank double-checked everything Paloli did, using a grease pencil to check off items on a laminated checklist. Paloli, then Frank, returned to the control room where the captain, the only person there still wearing khakis, was waiting. Everyone else has changed after lunch into their blue coveralls, called "poopy suits." Frank was winded. It was quite a workout, closing the hatches and rigging the sail for dive.

Frank took a deep breath and said, "Captain and Officer of the Deck, the sail is rigged for dive."

"Very well, Lieutenant Wright. Officer of the Deck, is the ship rigged for dive?"

Eric Armstrong—the ex-wrestler, current OOD—replied, "Captain, the ship is rigged for dive."

"Very well, Officer of the Deck, dive the submarine," said the captain.

"Aye aye, Captain. Dive the submarine. All stations submerging the ship."

All stations acknowledged.

Armstrong lowered all antennae and all but one periscope. The only periscope still up was the one he was looking through.

"Dive. Make your depth 300 feet."

The diving office acknowledged and added, "Chief of the Watch, sound the diving alarm and open the forward and aft main ballast tank vents."

The chief of the watch acknowledged the order and announced to the ship: "*Dive, dive*!"

The dive alarm sounded, a klaxon two times: "Arrogha. Arrogha." It was so loud it echoed.

Armstrong looked forward through his periscope and said, "Forward group venting." Looking aft, he added, "After group venting."

The remote opening of the vent valves on top of the main ballast tanks allowed the tanks to fill with water and submerge the submarine.

The diving officer called out depths. The figures signified the depth of the keel below the surface of the water. The submarine was not officially submerged until it was greater than fifty feet down, which was the distance from the keel to the top of the sail.

"Fifty-two feet, fifty-four feet."

Armstrong said, "Number two periscope is submerged. Lowering number two periscope."

The diving officer said, "Chief of the Watch, close the main ballast tank vents."

The chief of the watch acknowledged and the submarine dropped to 300 feet.

The captain picked up the mic and delivered his familiar "just-submerged" speech: "This is the captain speaking. Once again, the officers and crew of the USS *Quincy* got this vital strategic and tactical asset of the United States Navy and the U.S. government underway in an extremely professional manner. I am proud of all of you and I am honored to have such a great crew. We will be transiting across the Atlantic to points unknown. I will let you know our destination when the time is appropriate. After dinner, we will be conducting angles and dangles drills. Thank you and *carpe diem.*"

"Angles and dangles" was an exercise to make sure everything was stowed well, and would stay where it belonged even during extreme climbs or dives. A radio crashing to the deck could make enough noise to be heard by another submarine.

Dinner was served at 1700. Morale was high, as tonight was a crew favorite, Philly cheesesteaks made to order.

"Go with the Cheese Whiz," the captain always advised. "That's the way they eat 'em in Philadelphia."

The first meals after getting underway were quick preparations like sandwiches. After a few days, when everyone was settled in, more impressive meals would be prepared. Prime rib. Lobster. Submariners didn't get much Vitamin D from the sun, but they ate great!

Food preppers reviewed their menu, editing it to take into account both the short- and long-term. For the first few weeks, there were fresh vegetable salads with every meal. Once the lettuce and vegetables were used up, they served fresh fruit salads for a couple of weeks. After about a month, if no fresh supplies were acquired, everything came out of a can.

Officers ate in the wardroom. The captain, XO and department heads sat in the same seat for every meal. The captain sat at the head of the table, Jay just to his right, the right-hand man. The senior department head, in this case the Weps, sat to the captain's left. The others filled in by seniority, with the exception of the suppo—the supply officer—who always sat at the other end of the table, across from the captain, regardless of his rank. They stood until the captain entered and took his seat.

Department heads (again, with the exception of the supply officer) took orders from both the captain and the XO. The rule read that officers reported operationally to the captain and administratively to the XO. In other words, the captain told them what to do, and the XO made sure they did it. The XO was also responsible for all of the paperwork and administration on the ship. The supply officer reported *both* operationally and administratively to the XO.

The navigator, Lieutenant Adam Radzemski, had been on the *Quincy* longer than any of the other department heads, yet he remained junior in rank. Obviously, he started young. He'd gone from his first sea tour as a division officer directly to his department head tour without a shore assignment in between. They called him Radman. Captain Davis had been his instructor in basic submarine officer school as an ensign. Radman requested to be the captain's navigator, and got the assignment. Radman took a lot of crap during nuclear training. Not only was his first name Adam—like atom—but his nickname, Radman, changed meaning in nuke-land, where a rad was a measure of exposure to radioactivity. Radman came from Presque Isle, Maine, which everyone figured out the first time he pronounced any vowel. He attended Maine Maritime Academy, studied to become a deck officer, became a naval officer, surface and submarines, and practiced both engineering and deck officer roles. Now Radman was finally doing the job he'd learned to do in college. He was a skilled navigator and deck officer, and wasn't a bad engineer in a pinch.

The suppo was Lieutenant Raymond Subtles. Of the officers, he was the only non-nuke. He was in charge of all supplies on the ship and all the meals. Just about everyone pronounced his name with a silent B. Everyone except Subtles himself, who, if you listened closely, put just a little B in there. His nickname was Rainman because of his gift for memorization. Luckily for the *Quincy*, Subtles was as good with supply inventories as he was with baseball statistics. This was Rainman's second time as a suppo. He wore gold supply officer dolphins and sat facing the captain during meals. Nobody was certain why. Word was, it was so the suppo could see the expression on his most-important customer's face.

While it might be true that submariners are a mixed bag of nuts, they are not lazy. On naval ships—surface ships, that is—there were two divisions: a repair division, and an operations division. But, on a submarine there was only one division. Everyone did both. It was tough work. Therefore, the submarine qualification process was rigorous and weeded out the wimps.

After dinner, the captain and XO grabbed a fresh cup of coffee and headed to the control room for angles and dangles. The proper name for this process was "verification that the submarine is stowed for submerged operations," thus the slightly suggestive internal rhyme.

The Weps was relieved by Radman, the Navigator (NAV), as the officer of the deck. The Weps told the NAV course speed, contacts, and anything else noteworthy. It took several minutes to provide a proper turnover. When it was through, the Weps finally got to eat.

Radman assumed the duties of officer of the deck: "All stations, this is the navigator. I have the deck and the conn."

The captain told Radman to take the submarine to periscope depth. The NAV acknowledged the captain's orders and carried them out over the next twenty minutes, while the captain and XO retired to the captain's stateroom for more coffee.

"Damn good meal."

"Roger that, sir. Do you want a movie tonight?"

"I'll pass tonight. Roll whatever you want. I'm going to take the night shift, so I may nap after angles and dangles."

The captain and XO rarely slept simultaneously. One or the other was up all the time. Sure, the NAV was capable of safely operating the submarine, but the captain believed in remaining at all times fit to fight.

The after-dinner weekday movies, with popcorn and punch (called bug juice), were a *Quincy* tradition—only broken if an operation prohibited it. Friday and Saturday nights were poker nights.

The captain and XO listened to the open mic and looked at the periscope video repeater in the captain's stateroom to keep tabs on the periscope depth evolution.

Radman: "All stations, conn, going deep."

Freshly caffeinated, the captain and XO returned to the control room.

"Navigator, what is in the mail?" the captain asked.

"There is one 'your eyes only' message."

"Contacts?"

"No one within a hundred miles, Captain."

"Very well, NAV, I'll check out the message after angles and dangles. With no contacts, this seems like a good training opportunity." In other words, if the submarine accidentally surfaced during angles and dangles, there was no chance of hitting anything.

The captain took the conn from the NAV and made an announcement to that effect. "The navigator continues to have the deck," the captain said. Once again, the captain preferred to be in control during potentially hazardous maneuvers.

Angles and dangles, Captain Davis thought, was an excellent training opportunity for junior diving officers, helmsmen and planesmen. He made sure the correct people were in place, and said: "All stations, prepare for extreme angles. Diver, make your depth 600 feet with a twenty-five-degree down angle."

Petty Officer Raymond Bander had shaky knees as he manned the diving officer position. The guy had "under-instruction" written all over his deeply furrowed brow.

Diving officer was the position that most senior enlisted men qualified on. Usually they were a first-class petty officer or above. Bander was a newly promoted first-class fire control technician. Fire control technicians were in charge of the electronics that supported tracking and possibly destroying a target. Ray was a computer wiz—but (obviously!)

controlling the submarine was not in his comfort zone. He was a corn-fed Nebraska farm boy, strong as an ox but meek as a mouse.

The captain ran the training session crisply, giving the student his orders to take the *Quincy* up and down, up and down, up and down. Six-hundred feet, 150 feet, 600 feet, 150 feet. And with each repetition, the captain ordered that the angle of descent and ascent increase by five degrees, until the *Quincy* was climbing and plummeting at a forty-degree angle. This maneuver took all of the diving officer's skills. The trick was to end the dive, or climb, without overshooting the desired depth. The first two repetitions went well, but there was trouble with the forty-degree climb. The student passed 150 feet and took the submarine to the surface.

The crew felt like it had gone airborne.

Accidentally surfacing a submarine was called broaching. When a whale did it, it was called breaching.

The captain joked, "Dive, you just earned your wings."

Punishment for broaching the submarine was wearing aviator wings on a ceremonial leather vest while on watch duty. The student would wear it until the next time an officer broached the submarine.

Bander got the submarine settled at 150 feet.

The vest and wings were brought to him, and he donned them. Bander started to leave the diving officer station.

The captain said, "Where do you think you are going, Dive?"

The young man replied, "Sir, I am taking my flight vest and going where I won't cause any more damage."

"Like hell you are, sailor. You are going to do it until you get it right. You've got nothing to lose—you already have the vest."

"Aye aye, Captain," said Bander nervously.

The submarine returned to 600 feet.

The captain said, "Rise to 150 feet at a forty-degree angle."

The submarine broached again. Some of the watch standers snickered in the control room, including Bander's immediate supervisor, Chief Lionel Ledbetter.

The captain angered, "I don't know what you assholes are laughing at. We are a team, and we are fucking this up together."

The captain put his hand on the young diving officer's shoulder and whispered: "Ray, *listen to me*, you are holding the forty degrees too long. The minute you hit a bubble of forty, flatten out to a down angle if you have to. *You can do this.*"

The diving officer returned the submarine back to 150 feet, then 600 feet. He was poised for his third try, and breathing heavy.

"Dive, make your depth 150 feet with a forty-degree up angle." The captain turned his back to the diving officer to look at the chart.

The diving officer repeated the order, and added, "Captain, we have a forty-degree up angle, coming to 150 feet." He leveled off the submarine at 150 feet perfectly, and let out a deep and audible sigh of relief.

The control room clapped. Bander looked relieved and got up to leave his station.

The captain said, "Bander, where do you think you're going?"

"I was going back to my normal duties in fire control, sir."

"You are now fully qualified as diving officer. Stay in the chair. Chief Ledbetter can take your watch."

"Aye aye, sir."

"Diving Officer, why don't you have the FT of the watch get us all coffee?" This was payback for laughing earlier, everyone understood.

"Aye aye, Captain. Chief Ledbetter, you heard the captain," said Bander.

Once the captain got his coffee, he returned control to the NAV.

"Navigator, please have my message printed and brought to me in my stateroom."

"Aye aye, Captain."

The radioman presently brought two covered clipboards to the captain, one red (captain's eyes only), and a second one blue with the ship's routine communications. The radioman quickly left to allow Captain Davis privacy to decrypt and read the message.

The captain was quickly on the microphone: "XO to the captain's stateroom." The captain did not often call people to his stateroom in this way.

The NAV acknowledged, adding that the XO was on his way. Jay had to admit a charge of fear when he heard the announcement. So soon after his dad's death, was it Mom? Had something happened? But he could tell the instant he saw the captain's expression that the news was not grim, and he felt his shoulders relax.

Jay entered and closed the door behind him. For a moment he began to read the message on the captain's desk upside down, but he quickly pulled his eyes away.

"Relax, XO, this is for you, too. You are not going to believe this. Look at what port we are heading to in the Ukraine. Moreover, we are picking up riders on the way via Holy Loch, Scotland. And what riders!"

VIII

September 7th, 1992

USS *Quincy* To Holy Loch

"I can't believe we have to go to a boomer port. Those blue and gold *prima donnas*!" Jay said. The *Quincy* was a fast attack submarine, manned by one and only one crew—and they were headed to a ballistic missile submarine base in Holy Loch, Scotland. Ballistic missile submarines were also called boomers since their mission was as a floating underwater missile silo with twenty-four strategic nuclear missiles that could each blow up a city. Therefore: "BOOM!" The boomer's two crews, blue and gold, served for alternate three-month periods. During the three months that the off crew wasn't onboard, the men trained in port, and there was plentiful R&R. It was a bone of contention for sailors on fast attack submarines who received R&R once in a blue moon.

"Yes, XO, a boomer base, but that is not what I am finding unbelievable. Read on."

Jay said, "Ah, we are loading a woman spook in Holy Loch and ultimately going to the port of Saint Petersburg, formerly known as Leningrad."

"Bingo, XO. Woman on a submarine! Going to Russia! I do not think a U.S. submarine has ever visited a Russian port. Two skimmers, the *Princeton* and the *Reuben James* visited Vladivostok in 1990."

Jay gave his surroundings a mock looking over. "Um, where is the woman going to stay, Captain?"

"In your stateroom, XO. She is a lieutenant commander in the United Sates Navy. Your stateroom is appropriate."

"It's awkward. Sharing a room with a woman!"

"It won't be awkward at all. Because you are going to move out. Pick a junior officer and take over his bunk. Leave the department heads alone. I'm the one who has it awkward."

"How so, Captain?"

"I have to share a head with a woman that is not my wife."

"Captain, you may want to make sure she is on watch for the entire twenty-four hours after chili night."

The captain laughed. "Goddamn it, XO, that was one time. Hot chili on a submarine. What were they thinking?"

"Captain, maybe I can hot bunk with her. We are all professionals here." That is, share the bed and sleep in shifts.

Dormitory space on a submarine was limited. There were not enough racks for every member of the crew. Bunks were shared by first-tour sailors. The sailors, it should be noted, each had their own pillow and slender bed roll that went on top of the rack.

The captain again shot down Jay's suggestion, adding, "You are starting to piss me off."

"I'll start packing," said Jay.

"And no romances on my submarine, real or perceived. Or even fantasized!"

"Aye aye, Captain. I don't need a new girlfriend; I already have one in Leningrad. I was there once."

"Really, Jay?"

"Yeah, but she wasn't really my girlfriend, Captain. I just wished she was my girlfriend. I was in music school. She had these magic floating fingers."

"You've gone from pissing me off to creeping me out."

"I just played guitar with her."

"Another guitar reference. A very bad sign."

"I played the guitar with her in her dad's guitar shop. With her rather awesome Russian dad in the room. I was nineteen. She might've been younger. Her dad had been a former Victor Three class submarine captain. I sort of connected with the old man. Vlad. He was like one of my Brown elders, only with a Russian accent. It was the old cliché. He told me to follow my heart and I knew I wanted to be a submariner. I set the guitar down—until now. My musical muse has returned just to annoy you."

"I take you at your word that the instrument is for port-use only."

"Yes, sir."

"It's all about doing what you love, XO. We may want to pay your buddy Vlad a visit. For human intelligence purposes. Up for a little humint?"

"This is a diplomatic mission."

"We are *always* gathering intelligence, XO." The captain grabbed the mic. "Crew of the USS *Quincy*, this is your captain speaking. We have received orders to be the first U.S. nuclear powered submarine to dock in Saint Petersburg, Russia. We will be visiting as friends of the newly independent state of Russia. We will be picking up three guests from the U.S. diplomatic corps in Holy Loch, Scotland. They will be our guests on the *Quincy* as we travel to and from Saint Petersburg. The senior officer among our guests is a female U.S. Navy officer. I am very confident she will be treated with the utmost respect and courtesy. You should be very proud to be part of this very exciting chapter in history. I am proud to be part of such a great crew. Continue to make me proud. Carry on."

The captain's announcement was upbeat, perhaps deceptively so. There were many smart sailors on the submarine who thought things through and figured there were whole levels the captain wasn't addressing. Diplomatic corps members frequently had other responsibilities. A little bit of the cloak and dagger. Guys handcuffed to their briefcases. Babes who work as sex lures to loosen the lips of the enemy. They didn't say anything out loud, of course, but internally those smart sailors felt their mission probably had in it an element of espionage.

The captain's warning about the woman—that was pure optimism. Please don't be animals, he was pleading.

When Jay learned of his father's passing, he had expected to be haunted by the man's ghost. He figured his dreams would bring his father "back to life" on a nightly basis, if only in his dreams.

But on the third "night" of the *Quincy*'s journey across the Atlantic, Jay's father appeared for the first time in Jay's dream. It wouldn't be the last. As usual, whether conscious or unconscious, when Jay recalled his dad, Jay was a young boy and was answering a rapid-fire quiz from the old man.

"What was the first nuke?"

"The *Nautilus*, sir."

"Whose concept was the first nuclear-powered submarine?"

"It was conceived by Admiral Hyman Rickover."

"What was his vision regarding atomic research?"

"He saw the atom as a source of energy, not destruction."

"In what year was the *Nautilus* launched, Jay?"

"1954, sir."

"Here's one from left field. Who christened the *Nautilus*?"

"It was the custom to have the First Lady break the bottle. Mamie Eisenhower."

"Getting back to Admiral Rickover, what was his theory of psychodrama?"

"He believed that submarine crews needed to be trained not just how to do the routine things, but how to react in the event of a real crisis."

"Give me an example of Rickover's psychodrama technique."

"During an exercise, he would place a hand on an officer's shoulder and say, 'You're dead.' The man closest, regardless of his rank, then had to take over for the dead man. If men reacted poorly to his psychodrama, they were off the boat."

"One last question, Jay."

"Yes, Dad?"

"Why would I kill myself? It doesn't make any sense, does it?"

Jay woke up, his forehead beaded up with sweat.

That was not Jay's only nightmare of the transit of the Atlantic. But the great majority of his other dreams were happy and, when symbolic, easily interpreted—he was a hot dog chasing a bagel while Abraham Lincoln watched holding a beaver, for example. The days were filled with standard operations, training and drills. No psychodrama. The *Quincy* approached the surface point at 0255 GMT, Thursday, the 10th of September. The captain felt as if the trip had lasted one wonderful day. Jay thought it was a long drawn-out week. Jay moved out of his stateroom. The captain ordered the stewards to make the head cleaner than clean. Jay took Lieutenant Wright's bunk, figuring Wright would gripe the least, and Wright got a rack down in nine-man berthing. As anticipated, Wright did gripe, but not that much. The men quickly struck a deal.

As the captain and XO entered the control room, Wright was suiting up, and sounded aggravated: "How is my bunk working out for you, XO? I hope you changed the sheets."

"Sheets are changed. Thanks for volunteering. I'll make it up to you."

"Thanks, XO. You going to take my sail watch for me?"

"You know what, Ferris?" Jay said. "I can't take your watch right now, but the first round in Holy Loch is on me."

"How about the first two, XO? Then you won't hear me bitch again."

"Sure. Why not?" Jay replied.

While at periscope depth, the captain examined the chart and took a look around. The Weps was officer of the deck.

"Officer of the Deck, surface the ship!" The captain made the announcement with tons of theatricality, almost singing it, and it made every sailor on the boat just a little bit more alert.

"Aye aye, Captain. Surface the ship," replied the Weps. Into the mic, he announced, "Prepare to surface."

When all stations acknowledged their preparedness, the Weps ordered the diving officer to surface the ship. The diving officer chanted rhythmically: "Surface, surface, surface."

The chief of the watch thrice sounded the diving alarm. The submarine drove to the surface.

The captain announced from the periscope, "Decks awash." That was a signal for the chief of the watch to blow the water out of the main ballast tanks. It was important to ensure buoyancy before opening hatches or allowing anyone in the sail.

They remained on the surface overnight. The *Quincy* was scheduled to dock at location code-named "Site One" at 0700.

0610. A half-hour before sunrise. The captain joined the Eng at the top of the sail, where he was standing the officer of the deck watch.

"So Eng, I bet you forget what it's like to dock or undock a submarine."

Eng, earth name Joe Silio, admitted he remembered little. He was usually in the engine room overseeing the startup and shutdown of the reactor during docking and undocking.

The captain said, "The *Quincy* will be tying up to the submarine tender the USS *Simon Lake*, AS-33." The *Simon Lake* was crewed by 1,400 sailors, the captain explained, one-third of them women. It had machine shops, electronics labs, extensive radiological controls capabilities, and rigging to load and unload weapons and equipment onto an adjacent submarine.

The Eng just looked at him wide-eyed.

"This will be good practice for you, Eng. You'll be running your own ship before you know it."

The Eng griped: "If I ever get a command, the tours might be down to six months long with all the downsizing. They say the Cold War is over and we can slack. My gut tells me it ain't so."

The captain sounded soothing as he said: "We'll find a new enemy. We are the world's police force. Somewhere, sooner rather than later, there will be tyranny we must deal with. I'm guessing sooner."

The folks who make money off of war will see to it, the captain thought silently. Captain Davis was a closet conspiracy theorist. Illuminati. Vrill Overlords. Stuff like that. He told no one.

"The Pentagon doesn't know what to do with a submarine these days," said the Eng.

The captain patted him on the shoulder and maintained his comforting tone: "You know, Eng, just like every business, the submarine service ebbs and flows. We are definitely ebbing these days, but if you like what you are doing, keep doing it. And don't worry about what the future holds—it will work itself out."

"Sage advice, Captain. Thank you."

"Have you told your guys to behave with the tender crew?"

"I told them, Captain, but it's always good to hear it from the old man, too."

"You're right. It's time for another pep talk to the crew. Hand me the 1MC."

The Eng was fascinated by the captain's ability to eloquently address a crew of 120 men at the drop of a hat.

"Crew of the USS *Quincy*, this is your captain speaking. We will be docking alongside the USS *Simon Lake* within the next hour. This is a working port of call. We will be making final preparations for our historic port call to Russia and loading our guests. It is imperative that we remain razor sharp focused on getting the ship ready for our diplomatic mission and we continue to maintain the professionalism expected of a world-class cadre of submarine sailors. I am proud to be part of such a great crew. Continue to make me proud. Carry on."

"Captain, Site One is in sight," the Eng said from the playpen, binoculars to his eyes.

The captain looked through his own binoculars. "I see two boomers on the port side and nothing on the starboard side. Call Site One on the radio and find out where they want us, Eng."

"Aye aye, Captain." On the radio, the Eng said, "Site One, this is inbound vessel seeking docking information, over."

The radio crackled. "Inbound vessel, this is Site One. You will be docking on our starboard side with your port side to Site One, over."

The Eng replied, "Roger, Site One, I copy. Inbound vessel to dock on your starboard side with our port side to, over."

"Inbound vessel, do you require tugs or pusher boat assistance, over?"

The captain shook his head no.

Mildly concerned, the Eng said, "Site One, we will need no assistance other than line handlers, over."

"Inbound vessel, line handlers are standing by, out."

"I hope this goes well," said the Eng to the captain.

"You will do just fine. I'll help you only if I have to. Stay calm, move slow, and think about how much of a badass you will be in front of these boomer sailors that get underway and dock only eight times a year—always with tugs. It's a beautiful day, the sun in shining and conditions are perfect."

"Well, if you put it that way, let's do it, sir." The Eng noticed a fifteen-knot wind and cloudy skies. Conditions were not perfect, but he wasn't going to let facts get in the way of the captain's inspirational words.

0700. First line thrown over to the crew of the tender. Thirty minutes later, the *Quincy* was tied up with a gangway installed. Wearing his underway coveralls, Captain Davis was first across the gangway. Awaiting him in the quarterdeck of the tender was a number of officers, also in coveralls, some wearing submarine sweaters on top. Included in the group was the Group 2 commander, Admiral Bennett, the commodore of Ballistic Submarine Squadron 14, Captain James Riffer, and the captain of the *Simon Lake*, Captain Gumbert. Also awaiting Captain Davis was the captain of the USS *Will Rogers*, Captain Robert Young "Yogi" Kaufman, and the captain of the USS *Daniel Boone*, Captain Bruce W. Cavey.

Captain Davis exchanged greetings with the men. Admiral Bennett explained that the brass was there because Site One was shutting down.

A decommissioning ceremony was scheduled for the next night, but Davis wouldn't be there to enjoy it.

"You are heading out first thing tomorrow morning. We have a busy day planned for you. This morning will be technical briefings. This afternoon you will be getting your mission briefing. You should be done around 1600 for a little R&R, then back onboard at 2000 for an 0900 underway in the morning. Get your officers and the chief of the boat to the quarterdeck at 0900. There will be escorts to take you to the morning briefing room."

Four hours of R&R seemed slight, Captain Davis thought, but he kept his lip zipped. He was less polite when addressing the boomer captains—as he was friends with Yogi Kaufman and Bruce Cavey from back in the Groton days—once referring to them, because of their comparatively light schedule, as a pair of "girls".

Admiral Bennett didn't like that. This was no time for anything that might have the slightest scent of sexism: "Watch it, Captain Davis! This ship is one-third women, and you are about to take on a woman rider. I hear another crack like that, I'll give Yogi command of the USS *Quincy* and you can take his boat on patrol."

"Sorry, Admiral. We were being familiar, but I understand. That's no excuse." The boomer captains openly enjoyed Captain Davis's dressing down.

Captain Kaufman turned to Davis, and said, "We will exchange crews in Kings Bay, Georgia, when we get back."

Captain Davis asked, "Are you moving down there?"

Captain Kaufman replied, "We are going to keep Squadron 14 in place in Groton for a year, and transition Site One ballistic missile subs in Kings Bay and Bangor. The *Boone* and the *Rogers* are transitioning to Kings Bay."

Davis offered his sympathy. The boomer captains had families in Groton that were disrupted again by the navy. He suggested they meet right there at 1601. "We can head ashore together and grab a beer."

"Sounds good," they replied.

To the admiral, Captain Davis said, "I'm guessing we won't see the Cowal Peninsula again anytime soon after this week, sir."

"We may not," Admiral Bennett said. "But you will. You'll learn more in the afternoon briefing."

IX

Friday, September 11th, 1992
USS *Quincy* In Holy Loch

0910. The officers of the USS *Quincy* were gathered in the refit briefing room of the USS *Simon Lake.* The room was located amidships in the forward portion of the *Simon Lake* on the 02 level, a few decks below the bridge.

Jay's eyes scanned. There was a large blackboard with a folding table in front. Four navy personnel sat at the front of the room: one female commander, Admiral Bennett, a lieutenant commander, and a master chief petty officer.

Everyone wore underway coveralls. On the right side of the blackboard was a U.S. flag on a stand. The U.S. Navy flag was to the left. There were folding chairs for the visiting officers. All but two of the *Quincy*'s officers were in the room. Only the in port command duty officer (CDO) and the Eng were holding down the fort. Jay turned his neck around. In the back of the room was another folding table with a Bunn coffee maker, three metal pots of navy coffee (zing!), and paper cups. Sugar and powdered creamer were available. Next to the coffee maker was a two-foot tall urn with a sight glass showing the level of hot water for cocoa, tea or decaf instant Sanka. The table was doing brisk business, everyone with a cup of something, so Jay poured himself a black coffee and took a seat. The officers sat more-or-less in order of rank, with the admiral charmingly allowing the captain of the vessel the best seat. The *Quincy*'s officers tried not to stare at the woman in the room, with only partial success. It had only been a week, but a new gender was startling.

Lieutenant Wright sat in the row behind Captain Davis and so had to lean forward to ask in a stage whisper, "Is that her, Captain?"

The captain shrugged as if he neither knew nor cared.

The admiral stood in front of the blackboard and began the briefing: "Captain Davis and men of the USS *Quincy*, welcome to the USS *Simon Lake*." The admiral offered a brief history of Site One and explained that the *Simon Lake* would be leaving that week. "The *Simon Lake* remains here on station this day to support preparing the USS *Quincy* for their historic mission to Russia. The decision to decommission Site One was made last year and it was very important to have the *Lake* here to calibrate and test the special equipment that has been installed on the *Quincy*." The admiral paused for a sip of his coffee. "Your mission is three-fold. In addition to a diplomatic mission and assisting in the monitoring and control of nuclear material by our now Russian allies, the *Quincy* will conduct baseline monitoring of the background radiation level of Site One tomorrow. When you return, your mission in Russia complete, you will return and monitor this same site without the *Simon Lake* present. The data you gather will provide vital data to assure the United Kingdom that we left Site One in the same condition we found it in when we arrived in 1961. This morning, you will be briefed on the final testing and calibration, as well as the monitoring procedures of the background radiation and contamination monitoring equipment installed on the *Quincy*."

"Touch and sniff," John Little blurted out.

"Excuse me?" said the admiral. His briefings were not usually heckled.

"Sorry to interrupt, Admiral, sir," Little said. "It's the code name we came up with for the mission. 'Touch' being the background radiation detection and 'sniff' being the contamination monitoring."

"Scratch and sniff, what's your name?"

"Little, sir, Lieutenant Junior Grade Little, sir—and it's touch and sniff, sir. I am not sure where people get this scratch idea from."

The admiral had heard enough. "Touch and sniff, it is!" he said. "It beats our name, RACTAM for radiation and contamination testing and monitoring." The admiral continued. Who would be the first to laugh aloud? "We had RACTAM 1 for radiation, and RACTAM 2 for contamination. Let's call it RACTAM touch—or touch for short—for monitoring, and RACTAM sniff—or sniff for short—for contamination detection."

That did it. The room dissolved into laughter.

The admiral pretended not to get it, but waited for the laughter to subside before he said to the officer taking the minutes, "Lets revise the Navy Warfare Publication for RACTAM to include this terminology and make sure we credit Lieutenant Junior Grade Little. Let's be prepared to make other revisions as we brief the *Quincy* this morning."

The admiral raced through an itinerary: "Your morning briefings will last approximately two hours, then we will conduct some tests of the RACTAM touch and sniff gear. You are all invited to have lunch in the *Simon Lake* wardroom. The afternoon briefings will be limited to the captain, XO, and the officers of the NAV/OPS, and Weps department. The briefing will commence at 1330 in the war room located directly above this one."

The admiral turned his attention to Captain Davis, "Joe, in the afternoon briefing you will meet your riders and get further instructions on your mission."

To the larger group he said, "The rest of you will prepare the *Quincy* for tomorrow's underway. Let me introduce the three individuals that will be speaking to you this morning. First is Lieutenant Commander Joel Forrester. Joel is the program manager for the RACTAM project."

Forrester interjected, "Touch and sniff is fine with me. I like it."

That got a mild laugh.

The admiral continued, "Commander Forrester holds more degrees than I can cover in the hour and a half we have remaining. He is going to brief you on the engineering and design behind the equipment. He has promised to keep his overview brief and will avoid the use of differential equations in his discussion."

That received a more confident laugh.

"After Commander Forrester, the briefing will be conducted by Master Chief Riggs. He is a nuclear machinist mate, engineering laboratory technician and a former COB for three fast attack submarines much like the *Quincy*," said the admiral.

The men of the *Quincy* made "ourah" sounds as Riggs took a bow.

"The master chief is going to discuss operation of the equipment and review the NWP that you will leave with today. He will answer any questions you might have on the equipment and will spend the afternoon with those of you that will conduct the final tests and calibrations.

"Last but not least, we have Commander Laurel Salton or Doc Salton, as everyone calls her. Doc is qualified as a diving medical officer and submarine medical officer. She is a radiation health officer and undersea medical officer for Site One. She is the issuer and controller of the nuclear material you will be using to test and calibrate the equipment. Doc Salton will also be assisting in the testing and calibration of the equipment."

The men of the *Quincy* were confused. There was increased whispering and chatter among them.

The low-level hubbub in the room continued until Doc herself spoke up in a clear alto voice: "You will understand my role better after Commander Forrester and Master Chief Riggs deliver their briefings. Basically, I'll be using special radiation and contamination sources to calibrate the new gear. Bottom line, I am going to make sure no one gets an excessive radiation dose or gets contaminated."

The morning briefings continued until 1130, at which time Riggs and Doc Salton accompanied officers back to the *Quincy* to walk through the test. The officers remaining onboard the *Simon Lake* had lunch in the wardroom at a large table with the admiral, and captains Riffer and Gumbert.

Salton, Riggs and Forrester, having delivered their briefing, left without fanfare.

After lunch, six officers—Davis, Brown, Armstrong, Radzemski, Wright and Little—huddled in the corner of the *Simon Lake*'s wardroom. The captain was the quarterback: "There is a reason that it's called special compartmented information. Whatever we hear this afternoon, the XO or I will let you know if you can know it, and, if you can know it, to whom you can tell it. It might seem innocent, but there is a reason only we are getting briefed. Understood?"

Everyone mumbled, "Understood."

Although every officer and many of the enlisted men onboard a submarine held top secret security clearances, special compartmented information (SCI) meant only individuals with a "need to know" were provided certain information.

Admiral Bennett interrupted, "You guys ready to head to the war room?"

"Yes, sir," the *Quincy* officers replied, more or less in unison. They followed the admiral through a few short passages and ladder wells to arrive at an unmarked steel grey door that had a circular button pad above the doorknob. The admiral opened the door to a small room, twelve by twelve feet with two uniformed and side-armed marines at the far-end security desk.

The admiral said, "All right, gents, step up to the desk with your IDs in hand and be prepared to be photographed and electronically fingerprinted."

After that was done, the marines explained that they were to enter the briefing room one person at a time using a hand scanner to enter and a hand scanner to depart.

Little asked, "What if there is a power failure, do the locks fail open?"

The marine Gunnery Sergeant replied, "No sir, the doors fail in the locked position. In the event of a fire or emergency, we will unlock the door and let you out."

"What if you guys are incapacitated during a fire?" asked Little.

"Sir, this space is highly insulated, flame retardant, and has its own ventilation and power supply. In that unlikely event you have described you would all succumb to the elements and breathe your last breath in this compartment. Sir, aren't you attached to a submarine?"

Little looked a little disturbed and replied, "Yes, I am. Thank you, Gunny Sergeant."

"My pleasure, sir," replied the gunny.

The rest of the officers looked much less concerned.

Captain Davis said, "Come on, Little, let's get on with our death march."

The admiral and the officers filed into the war room. It was unexpectedly dark, with blue lights, and at the front was an oversized and internally illuminated map, ten feet wide with markings on it. Dark screens flanked the well-lit chart on either side. One area of the chart was spotlighted: Western Europe from the Mediterranean to the Barents Sea, and the U.K. to Saint Petersburg.

The chairs were padded like theater seats. Jay noticed there was no coffee—but a futuristic assemblage of electronics. Before the map was a round briefing table holding something that resembled, at first glance, a Monopoly game board, tilted slightly forward so they could see another much-smaller map, spotted with blue, yellow and red magnet pieces shaped like ships and military aircraft. Jay figured the blues were U.S. Four people sat at the briefing table. Riffer was one. The other three were difficult to make out. Perhaps after Jay's eyes dilated further he would recognize them.

The officers took seats in rank order. Captain Davis and the admiral chitchatted about lunch. Jay's eyes were dilating, and he was recognizing. His brain was flooded, in fact, with the recognition. He didn't move, blink or breathe.

It was a woman. (The second one of the day!)

No.

It couldn't be.

The captain and admiral noticed Jay's statue impression.

The captain said, "Gee, Admiral, I think the XO's in love already."

Jay didn't hear the comment. He was too busy staring at Cassie Voxer. Jay's mind raced. This meant the *Quincy*'s upcoming mission was likely tied to his father's work regarding the control of nuclear material in the former Soviet Union. Jay knew that compartmented information because of his personal relationship with Cassie. Jay finally managed to pull his eyes off the woman and recognized the man next to her as

Lieutenant Jeff Cody. The third officer, between Cody and the commodore, was an unknown lieutenant commander. Jay took a deep breath but still looked like the guy whose mouth was most apt to gape.

"XO, snap out of it," Captain Davis said.

"Sorry, sir. I went to the academy with the female lieutenant commander and just saw her at my dad's funeral," said Jay, master of the understatement. The mention of the funeral got the captain and admiral off his case, as they now merely nodded sympathetically.

Captain Riffer stood up. "Welcome, officers of the USS *Quincy*, and good afternoon."

"Good afternoon, sir," the officers echoed in a raggedy unison.

Riffer continued: "Gentlemen and lady, the briefing you are about to receive is SCI and for your eyes and ears only, not to be shared with anyone else." He added five minutes of unnecessary "loose lips sink ships" anecdotes. The officers got it. Their lips were zipped. "The mission of the *Quincy* is actually four-fold. Your primary mission is to be an ambassador for the U.S. and present yourself professionally and diplomatically to Russia in the city of Saint Petersburg, as well as project the power of the United States military."

Riffer gestured at the unknown officer seated at the briefing table. "Lieutenant Commander Mark Maximov is a deck officer in the Royal Submarine service. Mark is going to be temporarily assigned to the *Quincy* and is a Russian linguist, and culture and etiquette expert. He is also an expert in submerged operations in the North Atlanta and the Gulf of Finland."

His vast credentials got everyone from the *Quincy* buzzing a little.

Maximov said, "I am also part Russian and grew up in a Russian-speaking house. I am also completely Jewish—so hold the bacon."

It was a joke, and received a smattering of laughter, but Captain Davis took the comment seriously enough to say to the admiral, "Kosher stores, I hope. We don't have any conservative Jewish crew members."

The admiral whispered back, "You still don't. Mark is being a wiseass. And don't worry, I have you loaded with kosher goods, in case Maximov wants a traditional nosh."

"Very considerate of you, Admiral," Captain Davis said.

The admiral was still talking about Maximov: "The lieutenant commander will be the first briefing after I stop talking."

"Your secondary mission is to monitor, correlate and report background and contamination levels. This monitoring will take place everywhere you travel—from getting underway tomorrow until you return to Her Majesty's Naval Base Clyde in Faslane, Scotland," said Captain Riffer.

"Delivering me right back home, thank you very much," said Mark Maximov in his peculiar accent, a Scottish and Russian combo. He sounded to Jay like Illya Kuryakin on the old TV show *The Man from U.N.C.L.E.*

Captain Riffer said, "Just for you, Mark. Next, Lieutenant Commander Voxer will review strategically what we are looking for with the RACTAM equipment."

"I am just the warm-up for the Sneaky Beaky's," said Maximov, using royal navy slang for intelligence officers.

Riffer ignored Maximov and said, "She is a qualified naval intelligence officer whose extensive résumé is classified, but will make a hell of a book someday. The focus of her briefing is your secondary mission, gathering radiation and contamination readings at key formerly-Soviet sites and correlating them to known and expected levels."

The *Quincy*'s officers looked confused. Seemed like they would be shooting in the dark.

Voxer spoke up, "Gentlemen, don't worry. There is a method to our madness. We have evidence indicating that nuclear material is being smuggled out of Russia, and we are going to figure out how this is happening."

Riffer said, "Voxer will also brief you on your tertiary mission, to baseline Site One tomorrow, then scan it again when you come back to Faslane."

Voxer editorialized, "That's an easy mission. Just keep the RACTAM equipment on and follow the monitoring paths, and the equipment has everything it needs."

Little raised his hand.

Captain Riffer said, "I didn't know we had gotten to the question and answer period of our briefing. Oh, all right, Horshack, what's your question?"

"Aren't we calling it touch and sniff?" said Little.

Riffer looked perplexed.

Admiral Bennett spoke up, "Yes, Captain Riffer, we are calling RACTAM touch and sniff. I can explain later, if you care."

Voxer shrugged her lovely shoulders and said, "Touch and sniff it is."

Riffer raised his voice, "Everyone is getting a little giddy. One more introduction. This is Lieutenant Jeff Cody. Jeff is a cryptographic expert and, although very young, one of the best in the business. Jeff is not going to speak; he is here to observe and interpret."

Cody offered a shy wave. "I look forward to working with everyone," he mumbled.

Riffer must've needed the head. He quickly said, "With that, let's take a quick break. There is a head and a pantry through this door, so you don't have to hand scan in and out again. Let's give ourselves ten minutes and collect back here at 1330." Riffer shot through the door.

As everyone stood, Cassie and Jay tried not to look too excited. Cody was right behind Cassie.

"Holy mackerel," Jay said. "I can't believe you guys are here."

"I know," piped in Jeff Cody. Cassie and Jay ignored him.

"It's not a coincidence," Cassie said. "The *Quincy* was lined up to do this mission as a surprise for you from your dad. We, of course, couldn't say anything. I think Captain Douche Royce wanted to screw it up, but timing prevented us from lining up another submarine."

Jay thought, more things that didn't make sense. Why would his dad kill himself two weeks before beginning a mission with his kid?

"Are you free after this? We have liberty from 1600 to 2000," said Jay.

Cody replied, "Heck yeah, I'm free!"

Cassie said, "We have to bring our stuff down to the *Quincy*."

"That should take all of five minutes," Jay said. Now it was his turn to brief Cassie, on the sleeping arrangements. "You are in my stateroom on the top deck. Jeff is going to be in the nine-man berthing on lower level and Lieutenant Commander Maximov is also bunking in my stateroom," said Jay.

"I'm sharing a room with two men!"

"No, no, Cassie you are in my usual stateroom where I share a head with the captain."

"Join the navy and see the world," Cassie quipped.

Jay continued, "I have moved to officer's country next to the wardroom. Grab your stuff and bring it to the quarterdeck at 1600 and I'll show you where to put it," said Jay.

"So I'm sharing a head with the captain. How awkward!"

"Believe me, Cassie, the captain is more nervous about it than you are. You'll get into a routine. By the way, do you guys have what I had asked for back in D.C.?"

Cody said, "Yes, sir. I have the sheet music your dad had me analyzing and three cassette tapes with the background music from..." He stopped and corrected himself. "With the background music you requested."

"Good job," Jay said. "We will play with that on the way to Saint Petersburg. Did you bring any recording equipment?"

Cody said, "Yes, I brought the kit the admiral had told me to pull together. He told me he was going to have me deciphering my ass off."

"We'll look at the kit tomorrow after we get underway," said Jay.

The afternoon briefings resumed at 1330. Lieutenant Commander Mark Maximov went first, and gave a most entertaining presentation. He made fun of the Russian culture, but also respected it. He kept the punchlines coming as he displayed his familiarity with the waters to Saint Petersburg as well as those from Holy Loch to the Baltic Sea. He used the illuminated wall chart and the table for much of his briefing. For a time, everyone stood around the war room table while Maximov explained the naval forces in the area.

When it was Cassie's turn, she presented herself with confidence and force. The key to their mission was the correlation of many sensors: touch and sniff, sonar signatures, decrypted radio communication, time and location.

"Put together, this data will paint a picture," Cassie said. She also used the war room table but pulled out new magnetic pieces, tiny donkeys to illustrate the possible mules that might be hauling nuclear material out of Russia. (Cassie had considered getting the magnets shaped like high-heeled slippers, but didn't think her audience would get the joke.)

1530. Admiral Bennett stood and thanked the briefers for their notably professional presentations. "Let's gather around the table one more time. Captain Davis, you are going to need to be at your best for this transit to Saint Petersburg. As a show of strength and power projection—and just to be a general pain in the ass—you are directed to transit out of Holy Loch, submerge at the dive point, and not to surface again until you are at the border of Russian territorial waters. At that point, you will surface and ask permission from the Russians to enter territorial waters. Lieutenant Commander Maximov will hail Saint Pete in Russian on the radio. He knows the protocols."

Maximov spoke up, "So, Admiral, you don't mean the entire route submerged, right? I would think we would surface to transit the Danish Oresund."

The admiral was firm: "You would think wrong, Mr. Maximov. The *Quincy* is to transit that route at night while at periscope depth."

"That's a quite narrow and shallow bit."

"Yes, it is, but we don't want any imagery capturing the transit of the *Quincy*. We want to surprise Russia with our stealth."

"Aye aye, sir. We will surprise them, all right," Maximov said.

The admiral continued, "The *Quincy* is expected to arrive at the surface point at 1200, Wednesday, the 16th of September. You will then transit slowly on the surface and dock in Saint Petersburg at 0800, Thursday, the 17th. You will depart Monday, September 21st at 0800. You know what to do between submerging at noon tomorrow and surfacing. *Don't get detected.*"

"Aye aye, sir," said Captain Davis.

X

SATURDAY, SEPTEMBER 12TH, 1992 TRANSIT: HOLY LOCH TO ST. PETERSBURG

Many of the officers and crew of the *Quincy* enjoyed a nice meal ashore in Holy Loch, and all were back onboard by 2000. The submarine got underway exactly at 0900 with the three additional riders onboard. The *Quincy* transited northwest out of Scotland and reached the dive point at 1300.

Cassie, Cody and Maximov were in the control room for the initial dive. Cassie had been on a submarine before, but only for a day. Cody had never been underway or submerged on a submarine. To everyone's amusement, the abrupt diving alarm caused Cody to jump.

Maximov said to the captain, "I can't believe you Americans still have to walk around periscopes. Makes me dizzy watching you." Maximov explained that Royal Navy periscopes rotated with a motor. The person attending to the scope could straddle a seat that folded down from the scope like riding a horse.

Captain Davis agreed, "We're still using the same periscope technology we stole from the Germans during World War II."

"Why mess with success?" Maximov said with a smile.

The captain noticed Cody's white knuckles. "Why are you holding on for dear life, Cody?"

"I am just preparing for angles and dangles, sir. I want to be prepared for the barrel roll."

"The barrel roll? You're having your chain yanked, Cody. I'm going over in my mind the list of suspects," the captain said, not totally unamused. He scanned the room, but *everyone* looked guilty.

"Are you looking forward to angles and dangles, Cody?" the captain asked, taunting a little bit himself now. Everyone loved to pick on the nervous guy.

"No, captain. I'm am looking forward to angles and dangles being successfully completed."

"Then, let's not draw out your dread. That would be cruel. We will do angles and dangles now, and get it over with."

The captain picked up the mic and gave his usual underway pep talk. "We're about to conduct angles and dangles. One other thing: The *Quincy* will be rigged for quiet until the submarine surfaces again in four days. That would be, what? Wednesday, the 16th of September.

The officer of the deck was Armstrong.

"Weps, conduct angles and dangles."

Cody had a new anxiety: "Captain, how long can a nuclear submarine like the USS *Quincy* operate submerged?"

The captain warmed up to the question. This was one of his favorite subjects. "Cody, the USS *Quincy* can go three months without surfacing. We are limited only by our food supply."

Up thirty degrees.

"What's the longest you have been submerged personally?" Cody asked, a man of many fears, yet oddly unafraid to be inquisitive.

Down thirty degrees.

Captain Davis recalled from which office of the navy Cody came, and he felt a twinge of a conspiracy theory pang at the back of his mind.

Up thirty-five degrees.

"Three months," the captain said. "Did you feel that barrel roll?"

Cody's eyes went wide with amazement, "No. I'm feeling some big angles."

The captain changed his tone. "All right, Cody. I apologize. There is no barrel roll. Enough already. Depending on who got to you, there is also no bucket of relative bearing grease, there are no scales to weigh the anchor. There is definitely no net positive suction head for electrons."

Like a show-business veteran, the captain waited for everyone to stop laughing, then turned to the officers in the control room and said, "OK. We've had our fun, but our guests are here for a reason and I don't want them distracted or stressed. I have a feeling the next few days are going to be balls to the wall busy."

Cody turned to Cassie and said, "I would have known the electrons one was a joke, ma'am but balls to the wall?"

"Your not really asking me about balls are you?" Cassie said. She could roll her eyes with her voice alone.

Cody moved away quickly.

The USS *Quincy* remained submerged, heading north toward a course change point. They arrived at 1900 and went to periscope depth to obtain a fix, download the broadcast and take a look around. A quick peek, then they would submerge to a cruising depth, maintain a course of 123 and travel south of the Shetland Islands toward Norway.

The riders had settled into their underway routine. Maximov frequented the chart and control room. Cody holed up behind the locked doors of the radio room. Every time the *Quincy* headed to periscope depth, Cody saw to it that relevant radio communications were captured and recorded for future analysis.

Cassie became a fixture in the computer and electronic space just forward of her temporary stateroom. There was a rack in there that had a combination lock that only she, the Weps and the captain could unlock. Inside the rack was the correlation equipment for touch and sniff. Various inputs—from sonar, inertial navigation, electronic signals, video from the periscope, and the readings for both the touch and sniff sensors—all were stored in a two-gigabyte array in the bottom of the cabinet and processed by an HP-9020 tactical computer with a RISC processor. The modified HP-9020 had more processing and storage capacity than all the computing capabilities of the USS *Quincy* combined. There was also a Zenith laptop in the enclosure with a 3-1/2-inch floppy drive and a 100-megabyte hard drive.

Every time Jay looked at it, all that state-of-the-art stuff, he thought about the price tag. How much did it cost? Was it a figure he could even comprehend?

The laptop could be plugged in throughout the submarine via the many BNC connections available to the *Quincy*'s SNAP 2 networked computing system, a system primarily used by the supply department. Cassie's treasure trove of equipment was shipped to her and was stored in a round stainless steel trashcan with a Naugahyde cushion lid.

During a quiet moment in D.C., Cassie had flirted with Jay by confiding that her intelligence-gathering skills were based on her acute senses. At least it started out as flirting, but she had become serious when she told him she could hear like a bat and smell like a bloodhound. She didn't think of it as a God-given talent, however. She knew how hard it was, to focus like that. She considered her abilities tradecraft. On the *Quincy*, she was all ears, listening to everything she could hear, and even reading lips when she saw someone speaking from afar. She quickly picked up on the sub's odd combination of efficient protocol and prepubescent boy humor. When at her station, Cassie wore a headset that allowed her to listen to the control room. The headset had a small microphone, so she could communicate with the control room, if necessary. She heard things like, "Dusk. All upper level spaces rigged for red." It sounded like poetry, some of it.

While at periscope depth, Cassie said into her mic, "Officer of the Deck, request you raise the number one BRA-34 for *touch* operations." Sounded a little funny, but she figured she might as well go with it.

Radman, the NAV, was officer of the deck. "Raising number one BRA-34."

Cassie watched her program as the BRA-34 antennae poked out of the water. Reaction was immediate. There was an increase of expected background radiation. The touch sensor was directional. The front of the antennae was most sensitive.

Cassie said, “I have an increase in background radiation level. Request a course adjustment to the left or right to resolve directionality.”

That made the control room buzz. In two breaths, the captain and Weps were there with her, looking over her shoulder. Jay, a lone man, was left in the control room to operate the periscope and oversee safe operation of the submarine.

Jay proved he’d been paying attention at the briefing: “All stations, turning right with a three-degree rudder.” That slight rudder movement, Jay remembered, offered optimal radiation detection.

Cassie monitored a small view of the periscope, radiation levels, location, direction, speed and depth of the *Quincy*. As the submarine turned the radiation levels reduced.

The captain said to Cassie, “Tell them from the captain, ‘shift your rudder.’”

Cassie acknowledged the order from the captain and repeated as if she had been conning a submarine her entire career.

“Look, radiation levels are creeping back up. Looks like max level is on the course we were on, due north,” Cassie said.

The captain came up with a quick plan, and ordered that the submarine come back to due north, drop all antennae and scopes, except for the number two periscopes, and increase speed to ten knots.

Armstrong looked to the captain and said, “And why don’t we have women in submarines, Captain?”

“I can’t think of a reason right now,” the captain said, which made Cassie feel great.

Then she laughed lightly, and said, “No thanks for me. With all the respect in the world for what you guys do, I do not want to drive a submarine for a living. Partial doses like this are good enough for me—thank you, very much.”

Only moments later, as the submarine smoothly proceeded on course, a silhouette formed in the video from the periscope. The image was captured off the RACTAM console, and that low-light image could be enhanced, captured and blown up. It was amazing, mind-blowing technology. They closed to within one hundred yards of the image and it became clearer.

The enhanced image was startling. The silhouette now looked very much like a ballistic missile submarine on the surface. But it had a little something extra. The submarine had a bump coming out of the missile platform well aft of the sail.

The captain still standing behind Cassie and relaying his orders through her, said, "OK, Cassie, tell the conn to slow to five knots, raise the number one periscope for safety and bump the number one BRA-34 four feet out of the water. Keep the number two scope on the contact of interest."

The number one periscope was used to sweep around and around to make sure a quiet sailboat—or anything else that didn't make much noise—didn't sneak up on them. The number two periscope had the enhanced optics, night vision, magnification and built-in video camera.

After relaying the captain's orders, Cassie added, "We are getting a good sonar signature from the bearing, but it looks like they are submerging. Also, there are no radiation levels coming from the vessel anymore; they should have increased."

"Ask for sonar signature correlation."

Cassie did and reported back, "Sonar reports, ninety-five percent certain it is an India class submarine, over fifty percent certain it is the second of the class."

Hearing the words "India class" caused Jay to access his knowledge on the subject. The info was filed in quiz form, with the ghost of his dad firing the questions.

"NATO knows these submarines as India class subs. By what name do they refer to themselves?"

"The Soviets call their submarines Project 940 Lenok. A Lenok is a type of salmon, sir."

"And what is the primary mission of the India class submarine?"

"Sir, it is a mother ship for two Poseidon Deep Submergence Rescue Vehicles. They are commonly referred to as DSRVs, or mini subs."

Jay snapped back to the present. The captain was talking.

"It is so strange. The India class is a diesel-powered submarine. They carry two deep submergence rescue vehicles for submarine rescue and recovery. Why would it have rad levels?"

It was almost like an echo to Jay. He felt a strong sense of déjà vu.

Cassie replied, "Captain, the radiation levels are no longer detectable. Still, all indications are that this is a high-interest target for our mission. Sonar also reported it looked like the India had an accidental surfacing because of the sound of main ballast pumps operating."

Perhaps a young crew member was working on his angles and dangles and overshot his mark, the captain thought. "Any other contacts of interest in the area?"

Cassie replied, "From sonar and RACTAM, Captain, there are a couple of merchant ships and a high-speed luxury yacht. The merchants are in the opposite direction of our detection, and the yacht is in the general direction but was never on the same bearing as radiation detection."

"Interesting," said the captain. "I have a feeling this is one of the first pieces to the puzzle." He paused a beat to think, and then added, "All right, Cassie, pass the word to the conn to submerge. Let's quietly get away from our India friend."

"Aye aye, Captain," Cassie said. "Quietly getting away, sir."

After a busy first day at sea, everyone slept well. Everyone except Jay. His schedule had him sleeping during the day, which had his sleep cycle off. Not that there was a clear-cut day and night in a submerged submarine anyway. Normally, odd hours didn't bother him, but during this day's snooze, he had his sleep visitor again, his father, so real he felt he could reach out and touch him. As usual, Jay felt like a small child during the dream, but his father didn't look the way he did when Jay was a kid. Dad looked like the last time Jay saw him, the way he looked when he died.

"Today, we are going to talk about the toilets aboard a submarine," Dad said.

"Yes, sir."

"Describe for me how a submarine toilet works."

"Yes, sir. There is an eight-inch ball valve at the bottom. A one-inch pipe fills the bowl with seawater. To flush you pull the handle and the ball valve opens, connecting the toilet basin with the sanitary tank, and the waste flows down the pipe into the tank."

"And what happens when the sanitary tank is full?"

"The submarine blows sanitary. Do not flush the toilet during this process or you will get a face full of sewage."

"Very good, Grasshopper. How many strings on a classical Russian guitar?"

"Seven, sir."

"And what do they represent?"

"I don't know," little Jay said. He looked down and saw he was standing in his underwear. Looking back, his father was gone and replaced by Cassie, who was exquisite in her birthday suit. He woke with a start.

Jay tried to relax again and get some more shuteye but gave up after a few minutes and poured himself a cup of coffee. It was time for the after-dinner movie.

Sunday the 13th was quiet. There were no additional hits on the RACTAM unit. Jay had not missed a thing. The dream had him thinking. He tried to think of it symbolically. Dreams worked that way—there were codes that your subconscious understood. Or something. Jay had read an article about it once while waiting for a doctor's appointment. Did the first part of the dream mean that everything else was bullshit? And what *did* the seven strings represent?"

The movie in the wardroom after dinner was the *Prince of Tides* with Nick Nolte and Barbara Streisand. It reminded the captain of his southern roots.

At the end of the movie, it was time for Jay to relieve the captain.

Jay said to Cassie and Cody: "After I turnover with the captain, I would like to talk with you guys for a few minutes, if you have the time."

Cody said, "Are we in trouble?"

"No, you knucklehead. I just want to talk to you."

Cassie said, "No problem, Jay. How long will you be with the captain? We'll just meet you back here."

"Sounds good. Give me ten, no. Fifteen minutes."

Jay locked all of the wardroom doors and rigged the wardroom for max security.

The captain said, "Seems serious, XO. I was just going to tell you to keep heading toward Saint Petersburg and don't get detected. Then I was going to share with you today's football scores."

"Captain, I wanted to let you know that this mission is very nerve-racking for me. Both Cassie and Cody are from my dad's staff. My dad specifically selected the USS *Quincy* so that he could do some father-and-son bonding underway," said Jay. "It's a rather haunting sentiment, considering."

"Of course, Jay, I have known that all along. The admiral and the commodore wanted to yank you off the ship, but I advised them otherwise."

"Captain, I greatly appreciated your confidence in me. Thank you, sir."

"You're welcome, Jay."

"Captain, here's where it gets fishy." Jay told him the details of his time in D.C., about Royce and the special relinquishment of claims document he and his mother had to sign after the briefing with Admiral Conner. Jay told the captain about his request for tapes and sheet music from Cassie and Cody, a request made before he even knew they were all going on a mission together.

"OK, so your friends, the spooks, brought sheet music that the former director of naval intelligence was analyzing, as well as the tapes of the background music for the night of his demise."

"Yes, sir," Jay replied. He liked that word. Demise. It was so much better than death or suicide—or drippy euphemisms like unfortunate occurrence and unexpected departure.

"Have you told anyone else about the special relinquishment of claims?"

"I am sure Cassie knows based on conversations with me and being part of the office."

"I'm not worried about her. As far as I'm concerned, you never told me either." He paused and added, "So, if naval intelligence were to use the USS *Quincy*'s resources to conduct further analysis of an ongoing project that I have no need to know about, that's their business."

"Yes, sir," said Jay. "Which is not to say that you shouldn't remain informed of the situation to the best of your XO's ability."

"And if and when you find something out that I need to know, you will let me know?"

"Precisely, sir."

"Oops, looks like your Patriots lost again, to the L.A. Rams. Fourteen-zip. Cowboys won in overtime over the Giants. In baseball news, the Red Sox are still in dead last place in their division."

"Captain, I don't know what I did to deserve this taunting. I'm sorry there's no major league baseball in Louisiana. You know I come from a family that suffers from the Boston curse. The curse of the Bam-fucking-bino, pardon my French. My great grandfather saw the last World Series the Red Sox won in 1918. Babe Ruth pitched in that one, you know."

"Really?"

Jay thought about that for a moment and said, "Babe Ruth really pitched, yeah. Was my great grandfather there? Probably not. My great grandfather was a navy guy. Served in pig boats in World War I."

"Those guys are notorious distorters of the truth. Still, Babe Ruth, pitching! A lefty, I presume."

"Oh yeah. One of the greats, but he hit too well not to play every day."

"Amazing, Jay. Time for me to hit the hay. Don't keep our spooks up too late. I found our discussion very, very interesting. You ready to assume command, Duty Officer?"

"Yes sir, I have assumed the responsibilities as command duty officer, Captain."

"Very well, XO, good night."

"Good night, sir."

The three officers sat down at the wardroom table. Cody carried a green aviator's helmet bag that Jay assumed contained the sheet music and cassettes.

"Nice bag, Cody."

"Thank you, sir. It was a gift from your dad. He gave them to all the staff. It has the navy intelligence emblem on it and our names engraved," Cody said.

"All at tax payers' expense."

"I suppose so. Yes, sir."

"Don't let the captain see that bag. He thinks they are a source of waste, fraud, and abuse."

"Too late. He did seem interested."

"First off, how are you guys settling into submarine life?" Jay asked.

Cody shrugged.

Cassie said, "I have hardly seen you since we got underway. You sleep all day."

"Sleep all day for the party all night. You guys can't believe what you are missing," said Jay. "You have the tapes and music in the bag?"

Cody replied, "Nope. I actually have snacks in the bag. I am saving them to be prepared in case we run out. This submarine has the best food I have ever had. Commander Voxer has the tapes and the music in her pocket folder."

Tradecraft. Everything is a diversion. Jay wondered just how deep Cassie and Cody's hall of mirrors was. Was Cassie's seemingly sincere affection toward him merely a piece of sexy theater? Was it just more tradecraft? Jay shook those ideas out of his head. He was supposed to be working.

Cassie had the pocket folder on her lap and held it up over her head with a grin and said, "Exhibit A."

Jay said, "First of all, Cody, it is uncool to hoard stuff onboard the ship. If you must collect a few things for the future, lock them up in your bunk. I don't want to go into sonar and see you with your bag of snacks. You might find yourself duct-taped to the overhead by the sonar men."

Cody scampered out.

Jay said, "I want to get a moment alone with you."

"Really?"

"Yeah, I want you to know I've briefed the captain regarding the theoretical sheet music and recorded music cryptography," said Jay.

"That's it? I'm disappointed. Why did you get rid of Cody? I thought you wanted to be alone, you know, so we, uh, for another reason."

Jay sputtered, "What about Mr. Voxer?"

"Mr. Voxer wrote me a 'Dear Cassie' letter from deployment in the western Pacific in June. Talk about clichés. He's banging a nurse. I didn't want to tell you in D.C. I thought—anyway, now you know."

She looked up at him adoringly, her eyes looking as deeply as they could get into his.

"You are still wearing your wedding ring."

"I will wear it until I am officially divorced. It's a pest repellant. You, Jay Brown, are not a pest."

Cassie reached up and ran the fleshy part of her fingertips lightly across his cheek. Jay leaned in, and she turned her face to one side, exposing her jugular. She just felt the first breath on her neck when she heard it, and jabbed Jay with a surprisingly pointy elbow.

Cody had returned.

"Wow, there is a locker under my bunk. I was sleeping with my sea bag! Now it's all packed."

Cassie said, "Jay, that subject we discussed is probably not worth pursuing till other things are settled."

"All right, let's get this party started. I need you two to focus for a few minutes. I'll show you where the gear is so you can start analyzing these tapes and this music. I also want to explain some of the capabilities of the spectrum analyzer in sonar. The spectrum analyzer could filter out and remove background noise. The Weps created a hack on the analyzer's computer that generated a printout of the sheet music from music analyzed. The guys in sonar used it to analyze top hits like Eric Clapton's 'Tears in Heaven.' I want you to capture every note played during the reception on the last night of my father's life."

Cody said, "Sir, this sounds like something we already checked for and got nothing."

"Did you correlate the music to the actual instruments that play the music—like the button on the French horn or say the frets of a guitar?" asked Jay.

"Yes, sir," said Cody.

Cassie interjected, "Jay, perhaps you underestimate Jeff. You should know he is tenacious when it comes to this stuff. Mind-bogglingly tenacious."

Jay said, "OK, new angle. There is a guitar in the big locker in Cassie's stateroom with various tunings and sheet music for a traditional Russian seven-string guitar. There might be some correlation there."

"That I haven't tried," Cody said excitedly. "Let's look at it now, sir and ma'am," said Cody.

"No, we are looking at it tomorrow. I am hitting the rack after this. Beauty sleep, you know."

"Yes, ma'am. Maybe I can take a quick peek while you are getting ready for bed," said Cody.

"Do you hear the words that come out of your mouth, Jeff?" said Cassie.

Jay laughed. "Tell you what, Cody. I'll take you up to sonar, introduce you to some of the sonar techs and you can tackle this in the morning."

Jeff, Cassie and Jay got up to file out of the wardroom. As Jeff stepped out, Cassie gave him a little shove and closed the wardroom door behind him.

Cassie with her back still toward Jay, leaned back into him, and said, "Jay, by the way…"

It was the sexiest thing he'd ever heard.

"Yes, Cassie?" His voice was whispery.

"Captain Royce is going to meet us in Saint Petersburg."

"Really?"

"Really," replied Cassie as she reopened the wardroom door.

XI

SUNDAY, SEPTEMBER 13TH, 1992
TRANSITING THE BELT

The *Quincy*, at periscope depth, prepared to transit the Great Belt, Denmark. 2300. The captain, XO, NAV and Maximov were in the control room in the near pitch black. The control room was rigged for black to prevent light from shining through the periscope.

Cassie was at her station in the computer equipment space.

Jay thought geography: The Great Belt was a waterway with an island in the middle that passed between two main Danish islands, Sealand and Funen. The waterway was about thirty-seven miles long, ten to twenty miles wide in the northern passage, and as shallow as 150 feet at some points. A bridge was being constructed across the northern strait, to be called the East Bridge. A tunnel was also being drilled, so there was construction above and below.

Both periscopes were up—Maximov on number one, Jay on two.

Maximov wasn't happy with the game plan, and wasn't shy to say so in front of the captain. "You Americans are mad. We pass through here all the time on HMS submarines, but always on *the surface*, Captain. Between the shallow water and the bridge construction, and the extraordinary traffic, this is brutal, sir."

The captain replied, "So, what's your point, Mark?"

"I'm just stating the obvious, Captain."

"I hear you. We are just going to have to be careful. Ship's safety is paramount. If we have to emergency surface we will. Otherwise, we proceed with caution."

"Aye aye, Captain. I've seen those Wild West movies. I feel like I'm in one now. Heeeee haw!"

Everyone in the control room laughed, but the laughter was cut short.

"With all due respect to our member of the Royal Navy, instead of making a donkey sound, what the lieutenant commander meant to yell out was a cowboy sound: Yah-hoooo."

Maximov repeated, "Ahh. Got it, Captain. Yah-hoooo."

The captain got on the mic. His voice was filled with great drama. "All stations, this is the captain speaking. We are about to make a very challenging transit through The Great Belt. As we make this transit, all sensors will be operating. There will be a continuous Fathometer reading, secure active sonar for front-looking detection and radar for our surface contacts. We have to avoid the many surface vessels transiting the strait, as well as uncharted pilings that will support the giant bridge being erected to span The Great Belt straits. We also have to be continually mindful of how much water we have beneath us. The transit will begin in fifteen minutes and will take approximately four hours. There are no stupid questions. Maintain hyper vigilance, and let's do this. Captain, out."

Maximov said, "Yah-hoooo!"

Cassie called to the control room, "Captain, I am on station. I don't expect any activity but intend to remain for the entire transit."

The captain replied, "Commander Voxer, it is important for you to be available, but I do not think it is necessary for you to sit for four hours in CES. Feel free to join us in the control room. It will be good to have another officer to add to the periscope monitoring rotation."

"Aye aye, sir."

After a few minutes in the control room to allow her eyes to adjust to the dark, the captain said, "Voxer, relieve the XO on the number two periscope."

Jay wondered if his secret was out. Did the captain know he was hot for Cassie? Jay chastised himself for being such a bad officer as to have such thoughts. See? *See?* This was why it was bad to have relationships with shipmates—weird shit started going through your head. As she approached, Jay could smell her spring-like scent.

Cassie tapped Jay on his shoulder and said, "I am ready to relieve you on the number two periscope."

Jay thought, focus, *focus.*

He said, "OK, I am ready to be relieved."

Jay busied his mind by reviewing all the contacts and their relative location by bearing and distance to the spring-scented submarine.

The first three hours of the *Quincy*'s journey through the straits were tense but uneventful. Jay was on the number two periscope, the NAV on one. Cassie, Maximov, and the captain were standing by in the control room.

In a burst, Jay yelled out, "*Captain! I have a zero bearing rate contact barrel-assing directly at us.*"

Jay was not kidding when he said *directly.* It was dead ahead. The incoming vessel was aiming at them, at their periscope. He could see both the red and green running lights at the same time. Zero bearing rate contact is the technical term for collision course.

The NAV said, "I see it, too. He is approximately three nautical miles out. We have about six minutes to figure out what to do. Looks like a giant yacht."

The captain called out, "Fathometer, sounding."

"Sounding, 200 feet, Captain."

"Very well."

Cassie reported, "Captain, we are getting an intermittent RACTAM hit."

The captain replied, "Cassie, I need you to handle that on your own. My focus needs to be on avoiding a collision."

"Captain, what happens if the yacht hits us?" Cassie queried.

"We will go through them like butter," Captain Davis replied.

"Aye aye, sir. I'll take station in the computer equipment space."

"Thanks, Cassie."

Maximov said, "Captain, I recommend we submerge to 150 feet."

"But that would leave only fifty feet beneath us. Any up or down angle and we are hitting the bottom."

Maximov said, "I've been though here many, many times and these yachts are not manned by pillars of society. It's a party boat, sir. They are going to have a hard time seeing us, and at 0200, who knows how much attention the bridge of that yacht is paying. I think submerging is the least risk. Let's just avoid angles."

"I think you're right, Mark. Let's slow and get down to 150 feet and let this guy drive over us."

The captain announced the plan to all stations. He then asked, "Cassie, before submerging, any correlation information on the radiation hit?"

"Yes, sir. Direct correlation to the inbound yacht. But it is very weak and intermittent."

"The plot thickens," the captain said. "Anything we can do to maximize the intelligence gathering?"

"If we could keep the BRA-34s both bumped up slightly, that would be great. And, of course, the closer we can get to the contact the better."

The captain turned to Maximov and said, "How much do you think this guy draws?"

"Twelve feet, max."

"So, if we were to make our keel depth seventy feet, given the keel to the top of the sail is fifty feet, we should be safe."

"Captain, don't forget we are going to have the BRA-34s bumped out a foot or two."

The captain called out, "Dive, make your depth seventy-four feet with a zero down angle. Lower both BRA-34s to one foot of extension. Lower all remaining mast and antennae."

Jay reported, "Lowering number two periscope."

The NAV reported: "Lowering number one periscope."

Maximov, whose snotty tone was starting to wear on everyone, said, "Well, I feel better now that we are going to pass mere meters beneath this yacht."

The captain didn't appreciate the sarcasm, but he did appreciate the concern.

"What are the odds? What are the odds this guy is going to drive directly over us in this twenty-mile-wide channel?" Captain Davis inquired.

"I'm not Irish," Maximov said, "but I know Murphy's Law is absolute. What could go wrong, will go wrong, sir."

"We shall see, Mark. XO, go check out CES and check RACTAM."

"Aye aye, sir."

As Jay entered the CES, Cassie was intently focused on the many RACTAM displays.

"Jay, this inbound vessel is going to drive right smack over us."

"I can't imagine a yacht of that size drawing over ten feet. It looked to be around a hundred feet long. So, what do the radiation detections look like?"

"Still trace and intermittent. But there can be no question about the source. Still definitely coming from the bearing of the inbound contact."

"Could the detection be from a shore-based nuclear plant or facility in Denmark?"

"I thought of that, too. When I checked the database, I found Denmark is about as anti-nuke as you get. They have *nothing*."

"Here comes the moment of truth."

What were the odds? The yacht went directly over the *Quincy*. The buzz of its high-speed diesel engines was frighteningly loud inside the *Quincy*.

Fright turned to terror, as there was a jolt, then a new sound, both thunderous and screeching.

"They hit us," Jay said.

The screeching continued.

The captain called out, "Dive, make your depth seventy-five feet with a zero down angle, now."

The sound of the collision was so loud the crew could barely hear each other.

Dive: “Going to seventy-five feet.”

The screeching noise stopped. And once again the sound of the now receding yacht’s motor was predominant.

The captain grabbed the mic. “All stations, this is the captain. We have experienced a collision. All stations, look for leaks or damage and report to control ASAP.”

The lights were turned on in the control room and the captain looked around the periscope for leaks. All stations reported back: No leaks.

The captain turned to Maximov and the NAV and said, “We have to get up to periscope depth to see what kind of damage we did to that yacht and conduct rescue operations.”

Maximov said, “The admiral is not going to be happy.”

The captain replied, “Mark, I am more worried about injuries or deaths on the yacht we just cut down the middle. The fiberglass hull of a yacht is no match for the hardened steel sail of a nuclear submarine.”

“Sonar, conn, the yacht does not seem to be making any flooding sounds. In fact, it sounds exactly the same as it did before.”

The captain had the control room lights turned back off. “Periscope depth,” he said, taking up position on the number one periscope. The NAV got on number two.

The captain reported, “This is so strange. I see no signs of distress. And why did we collide in the first place? Were we closer to the surface than we thought, or were they riding lower?”

“No signs of distress?” Maximov asked. “None? You’ve got to be kidding me.”

“None! The yacht seems to be cruising away from us as if nothing happened.”

Maximov looked at the sonar display. “You are right. They didn’t even slow down, Captain. How is that possible? They had to hear that ungodly sound.”

Truth was, everyone onboard the *Quincy* was still feeling the effects of that sound. It was a sound that vibrated angrily into a human’s nervous system and stayed, like the ultimate fingernails-on-a-chalkboard moment.

Cassie in particular was affected by the nerve-jangler, but shook it off. She had work to do. "Captain, both touch and sniff are maxed out, maybe they got crushed and are malfunctioning after the collision."

"Very well, Cassie. I am going to take a look at the tops of the antennae before we move them. Dive, make your depth fifty feet." That depth allowed the captain to poke his periscope and both antennae out of the water. Looking at a night-vision image, the captain aimed the number two periscope at the two antennae, creating video that was instantaneously displayed at various stations throughout the submarine. "Everyone take a look. We definitely made contact. See the lighter colored stuff all over the cowling at the top of the antennae? Still, odd. They don't look mashed or damaged or bent. How is it possible?"

Maximov called out, "Captain, maybe the yacht has a slow leak, and in that case, the thinking will be that he hit a rock or something."

"Roger that, Mark. Party boat. It's their problem now. We couldn't catch up to them if we wanted to at this point. Mark, relieve the NAV on the scope. NAV, prepare a SITREP, reporting the collision. Let's make sure we can move the antennae without leaking. Dive, make your depth sixty feet."

Both antennae were tested and, although there was some rubbing that wasn't there before, they operated properly.

Then, a report from a forgotten voice! It was Jeff Cody who said, "Captain, I have intercepted some unique radio communications from the yacht."

"Radio, this is the captain. Unique as in how? Were they encrypted Russian military-like communications?"

"No, sir. They were in-the-clear amateur ham radio communications."

"All right, Cody. Let's talk about it in the morning once we get to deep water in the Gulf of Finland."

"Aye aye, Captain. Radio, conn, out."

The NAV asked, "Captain, do you want me to teach the lieutenant the difference between radio communications and internal communications?" Cody had said *out,* used for radio but not internal communications.

The captain said, "Commander Voxer, this is the captain. Please provide Lieutenant Cody with a naval communications briefing tomorrow morning after our debrief."

"Captain, computer, aye aye, sir."

The USS *Quincy* continued its treacherous transit of the remaining Great Belt straits.

0300. The tough part over, the captain told all non-watch standers to hit the rack.

"I will see you all in the wardroom at 0900. I've ordered breakfast to be extended to 0930, so people can eat during the meeting if they need the sleep. The XO has taken over as the command duty officer."

Jay ran for coffee while the other officers went to bed. He employed the ancient technique of leadership by wandering. Jay would meander from station to station and talk a combination of business and small talk. Sometimes he started in the engine room, other times, like tonight, in the control room. He entered with his flashlight out, looking at the area where the periscopes penetrated the hull. The Weps was there.

"How goes it, Weps?"

"All good, XO. I was looking up there, too. Not a drop. What a crazy night! I can't believe we hit that guy and he was still floating."

"Weps, you ever think about combining all of your fetishes?"

"I don't have fetishes. I have interests. I am not sick. I am an enthusiast."

"Whatever, you ever think about making a computer game about wrestling strippers?"

"Hey, I like waffles and I like sauerkraut. But I don't want sauerkraut on my waffles."

"I gotcha."

"Now that I think about it more, it might be an idea worth pursuing."

"Don't forget where you got it! Hey Weps, I don't know about you, but I can't get my head around this collision thing, can't make it make sense. Maybe the hull of the yacht was actually steel, but painted white. And so low. Why so low?"

"White paint. Hmmm. Hence the white stuff on the top of the antennas. Those BRA-34 cowlings did get munched a little. I jogged them up and down, and sonar reported a slight rubbing sound from sail sensors as they fully retracted."

"Start making a list of things to address for our briefing in the morning."

"XO, I've already started one."

"Good man."

The Weps pointed to a Mylar panel in the control room used for turnover notes. The list was written with a removable grease pencil. Mylar and grease pencil had been the chalk and blackboard of submarines for a long time. He'd made two columns: one in red called SHIP'S SAFETY, and the other in black titled RACTAM. Under SHIP'S SAFETY, the Weps had written:

HULL INTEGRITY (XO),
#1 BRA-34 (NAV),
#2 BRA-34 (NAV),
POSSIBLE CONTAMINATION OF SAIL (ENG),
REPLACE COWLINGS (NAV).

Under RACTAM, the Weps had written:

REPLACE SNIFF (WEPS),
ASSESS TOUCH (VOXER),
ASSESS SNIFF (VOXER),
CORRELATION NORTH SEA/GREAT BELT (VOXER).

Jay said, "Nice work, Weps. You are smarter than you look."

"That almost has to be true," Weps said with a laugh. "Actually, it was the captain's idea. He told me to start making a list while you were getting your coffee."

"Ah, sharing credit with your captain. Smarter yet!" Jay gave him a friendly smack on the shoulder.

The sonar room was connected to the forward end of the control room via a black curtain—just like the back room of the music shop in Leningrad.

How cold it was outside that night, and how warm inside. It was the contrasts in life that...

Jay snapped out of it, and pushed past the curtain. Even by distorted submarine standards, the sonar space was cramped—and always under low blue light to both sharpen the sonar operators' hearing and provide a better view of the many sonar displays.

Jay's coffee cup was still three-quarters full, although it was no longer visibly steaming.

When he wandered into sonar he always sat in the same seat, closest to the control room, in front of the analytics stack. On this visit Jay was on automatic pilot, turned his ass to sit in his usual seat, and came within inches of sitting in the lap of young Lieutenant Jeff Cody.

Jay's recovery lacked grace, and left observers with the distinct impression that the XO cared more about his coffee than he did about Cody. The sonar guys cracked up.

"It's all funny until my coffee gets spilled, then someone dies," Jay said. "Lucky for you, Cody, this time not a drop. What are you doing?"

"I am analyzing the music that was being broadcast from the boat we hit," said Cody.

"Cody, just call it the yacht. We are trying to downplay the whole collision concept." Jay's hands mimed an invisible globe when he said the word *whole.*

"Roger that, sir," said Cody.

There was no roger in face-to-face communications. These naval *faux pas* drove submariners nuts, but Jay gave Cody a break—this time.

"Sir," Cody continued, "I am about to have a break through! I hooked up the National Security Agency recorder/player that I brought onboard. The Weps was kind enough to give me the source code for the sheet music generation program that he built. That Weps is one smart cookie. You should see the nice code he wrote," said Cody.

The Weps overheard and offered, "Yeah, Cody. I am much smarter than I look. But, hey, Cody! What was our deal?"

"Yes, yes, our deal was that the Weps would give me the source code if I left him the NSA tape recorder. It has special capabilities to record up to sixteen tracks on a simple cassette tape.

"You could record *Sgt. Pepper* on that thing," the Weps said with a toothy grin.

Cody continued, "It has light-speed rewind and forward, and a number of other features that are not available to the stock cassette player recorder you have here. The Weps even told me how we can fill out the paperwork to pretend it was lost..."

Weps said, "No need to get into that. Cody, tell the XO about the cool hack you made to my program."

"Cool hack?" Jay said. He could feel the conversation going tech, and tried to sharpen his focus.

"OK," Cody said, sounding very boyish with his enthusiasm. "The program provides an output of sheet music to the thermal printer. What I did was make it so you could get a digital display of the music in addition to the thermal printout."

Despite his sharpened focus, Jay didn't get it. Not even close. He decided to blame it on the lieutenant: "Cody, I am quickly getting unimpressed."

Sonar operator MacIntyre Symms piped in, "XO, you gotta see what he built! I can't wait till Ferris wakes up to show him!"

Cody continued, "I created another routine that outputs digitally and on the thermal printer the guitar tabs for the music. You know what guitar tabs are, right, XO? Tiny fret and finger-placement illustrations for people who can't read music."

"Yeah, Cody, I know. Get to the point."

The sonar operators snickered. Cody had clearly bonded with these guys in a short time. "Come on, Lieutenant, show him the tabs," Symms said.

"OK, the tabs. So you input the music through the nice cassette player. You can select six-string tuning or seven-string. I coded for the seven-string first, then added the six-string because some of the sonar operators play the guitar and could use the results," said Cody.

Symms said, "We have decided we are going to build a company with the lieutenant when we get out of the navy selling guitar tabs."

The Weps shouted in: "Hey, it is my original source code. I am expecting royalties from you guys."

Cody whispered, "Are they serious?"

Jay replied, "At this point in time, it doesn't matter. When did you guys start this?"

The Weps said, "Lieutenant Cody got my source code this morning at 0600."

Jay was impressed. "Wow, amazing work for a day."

"That is not all, XO. I also created an overlay analyzer to compare similar guitar tabs, and determine if there is some kind of code hidden in the music. Once you mentioned the seven-string guitar I thought, how convenient and easy, each string in like a bit, all seven strings make up a byte."

Jay felt the icy fingers of a chill course the length of his spine. Was this some kind of mind-boggling coincidence? Did his subconscious know things that his conscious mind didn't? And, if so, could the subconscious deliver that message through a dream? If none of that was true, then the only conclusion was that Jay's dead dad had visited him and pointed him toward the conclusion that Russian guitars with seven strings were being used to send code. Jay's body hairs stood up as if he were electrically charged. He felt goosebumps on his arms. His father had asked him in the dream. What did the seven strings mean? Now, he knew.

Cody continued: "So you have 128 combinations representing an ASCII Character. I think we have something here. The ham radio broadcast last night was 'Along the River,' the same classical Russian guitar music played the night of the reception."

"OK, Cody, I take back half of the bad things I've said about you today," said Jay. He was thinking: Holy shit, Cody is a fucking genius! "Superb work. Don't make yourself sick with no sleep."

"Thank you, XO. I just want to overlay the music I heard today with what I was already analyzing. I am really close to getting something here."

"Bring your results to the morning meeting. Really nice job." Jay walked to the control room and grabbed the black grease pencil.

He wrote on the Mylar sheet under the last item in the RACTAM list:

AMATEUR RADIO CIPHER (CODY)

XII

Monday, September 14th, 1992

Gulf Of Finland

0900. Transiting submerged toward the surface point. In the wardroom, the off watch officers gathered: Maximov, Voxer and Cody. Others filtered in for the morning meeting. Eng, NAV, Weps. The Weps brought the Mylar sheet list, which doled out post-collision responsibilities. Little scooted into the room just ahead of the captain, who arrived already talking: "OK, boys and girls, we have had quite a night. First thing we have to address is hull integrity and ship's safety. Weps and XO, you guys have been up all night checking. What do you know?"

Cassie noticed and appreciated the reference to girls. Even though she was the only one, close enough. Unless, of course, the captain was using the word to insult the male officers, in which case she did not appreciate it.

The Weps presented a detailed, downright thorough, damage assessment with all of the things he inspected and reviewed. When the Weps was done, the captain complimented his report and agreed with his priority assessment. One, address the damaged cowlings on top of the BRA-34s, and two, check for possible contamination of the sail.

Little asked, "Captain, do you really think we have contamination after getting hit? Doesn't it seem like the RACTAM is pegged because it got crushed?"

"XO, explain to Little why are we going to proceed as if the sail is contaminated."

It was almost a Rickover moment, the psychodrama technique of training a submarine crew. Jay was put on the spot, and his mind scrambled in search of an intelligent-sounding answer. Just when panic was about to set in, he realized the answer came from his childhood, again from a quizzing his dad had given him. The lightbulb over Jay's head went on and he said, with an emotional conviction, "*Believe your indications.*"

"Bingo, XO. Absolutely. *Believe your indications.* What harm does it do to proceed as if the sail is contaminated? If it isn't, we just took a little extra precaution."

The Weps said, "Captain, of course I agree and support your thoughts on this, but I think it is highly unlikely that contamination actually exists."

"I share your opinion, Weps, but let's be prepared regardless. NAV, do we have spare cowlings?"

The NAV looked toward the supply officer.

Suppo said, "Yes, sir. We have three—in a box under the main condenser in the engine room."

The Eng said, "I have my guys pulling the parts now."

"For how many?" the captain asked.

"All three," the Eng said.

"Excellent, Eng."

"I have also crafted the message for inventory replacement to be released by you, sir, at our next periscope depth."

A submarine had a sophisticated spare parts inventory. Parts that were critical but not frequently needed were stored in isolated, sometimes hard-to-get-at locations. A plastic antenna-top cowling would not be a critical part on a surface ship, but on a submarine it was. It reduced the sound of the submerged submarine passing through the water, and thus made the submarine harder to detect. A lost cowling could create a hole in the sail. If water flowed over it and created cavitation, there would result a hard-to-miss underwater whistling sound.

The captain said, "Good call, Suppo. Get three. Do you think we will be able to get replacement parts in Russia?"

The suppo replied, "I don't think so, Captain, unless we turn the order into a mission critical replacement part. Then they will cannibalize the part of a ship in port and deliver it to us with a courier."

The captain didn't like the sound of that. "That won't be necessary. NAV, try not to drop one of those over the side."

"No butterfingers. Aye, sir." Then the NAV got serious, "I will make sure we tie everything down and put some bumpers and lights up there when we do the work. When should we start?"

"Right after we surface at noon on Wednesday."

Maximov could remain quiet no longer. "Captain, I strongly recommend doing the work under some kind of cover. The Russians surveil the hell out of the Gulf of Finland with spy planes and satellite imagery. I am not trying to make things harder. This is a real threat."

The NAV said, "No big deal. We will drape the top of the sail with some navy-issue blankets. After we survey it, of course. Mark, you know these waters better than us."

The captain dished out the kudos, "Well said, NAV. Good call, Mark. So, Weps and Cassie, do you have the parts we need to repair the RACTAM?"

Cassie said, "Captain, just a matter of note, the RACTAM unit is designed to fail pegged high. We did that intentionally just to be on the safe side. Furthermore, sir, the sniff side of the RACTAM is a self-contained unit so that should be easily replaced. The touch sensor is an extremely sensitive piece of radiation detection engineering. We are probably going to have to take that below and repair it, but we do have spare parts."

With an efficiency that made the captain glow with pride, the officers orchestrated a minute-by-minute plan for repairs. Jay, whose pencil was quick, was given the job of keeping a list of everyone's responsibilities. It developed into a more detailed version of the Mylar list. In addition, Jay made a list of all the equipment and parts they needed.

The repair program:

Step one, the surfacing of the submarine at 1200.

Two, conduct radiation scans of the sail.

Three, prepare the worksite by covering it with black blankets, and provide lighting.

Four, remove the damaged cowlings and slightly munched RACTAM equipment.

And five, the final step, repair/replace RACTAM. This included the replacement of the sniff unit, the repair below deck of the touch unit, and the ultimate replacement of that unit on top of the antennae.

By the time this discussion was completed, it was almost 1100, and it was time to prepare the wardroom for early lunch. The oncoming watch relief process began around 1130. The oncoming watch took over from 1145 to 1745.

The captain said, "OK, we scratched the RACTAM list."

The officers, relaxed with a sense that the meeting was just about over and that it had been a great meeting, couldn't take it anymore and burst out laughing at that one.

The captain said, "All right, all right, on that note let's break for lunch. We will regroup with a smaller crowd right here in the wardroom at 1330. That group includes the XO, our riders, NAV and the ever-lovin' Weps. We will discuss our findings to date. Don't worry, engineers, you aren't going to be missing much!"

Lunch was comprised of sliders, French fries, and beans. One officer joked that beans were part of the navy's submarine methane recycling system. The system was code named "Don't-light-a-match."

The wardroom was cleaned up after lunch by 1300. Cassie and Cody were first to arrive for the 1330 briefing. This was by design as they had setting-up to do. Cassie covered a portion of the table with a large Mercator projection chart of Europe and portions of western Asia. Cody had a number of pages filled out on a large flip chart mounted on the wardroom bulkhead. The front page of his flip charts said, "Amateur Radio Cipher." A blank set of flip charts was also clipped against the bulkhead.

Little came in and clearly wanted no social interaction with the spooks. He got a cup of coffee and avoided eye contact. Jay walked in and noticed Little's body language toward the visitors from the intelligence office. He didn't like it. After that, everyone came at once: Maximov, the Weps and NAV. Radman and Wright entered just ahead of the captain, who was already in mid-sentence.

"OK, folks, lets start with listing our observations. Voxer, you start."

"Thank you, sir. I have plotted our two RACTAM detections on this chart. Lieutenant Cody, let's make you the scribe and you can take notes on the blank flip chart."

Jay interjected, "I think Little would be a much better scribe."

Little looked picked-on as he took the flip chart.

Cassie continued, "Our first observation was of the India class submarine at 1900 on Saturday the 12th of September. Let's call this 'flash'—like a flash in the pan, now you see it, now you don't." She described, slowly so Little could get it all, her observations regarding the surface contact's sound signatures and electronic signals that were detected.

"I call our second observation, I'll call it the 'bump'." Again she described it in mind-numbing detail.

The captain interjected, "Cassie, what are we missing? What is it that doesn't smell right?"

"Both of the India class submarines were supposed to be decommissioned earlier this year. They are diesel powered. Why did we get a radiation detection on the bearing of the submarine? And why was it on the surface? Seems very unsubmarine-like to me."

"Excellent observations, Commander Voxer. What else folks, what else?"

Wright gave the sonar perspective: "We analyzed the recordings of the India and are ninety-nine percent certain it was the second India of the class, two screws, a gnarly harmonic—more of a cacophonic, to tell the truth—found only on that class of submarine. Interestingly, the submarine was operating on battery power on the surface and the main ballast tanks remained full. There were no bubbling sounds from blowing the main ballast tanks."

Jay said, “An unintentional broach? Maybe a junior diving officer?”

Wright replied, “A very junior diving officer. That sucker was stuck on the surface for a while before getting negative enough to submerge.”

The captain replied, “Of course, what is special about the India class submarine?” The captain knew the XO was mad at, and was punishing Little. He didn’t know why but decided to be supportive. “Little, what is special?”

Little, who luckily had been paying attention, said, “Captain, the India carries two deep submergence rescue vehicles, DSRVs, mini subs on its back.”

“You’re exactly right, Little. And what happens when you off-load a mini sub?”

“Sir, you get a heck of a lot lighter.”

“One could deduce, an inexperienced submarine crew that just off-loaded one or two DSRVs could severely struggle with depth control and have an unintentional surface.”

Jay said, “Captain, I looked up the range of travel of these mini subs. They are really designed more for going deep than going far. Max range is only about two miles!”

The captain said, “NAV, draw a two-mile radius circle around our contact. Let’s plot any contacts that could have passed within that circle.”

Cassie said, “Captain, there is only one. The yacht.”

“Let’s plot that vessel and note any unique acoustic characteristics.”

Wright said, “I may be jumping ahead, but that yacht and our bump encounter had some super-strange wavelength characteristics, some that are not normally found on fiberglass yachts. From that sound, and I know we all remember that sound…”

Everyone shivered with the recollection.

“…I would guess that what we really hit was a rigid steel hull.”

The NAV said, “Maybe our Russian friends have taken to building luxury yachts with steel hulls?”

Maximov said, “NAV, it’s highly unlikely. The Russians are cheaper than Scotsmen—and I can say that because I am one of them. They aren't going to build anything that is going to cost extra. No way a luxury yacht would be made with a steel hull unless it was for a reason. It had traditional yacht lines. It's hard to imagine it was a military patrol craft converted to a yacht."

Cody said, "The amateur radio has some applicability here. But it might get into areas that are not appropriate for this room."

The captain said, "All right, let's take a ten-minute break. Executive Officer Brown, Lieutenant Commander Voxer, Lieutenant Cody and I are going to reconnoiter in my stateroom."

"Lieutenant Cody, please explain your security concerns."

"Some of my findings are explainable due to data introduced from naval intelligence."

"So, your little science project has some applicability here?" the captain said, more at Jay than Cody. "Candidly, I am not surprised. Why else would your dad want to be out here with us? If not for you guys, the work would have just ended. I want the entire team to hear your report. Just don't discuss the source of any data. I have to hit the head. I'll meet you back in the wardroom."

Cassie, Jay and Jeff skedaddled. Out of the captain's earshot, Cody said, "I am surprised the captain didn't want to get my full briefing before presenting it to the larger group."

Jay said, "The old man likes to hear the pros and cons of an issue up front. If we pre-brief him, he'll have the pros but no cons. It's his way of being fair." Jay also suspected the captain did not want to let on he already knew all about the ongoing musical analysis, having been previously briefed in private by his XO.

Cody looked toward Cassie and said, "A lot like someone else we used to know."

Ah, back to Dad talk. OK. Jay said, "My dad used to say we submariners are one trick ponies. Figure out and apply what works. Doesn't have to be sexy, just needs to work."

1500. Wardroom, USS *Quincy*, a full complement of officers were attending Cody's briefing, titled "The Amateur Radio Cipher." Cody was crisp and ready. He began by explaining how he modified the Weps' program to generate guitar tabs for both seven- and six-string guitars. His presentation bogged down in the details of the computer program.

The captain interrupted, "Cody, how does this apply to our mission?"

Cody started in again, but despite his eloquent oratory, he couldn't come to the point. He sagged in the shoulders with the knowledge that his presentation was tanking. Cassie came to his recue.

"Cody, you've done a great job. But, to preserve your naval career, I am going to take it from here. Feel free to interject if I make any mistakes. Why don't you stand by your flip charts so we can explain what we know."

Cody said, "Yes, ma'am."

Cassie nodded to Cody to flip the first page. Written was: "Baseline, reference one, India encounter and yacht encounter."

Cassie said, "Cody's program allowed us to overlay a certain piece of music that we have found playing in public places and over amateur radio broadcasts. The musical piece is a classic Russian folk song played on a seven-string guitar called 'Along the River' by Michael Visotsky."

Mark Maximov spoke up, "It is a classic from the early 1800s, Mikhail Vysotsky."

Cassie noticed the subtle correction of the composer's name, and continued, "Cody had analyzed this musical piece already in the Pentagon and, strangely enough, it was being transmitted from our close-encounter yacht. Let me go to my notes here—this musical piece was being transmitted on the amateur radio frequency 28.001 MHz." Cody wrote the number down.

The NAV asked, "Was the music transmitted in the clear?"

Cody answered, "Yes, sir. Almost like a music radio station broadcast."

The NAV followed up, "Is that common? To transmit music over amateur radio?"

Cassie said, "It is not uncommon, but that frequency is used for very long-distance communications. Like halfway-around-the-world communications. So, here's where Cody earned his pay. He had already been analyzing baseline against reference one with the guitar tab program, and he'd determined that a code was generated and that code was, 028001."

The captain said, "OK, Cody, give me the abridged version of how you got this."

"Yes, Captain. Each of the seven strings on a classical Russian guitar is like a binary digit. The bottom string is zero or one equating to a decimal zero or one while the top string represented as zero or one equates to a decimal sixty-four. The cipher is captured in two-bar blocks (two-measure blocks, musically speaking, that is) so any string, one to seven, played differently from the baseline registers a blip, what I am calling a binary tick. If string one is played differently than the baseline one in the two bars, position one gets a one. If it is played differently than the baseline twice in the first it goes back to zero, three times, back to one. You guys are a bunch of nuclear engineers—I am sure you get it. Although you could capture zero to 128, they only seem to be using zero to ninety-nine."

The captain said, "How the hell did you figure this out?"

Cody replied, "Well, sir, it didn't click until I heard the music on that frequency. I had tried translating to ASCII characters and a bunch of things. I pushed the reference-one guitar music through the program, compared it to baseline, and got 0000010 from the first two bars equating to 02 and 1010000 from the second two bars, which equates to 80 and finally 0000001 from the third two bars equating to 01. Assembled, you get 028001, which I am assuming represents 028001 kHz or 28.001 MHz, the exact frequency the yacht was transmitting the code carrying music. Too coincidental to be a coincidence."

Little asked, "Where did the reference-one music come from?"

The captain interjected, "Sorry, Little, you can't ask that. Outside the scope of our mission."

Jay said, "So, Jeff, did you find anything encoded in the broadcasted yacht?"

Cody spoke rapidly, "Yes, sir. There were many more numbers generated from the yacht. The reference music provided 02, 80 and 01 every six bars, with two bars of 00 followed by 02, 80 and 01. I think the 00 bars are like spaces. I am connecting the numbers coming out of each two-bar sequence, then I make a space for each no-change two-bar sequence."

Cassie said, "And the numbers derived from the yacht transmission are..."

Cody replied, "I'll write them down for you. These numbers are a mystery to us as to the meaning, but they were clearly articulated in six-bar blocks with six numbers this time. The numbers are 026012, 623630 and 005150."

The captain asked, "They might have reverted to a different code."

Cody replied, "Captain, I thought the same thing so I went back to all the ELINT (electronic intelligence) data we gathered during the India encounter. Interestingly enough, there was a transmission of the same music from some faraway place transmitting on 28.001 MHZ, and numbers, similar in magnitude, were being communicated. On Saturday morning, September 12th at 1900, the following numbers were being broadcast, hidden in the Russian classical guitar music: 026212, 295530 and 462644."

Cody wrote these numbers down under India encounter.

The captain said, "Cody, your work is incredible."

"Thank you, Captain."

Jay said, "Cody, stick that sheet with all the numbers on it up on the bulkhead and lets get a blank sheet out to try to sort this out."

During the brainstorming session, different theories popped up. Did the numbers mean additional frequencies? Possible FIDO Net addresses, such as those commonly used for electronic bulletin board communications?

It was decided that, similar to the first cipher, the first number was a frequency.

"But it's outside the amateur band, 26 MHZ, must be a commercial broadcast," Cody said.

"Why don't we tune in?" said Ferris Wright. "The next periscope depth, we tune into 26.212 and 26.012 MHZ and see what's playing."

"I can only pray that it isn't disco," Jay said. He was a rock and jazz man. Fusion. That was something that he and Cassie had in common. Jazz, although she didn't like the modern stuff. She liked the jazz of the 1950s when the musicians wore skinny ties.

While Jay's head wandered a bit, Maximov had his head in the puzzle. He said, "Could the last two numbers be latitude and longitude? Let's see where they plot."

The officers gathered snugly so they could all see. The numbers from the India encounter plotted at a location in the very limited seacoast of Iraq.

"We're assuming they are north and east latitudes and longitudes," the NAV pointed out. The second set of digits was plotted. More Iraqi coast.

"Good work, Mark. I think we have some information that needs to be followed up on. I don't think we are going to figure it all out today. Let's take a break and revisit this tomorrow, at 0830. Keep your thinking caps on but please only discuss this with the people in this room. Let's put everything away so the cooks can set up for dinner."

The wardroom was vacated except for Cassie, Cody, Jay and the captain. The captain said, "Cody, lock up the wardroom for a second. I want to ask you a question."

Jeff complied. "Yes, sir."

"First of all," the captain said. "I want to apologize for my impatience with your initial briefing. You are clearly a gifted and hard-working young man."

Cody replied, "No problem, sir. Compared to the Pentagon, everyone is really nice to me here." Cassie and Jay chuckled.

The captain wasn't smiling. "Cody, tell me more about the baseline and reference one."

"Captain, the baseline was something I was working on for Admiral Brown. Reference one was obtained from the reception at the Pentagon the evening of the admiral's death. That music was obtained and analyzed at Jay's request."

Jay said, "I thought it was a remarkable coincidence that my old man had Jeff analyzing that piece of music and it was also playing at his last reception."

The captain asked, "How did you know it was the same music, Jay?"

"Captain, as perhaps some of you know, I used to be a classical guitar player. I traveled overseas with my school band. This was all prior to going to the Naval Academy. I have a bit of an expertise here."

The captain found it easy to smile when he thought of Jay as a musician. "I would expect nothing less from a nuke. Mixed bag of nuts. I just decided, Jay, we are having a talent night tomorrow. And you are playing, XO."

"Is that an order, sir?"

"You know it is, XO."

Cassie spoke, "We're all looking forward to that, Captain. But there is one more thing you should know. There is some non-coded intelligence on the reception audio. There was some bad shit going down in that reception. Someone is heard relaying a message regarding which 'amateur frequency to monitor.'"

Jay added, "And I think I know who that someone is!"

XIII

TUESDAY, SEPTEMBER 15TH, 1992
THE GULF OF FINLAND

0830. Wardroom, USS *Quincy*. The mess specialists had cleaned up after breakfast, and the officers were reconvening.

The captain began, "Cassie and Cody, why don't you get the charts and notes out? I need to make an announcement to the ship." Into a phone, the captain said, "Conn, this is the captain. Patch my mic through to the one MC circuit." He hung up the phone and picked up the mic. "Officers and crew of the USS *Quincy,* this is your captain speaking. Today we must make preparations for our historic surface at noon tomorrow at the border of Russian territorial waters. We have much to do today, but I am confident we will get it done. We must ensure the ship is clean and presentable for this historic event. We will be making some sail repairs on the surface as we transit into Saint Petersburg harbor. After dinner tonight, we will be conducting a talent show in the crew's mess. There will be six fifteen-minute acts made up of at least four crew members. Navigation and weapons departments will each have one act. Because they are exceedingly clever, engineering will have two acts. The officers and chiefs will each have one act. I hope that adds up to six. Our riders will be the judges unless, of course, they would like to participate." The captain looked toward Cassie and Mark. They shook their heads no vigorously. Cody was a little slow on the uptake, but eventually shook his head as well. "The talent show will start after dinner at 1900. Bring your humor and your skill, but keep it clean. Carry on."

The submarine buzzed. What to do? What to do? The ever popular "Blues Brothers lip sync" was mentioned. Impersonating the chiefs was suggested, and that squeezed out a little enthusiasm.

"OK, we'll figure out the skits later," the captain said. "The only coming attraction I will reveal is the XO will play guitar."

Jay piped up, "As the captain said, we will sort it out later. Let's get this meeting started. I need to take a nap before my command performance tonight."

"Don't fret," Little said, and everyone groaned. Without missing a beat, Little passed around the unclassified message clipboard, containing routine navy communications, news and sports. When the clipboard got to Lieutenant Wright, the chief of sonar let loose with a humorously creative string of Anglo-Saxon expletives. The Weps asked what the hell was the matter.

Wright said, "Look at the date time group for this message." He handed the message board to the Weps.

"2610730! It means 0730 of the 261st day of the year, today."

Cody exclaimed, "Of course, of course. Way to go, Lieutenant Wright! The first number is a date and time. Of course, of course." Cody's mind scuttled off into cipher-land.

Cassie was already plotting the points with times from the music decipher. "The communication we received in the North Sea translates to a port in Iraq on September 18th at 1200, noon. And the yacht we encountered in the Gulf of Finland was broadcasting a location in the North Sea very close to our encounter tomorrow: September 16th at noon."

"That's the same time we are surfacing," the captain said.

Jay asked, "GMT or local time?"

The NAV offered, "Saint Petersburg is GMT plus four."

"We need to get surveillance on these locations," the captain said. "NAV, draft a top secret SITREP that requests surveillance on these locations at both noon Zulu and noon Saint Petersburg local time, which will be 0800 Zulu."

NAV paused, double-checking the captain's time-zone math, then said, "Aye aye, sir."

"Once we get the surveillance reports back we will have a better idea what the heck is going on. Cody, monitor the amateur radio bands every time we go to periscope depth. Jay, it seems we don't know what we are looking for, but we know where it's going to be."

The captain left.

Jay said, "OK, let's figure out how we are going to entertain the crew. I tell you right now, I don't do country or disco."

Wright said, "Shucks, XO, I thought we were going to do a *Saturday Night Fever* skit."

"No," Jay replied. "I was thinking more *Saturday Night Live*."

1900. Crew's mess, USS *Quincy*. Everyone who wasn't on watch was in the room. Some were standing. Cassie, Jeff and Mark—in honor of their role as arbiters of talent—got to wear red ball caps and hold official-looking clipboards. The captain had ordered the acts to rehearse their bits lightly, if at all, and to do it simultaneously, so the racket would cancel each other out. It was a small space, and if rehearsals had taken place one at a time, everyone would have known everyone else's act ahead of time, and that was no fun.

The emcee was chief of the boat, Eduardo Haskell. The COB. He was nothing but class up there on the imaginary stage.

He'd drawn on a pencil-thin moustache and had enough oil in his hair to lube up the *Quincy*'s works.

"Good evening, ladies and germs," he said.

"Ed-die! Ed-die! Ed-die!" the crew chanted.

The COB felt like a hero of the people. He stood in the forward part of the mess holding a toilet cleaning brush as a pretend microphone. Atop his oily head was a Lincoln-esque top hat. No one knew where he got it, but it was beautiful.

The six acts hid in the kitchen, on the starboard side of the mess, noisily protecting the surprise factor.

The COB said, "Welcome to the first—and, with any luck, last—USS *Quincy* diplomacy mission to Russia talent show. Six big, big talent-packed teams representing all members of our crew, to be judged by our esteemed riders."

He introduced the judges. When Cassie was introduced, there were hoots and hollers and one deafening wolf whistle. She elaborately curtsied.

When Maximov was introduced, he stepped forward and yelled with his Scottish accent, "Thick as a brick!" Everyone stared at him. "Jethro Tull? Scottish band? Very big. Aqualung? No? Damn." He paused, then sang! "And the wise man don't know how it fee-hee-hee-hee-hehehe he-heels, to be thick as a brick…." He whistled the flute part and received a smattering of applause.

When Cody was introduced, he gave a shy wave, and received a couple of loud cheers from his pals in sonar.

The COB continued, "In the event of any violations of proper navy conduct, or if they stink it up so bad that the captain gives them the hook, this horn will be sounded. The act will end immediately and those responsible for it will be shoved into the trash disposal unit to be ejected as vermin to the bottom of the ocean at the next trash disposal operation."

The COB tooted the horn, and continued.

"OK, the acts are going to be in alphabetical order by height, or as I see fit. The engineers will go first, followed by NAV/OPS, Weps and the engineers' second team. Second to last, allowing age before beauty, and last but not least, the officers. Everybody got that? So sit back, relax and enjoy the show." The COB went to an index card. "So, here they are, ladies and germs, with their parody of *Basic Instinct*, the en-gin-eeeeeeeeers!"

Wild applause and rowdy laughter greeted the four engineers that came out of the kitchen, three in regulation coveralls, the fourth in white coveralls cut off really short. He wore a wig made from a mop, and said things like, "I will *not* be ignored!" That was the only joke they had, but they made it last almost eight minutes. Good opening act. Warmed up the crowd. Kept expectations low.

NAV/OPS presented that old show-biz wheeze: pretending to be the officers. The reason it got to be an old show-biz wheeze was that it worked every time. The officers laughed through tears as they watched their comically inept doppelgangers cavorting for all to see. There was a fake Captain Davis, XO, NAV, Weps, Eng and Suppo. And they were doing a song and dance number with some Busby Berkeley choreography. After the song there was a skit in which the officers discussed what the crew should do for entertainment in Russia. After dancing around a wide variety of options, from "red light" houses of hospitality to museums, it was decided it was too much risk to let anyone ashore. A fellow could kiss a bad girl and get the drip.

Perhaps not to an outsider, but to those cooped up in a tube underwater, it was hysterically funny.

Eight members of the Weapons department took "the stage." The group consisted of a nice racial mix, which warmed the captain's heart because he was big on blending, avoiding cliques onboard. Three black guys, two Hispanic, two Asians, one white guy, and a boom box. They wore their coveralls unzipped to their belly button, ball caps turned backwards and necklaces made of chains. The smallest guy got to carry the boom box, so it would look huge. He pushed play and out came LL Cool J: "I Can't Live Without My Radio". While one sailor lip-synched, and they took turns, the others were back-up dancers.

The engineers' second act featured one fellow juggling, and three others clapping and exchanging things for him to juggle. He started with three tennis balls, shifted to salt shakers, apples (that he sloppily ate while juggling) and finally sneakers.

"Something tells me we're getting applesauce tomorrow," a heckler called out.

Although the captive audience could not have been more entertained by the exceptional juggling skills, what they didn't know was that the juggler had to revamp his entire act (which, he had done many times when he was not on a submarine) because of the low overhead. But he never bobbled.

The four chief petty officers had penciled-on moustaches just like the COB. Those moustaches made them look like human reptiles, guys who would snooker blue-haired ladies out of their slot-machine money. Then, the COB himself came on stage, took his place alongside the others, and pulled a harmonica out of his pocket. "With the exception of my finely tuned harp, there gonna be no musical accompaniment with this vocal number. That's right, hepcats, they gonna sing it Acapulco!" On that cue, the four chiefs pulled three-by-five cards out of their pockets and held them in front of their eyes. The COB blew a note on the harmonica and the four chiefs all sang "me me me," warming up their velvet throats. Another note, this one sadder, bluesier, and the four chiefs, in perfect harmony, belted out, "*Is this the real life? Is this just fantasy*?"

"Bohemian Rhapsody." Very tough song to sing, especially Acapulco, but the chiefs nailed it.

Once the cheering settled down, the COB announced, "Last but not least, they put the F in official, here they are, you love 'em, you hate 'em, you follow their orders obediently even when they don't make sense, which is all the time because this is the navy, theeeeeee officers!"

Four men emerged from the kitchen in zipped up coveralls, hair slicked back with sunglasses on. Wright had a plastic bucket, a metal bowl, and two serving spoons he snitched. Little stood next to him with hands free. Jay took his place next to Little with his guitar around his neck. The captain had a bunch of different colored rags over his arm and maracas in his hand. Those with sharp eyes could see something written on the maracas. It said: "The *Quincy* Rumba Shakers."

Ferris Wright started a beat with his big spoons. Jay Brown came in on guitar, something slow and slinky at first, a behemoth approaching slowly and still quite far in the distance. Right on cue, Captain Davis came in on the maracas and the officers were in a tight groove. The crew was ecstatic as the beat grew more solid, a shift to rock and roll, by way of Mississippi and then Tennessee.

Little came out and said, "Thank you, thank you very much." Everyone knew what was coming: Elvis. But not cliché Elvis. There was no "Heartbreak Hotel", or "Jailhouse Rock". Little sang one of Elvis's great emotional vocals, slaying the number not just by staying in pitch over a wide range, but getting inside the song and feeling its pain.

Little sang, "*Treat me like a fool, treat me mean and cruel but...*" Little didn't just sing, either. He put on a show, wiggling his hips, giving them the old Elvis Pelvis. The captain placed the colored rags across the back of Little's neck. Little used them to wipe mock sweat from his face and then throw the rags into the crowd, where sailors would fight for them. Of course, one rag went to Cassie with a wink. She smelled it and wrapped it around her neck as if it were from Elvis himself. The crew loved it. (Jay noticed this and was pleased that Little was making great strides in staying comfortable when "the spooks" were in the room.)

"*Begging on m'knees. All I ask is please...*"

Jay could feel the crowd's *fascination*. Little was mind-bogglingly talented and no one knew. The song was raising the roof, so to speak. Ferris now put a little Latin American beat behind Elvis, and the XO was jammin'. Jay thought about playing a riff with his teeth but decided against it, mostly because he had no idea how to play a riff with his teeth. The captain now had his eyes closed and his maracas picked up the new Latin tone. Little blasted the last of the song, "Oh, yeah..."

The crowd went wild. The COB appeared, still talking into his toilet brush: "He may be the most junior officer in the wardroom, but from now on there can be no doubt, no doubt whatsoever, that he is also," the COB dropped his voice to a deep baritone, "the king of rock and roll!"

"Encore! Encore!" the crew yelled.

For the encore, Jay came out with his guitar. It looked like he was going to perform solo. The other officers remained on the side.

The captain took his sunglasses off and said, "I want to thank everyone that participated in the talent show. I reviewed the grades of our judges and it has been decided that it is too close to call, you are all winners and, with that, you can all work a half-day tomorrow."

The crew cheered.

The COB said, "You know a half day is just a twelve-hour day."

The crew cheered louder.

"To get in the spirit of where we are heading," the captain said, and some heard a new intensity in his voice, "the XO is going to play a special piece that I want everyone to listen to closely. If you hear this music playing anywhere when you are in Russia, I want to know about it. It is a very special piece."

The crew held their breath for a collective moment as they realized that this wasn't a normal introduction. They were being briefed!

"XO, hit it," the captain said.

The crew quieted into silence for Jay's big number. Jay's fingers felt light, guided by a higher force. He had never played that well even in college, and his fingers were rusty from lack of practice. For a second Jay thought it was his father helping him, but he pushed that notion aside and concentrated on the music. He was up and down every fret of the neck of his beat-up Russian seven-string. For the entire four-and-a-half-minute piece he felt a special energy that allowed him to play every note with precision. When he finished, his fingers throbbed with pain. Of course, Jay had played Mikhail Visotsky's "Along the River".

XIV

Wednesday, September 16th, 1992

Surface Point

1200. The USS *Quincy* surfaced precisely on time, and at the border of Russian territorial waters. The passageway forward of the control room was staged with a radiation contamination monitoring/decontamination station. Black blankets covered the sail and repair equipment. The radiation technicians were getting ready to go up on the sail and check for radiation. Maximov was in the radio room talking into a microphone with Russian officials ashore.

Maximov snapped the microphone back into place with a perceivable attitude. He looked furious as he left the radio room.

"How did it go?" the captain asked.

"We have insulted their country by violating territorial waters."

"Heck, we gave them fair warning. We had a damn talent show last night. I'm sure they heard us back in New London."

"After an initial burst of indignity, the Russian I talked to, a Colonel Nechiporenko, calmed down. He says they want us to stay in this general area. We are not trusted to enter Russian territorial waters until they send a ship out to test the water and radiation levels around us. They will then escort us into port."

"They will, will they? Hmmmmm. We are going to have to get moving," the captain said, his eyes filled with apple pie and mischief.

Maximov said, "I assume they will send some sort of frigate that could cruise at speeds up to 33 knots."

"Assuming they are getting underway from Saint Petersburg, about one hundred nautical miles away. Gives us three hours. Did they say they wanted to board us?

"They did not say. I have to believe a Bear is coming in the air, too." Bear was NATO-speak for Russia's Tupolev Tu-95 aircraft, often used for submarine surveillance. It was a large, four-engine, turboprop with an observation deck in its tail.

Captain Davis spoke up as he walked forward through the control room to the radiation technicians. "Gents, we have to get a move on. Be safe but be quick."

"Aye aye, sir."

Both techs were in full yellow contamination protection suits. One had a radiation-monitoring device while the other was checking for contamination with a bunch of little cloth swipes. The contamination checker led the way.

Anxious moments passed until news began to filter back downstairs. No contamination in the trunk of the sail. The clam shell—that is, the hatch at the top of the sail—was opened.

"Hot. I repeat, hot."

"Damn," the captain said. "Details?"

The tech yelled down now and was in direct communication with the captain. "Not that hot. Still, detectable beta radiation. About half of my swipes are getting a reading and they read about 5 m roentgen per swipe."

"Got it, thank you. Don't breathe that crap. Keep a good seal on your HEPA breathers," Captain Davis yelled back.

The NAV said, "What do you need me to do, Captain?"

"Please get the engineer. We need to decontaminate the sail before we do anything. Keep your guys standing by to do the repairs, but they can't do anything until that sail is clean."

Maximov said, "Captain, not to be a nudge, but I would say we have fifteen minutes before the Bear shows up."

"Quartermaster, mark the time and let me know when ten minutes has elapsed," the captain said. "Nudge away, Mark. That's what I need you to do." The captain called up the sail, "Come on down, guys. I want you to double-check that you are properly sealed and suited. Don't get contaminated, but bring me a sample."

A tech called down, "No problem, Captain. There is plenty up here."

"Jay, what could that stuff be?"

"Captain, we can figure that out later. How about right now I work with the techs? We'll throw the blankets overboard when we are done."

"All right, Jay. Do it," the captain said. "Throw the whole playpen overboard, if you have to. Get yourself suited up. Safety is first. If we get caught with our pants down, I'll take the heat. I don't want any member of my crew contaminated. You got that, XO?"

"Loud and clear, sir."

Jay noticed Eng was setting up for a decontamination.

"Quartermaster! Time check."

"Five minutes elapsed, Captain."

Jay efficiently donned a yellow decontamination suit and worked with the two radiation technicians. Both periscopes were up. The submarine was still being controlled from the control room. The sail contamination and traffic made it impossible to control the submarine from the bridge.

"Quartermaster?"

"Ten minutes, Captain."

Maximov, on periscope two, "Incoming Bear in the air. Inbound from bearing 070."

"They must've had the wind at their back," the captain said. "Let's get video and ELINT capture. It's not often we get to see one of these birds so up close and personal."

Maximov said, "Captain, we couldn't look guiltier with blankets all over the sail. We're getting caught with our hand in the cookie jar and pretending there is no cookie jar."

The captain joked, "Hey, those blankets are standard operating procedure. We're warming the sail after being chilled by the cold Gulf of Finland."

"Aye, Captain. Makes perfect sense to me."

With the sail covered with blankets, the decontamination team was frantically removing white powder. The Bear made a number of passes over the *Quincy*. The three men in yellow emerged from under the blankets and waved happily to the aircraft.

Jay said, "Fake it until you make it, men."

And they all waved just a little more enthusiastically.

With all visible powder off the sail, Jay and the radiation technicians came down from the sail and were replaced with a new three-man team equipped with wire brushes, decontamination materials, and sealed radiation detection equipment. Its job was to verify that the sail was clean.

Jay and the two techs removed their hazmat suits carefully, as per their training, under the watchful eye of the chief corpsman. They had a sample of the powder in a yellow borated polyethylene plastic bag that shielded low-level beta radiation.

Jay offered a summary. "Captain, this white powder is not like the residue from a fiberglass hull. It's chalky."

"White bottom paint?"

"Could be. But who uses white bottom paint? Maybe it's a Russian thing."

Maximov chimed in, "No, always black bottom paint. Even so, bottom paint is typically lead or copper based, highly unlikely to be radioactive."

The captain said, "You guys take it to the radiochemistry lab in the engine room and figure out what the heck it is."

As Jay and the techs were leaving, the radio room reported, "We are being hailed in Russian. Request Commander Maximov to radio."

Maximov disappeared into the radio room and after a few minutes reappeared.

The captain asked, "What was that about?"

"The port authority wanted to know why our sail was covered in blankets and why the men in the sail were in decontamination suits. I explained that we were conducting topside decontamination drills because it was rare for us to have so much time on the surface at such a slow speed while we wait for our esteemed Russian escort."

"Nice job, Maximov. Want a job on a U.S. submarine?"

"Sorry, Captain. I'm already spoken for by the Queen."

It took another hour, with much scrubbing, before the sail was determined to be completely clean. The Russian escort was due in about another hour and a half. The captain remained in the control room. The NAV, Cassie, and two men were standing by to make the sail repairs in the forward passageway. Jay was still in the engine room analyzing the powder. Wright was ready to stand watch in the sail as officer of the deck.

1330. "OK, Lieutenant Wright, shift the watch to the sail."

"Aye aye, Captain." Wright headed up the ladder.

"Captain," the NAV said, "once Wright is situated we will make repairs to the sail."

"NAV, you have one and a half hours and not a minute more. If repairs can't be made by then, we'll need plan B."

The NAV said, "B, Captain? I've forgotten plan B."

"That's because you haven't come up with it, yet."

"Aye aye, sir."

The NAV, Cassie and crew worked diligently in the sail under the blankets to remove the antennae cowlings and the number two RACTAM unit. The RACTAM repairs were done quickly and efficiently. No screwups. But it was complex and still required more than an hour.

Maximov, on periscope two, said, "Inbound Koni class frigate."

The captain said, "How nice of our Russian hosts to send an anti-submarine warfare ship to greet us? NAV, how long until you are done and we can take down the blanket covers up there? There is an inbound frigate within sight to meet us. They will likely board."

"Almost done. We should be fine, Captain."

"I don't want these guys to see the sail covered in blankets."

The navigator replied, "Promise, Captain. No blankets." NAV and his crew worked for a few more minutes then ran with surprisingly long strides to the bridge with their equipment.

By now the Koni class frigate was getting very close. Maximov and the captain watched the ship approach, a thirty- to forty-foot vessel heading directly at them.

"Captain, I think that inbound small craft is the launch of the Koni class frigate."

Wright said, "Captain, this inbound small craft is from our escort. They have hailed me on the radio and want to board."

"Very well, Officer of the Deck. You need to break down the cover on the bridge *now*, guys."

Wright replied, "Captain, the NAV and his crew are heading down. I am standing on the blankets. The small craft is already alongside. Request to open the weapons shipping hatch and send the NAV and two men topside to tie up the launch and escort them down below."

"Very well, open the hatch and send the men topside." The captain turned to Maximov, "Wow, Mark, that was fast." He picked up the mic and announced, "Officers and crew of the USS *Quincy*. Special guests from Russia are about to board and are likely to remain onboard until we arrive in Saint Petersburg this evening. Extend the same courtesy you would toward members of our own navy. We will be hosting these men and officers in the crew's mess and the wardroom respectively. That is all." In other words, do not expose anything you don't want exposed. Like damaged sail parts and decontamination materials, for instance. Where the not-to-be-exposed items went, the captain did not care, as long as they remained unexposed.

The captain assumed that the engine room of a nuclear vessel would be the universal safety area. The Russians knew they weren't allowed there. How many U.S. or NATO men have seen the engine room of a Russian sub? You could count them on no fingers.

The NAV met the members of the launch topside. "I'm Lieutenant Adam Radzemski," he said.

There was one Russian commander, a lieutenant, and a chief petty officer. Two other men remained on the launch. The NAV looked up at the sail to Wright and said, "Have Lieutenant Commander Voxer report topside."

Wright called below for Lieutenant Commander Voxer.

The captain overheard the Voxer request and it made him curious for a moment, then he focused on meeting the guests.

"Mark, I need you right by my side to interpret."

"Aye aye, sir. That's what I'm here for."

They stood by the weapons shipping hatch as the Russian crew came onboard, chief first, lieutenant, and then commander. Each saluted Captain Davis as they reached the bottom of the ladder, a custom unfamiliar to U.S. sailors that rarely salute inside a ship or submarine.

The Russian commander spoke English first, "Hello, Captain. My name is Captain Third Rank Stienov. I am the first officer of the *Rastoropnyy*. This is Lieutenant Gagarin, and this is Chief Wassov. We appreciate your hospitality and look forward to traveling with you."

The captain looked and smiled at each Russian officer with his introduction.

"Gagarin?" the captain said.

"No relative to Yuri," the Russian commander quickly said.

"Welcome. Welcome all of you. Come on in." Captain Davis sounded just a little tinny to the ears of those who knew him. "Would you like a tour of the ship or a cup of coffee or anything before we get down to business?"

The tone reminded Jay of saccharin.

Captain Stienov replied, also sweetly, "Captain, my English is not that good, if you could repeat yourself, slower, please."

That was Maximov's cue, and he repeated what the captain had said in Russian.

Stienov and Maximov exchanged some Russian dialogue. The captain had a nifty smile, although it was on the rigid side. In fact, it was starting to make his face hurt.

Maximov said, "Captain, they would like to visit the sail, now, as in right now, as in before we do anything else."

The captain replied with some concern, "OK, let's see if we can bring these men to the sail. We will start our tour with the control room."

Maximov translated. As the men headed toward the control room, Cassie headed topside.

The captain called up to Wright via the 27MC microphone: "Be prepared for visitors."

Wright acknowledged the order and looked down at the half a dozen black blankets he was standing on.

Cassie appeared topside. Wright did a classic doubletake and gasped. She had, for the first time since coming onboard, given clear pre-meditation to the presentation of her breasts. Topside of her coveralls were undone and she had done something… Wright tried to figure out what. There were different physics involving Cassie's breasts, not that they weren't always lovely but—oh, he didn't know what the hell he was thinking about. The point was, her breasts looked spectacular at that moment, reshaped and elevated by who knew what.

Cassie kept reminding herself that the things she did for the U.S. of A. as an intelligence agent were for a just cause and didn't make her a bad girl. The new exaggerated breast presentation was bold but calculated. She was wearing what she called, when in the proper company, her "secret weapon, her bullet bra."

Cassie checked the lines of the tender to the submarine. Wright, who knew what Cassie was up to, could see that the two men on the launch were fixated on the buxom woman. She found an excuse to bend *way down* at the waist while facing the Russian men, and then she stood and found an excuse to stoop *just as low* again with her back turned to them, the rear view being so very important when it came to Cassie's diversionary assets. With all Russian eyes diverted by Cassie's Mamie Van Doren rack and bum, Wright threw the blankets overboard on the port side of the sail. Wright flashed Cassie a thumbs up.

She returned the gesture, and zipped up her coveralls.

Moments later, Cassie said, "Captain, the vessel is properly configured for safe touring of the sail by guests."

"Thank you, Lieutenant Commander Voxer." There was something different about her. The captain could tell, even with her coveralls zipped.

Captain Stienov turned to Commander Maximov and spoke in Russian for what seemed like a long time.

Maximov explained, "Captain Stienov was surprised to see a woman serving on a U.S. nuclear submarine."

"Was that all he said?"

"No, sir. He offered commentary on how it's a bad idea to let men serve with women, and also, Captain, on the size and shape of Lieutenant Commander Voxer's tits and ass."

"Pro or con?"

"Very pro."

"Tell him there are many things about our navies that differ, but we all are here to serve our nation and preserve world peace."

Hearing the translated version of that, Stienov shrugged his shoulders and Captain Davis motioned for him to follow him up to the sail.

Captain Davis, Maximov, Wright and the three Russians perched on top of the sail in the playpen. They were so far inside each other's personal space that it was uncomfortable, almost comical. But the Americans kept their yaps zipped, their social instincts telling them that the Russians were not appreciators of fine humor.

Sure enough, Stienov was not in the mood for yuks. He began a solemn-sounding speech, which Maximov translated with an increasingly sour expression on his face.

"The *Quincy* will untie the launch. The launch will circle the *Quincy* and take water samples. If the *Quincy* is determined to be clean and safe, it will be allowed to enter Russian territorial waters. The *Quincy* will follow the launch to the *Rastoropnyy*. The *Rastoropnyy* will then escort the *Quincy* into Saint Petersburg. Lieutenant Gagarin will act as the pilot for the *Quincy* docking. Ah, he says, that deserves explanation. It is common practice to engage a harbor pilot when docking in any port. A harbor pilot is usually a licensed captain that has been tested on local hazards and idiosyncrasies of a port."

The captain listened. "Very well. Officer of the Deck, send line handlers topside to cast off the launch."

The captain knew the blankets were still floating out there, probably just below the surface of the water on the port side. There was a chance that those blankets were slightly contaminated—but there was nothing he could do about it now.

The launch was cast off and edged slowly around the ship. One Russian sailor was driving the launch and the other sailor was scooping up samples with a ladle and pouring the water into a stainless steel device. The launch passed down the starboard side of the *Quincy*, past the rudder, and up the port side. The Russian sailors performing the ladling and pouring looked bored. Strictly routine.

Captain Stienov yelled down to the nonchalant sailors. No translation was necessary. The sailors snapped to.

There was almost an incident. One of the two screws of the launch was snagged by something in the water. The launch lunged toward the *Quincy*. Luckily, the driver was alert and shifted the launch into reverse in the nick of time to avoid a collision.

Stienov screamed in anger, his hands flailing in the air.

"How shall the USS *Quincy* proceed?" Captain Davis asked. Maximov translated.

Stienov replied that he was pleased to announce that the *Quincy* was safe and clean to enter Russian territorial waters. The *Quincy* should proceed to the *Rastoropnyy*.

Captain Davis acknowledged, then turned to Maximov: "I wonder what they got tangled up in?"

"Very strange. I have no idea."

But they both had an idea—and were troubled that the launch was not escorting them to the *Rastoropnyy*, but was remaining at the spot of the snagged screw, to see what had caused the problem. Captain Davis cursed Murphy's Law, an absolute rule in all calls of life for certain, but, it seemed to the captain, particularly in the military.

The *Quincy* steamed behind the frigate *Rastoropnyy* for about 200 nautical miles. At 2200, the sub was instructed to anchor at a spot about 100 nm from the port of Saint Petersburg. Once the *Quincy* was at anchor the same launch as before came alongside to collect the three Russian riders. The plan was for everyone to get a good night's sleep so that the *Rastoropnyy* and the *Quincy* could parade into Saint Petersburg in the morning with all of the pomp and circumstance expected of an occasion with this much historic significance. One of the launch's two crew members now wore a wetsuit. The black blanket that fouled the screw was spread out rather neatly on the launch's deck.

2230. Officers of the *Quincy* collected in the wardroom.

The captain said, "Wow, what a day. Surfaced the submarine, decontaminated and repaired the sail, and accidentally crippled our host country's launch."

Everyone laughed.

Wright said, "Not to mention, Lieutenant Commander Voxer's burlesque show while I was tossing blankets over the side. Nicely done, ma'am."

"Just call me Sassy Cassie," she said good-naturedly. "The things a girl will do for Uncle Sam."

Those who had missed Cassie's show, which was already working its way into legend by the telling and re-telling, were bummed out. The Weps was already writing a thesis paper in his mind regarding the obvious parallels between Lieutenant Commander Voxer's act and that of the great Gypsy Rose Lee many years before.

The captain said, "All I can say, Cassie, is, good thing you're on our side."

Everyone cheered.

Jay changed the subject, "Captain, we have results to half life analysis of the white substance. It's titanium oxide, a low level gamma emitter."

"Not something I expected from a yacht," Cassie said. "Where is titanium usually found?"

The captain said, "Some of the deeper-diving Soviet submarines have titanium hulls. But just a few: Alpha, Sierra."

Jay said, "Deep submergence rescue vehicles like the mini subs found on the India could be titanium."

"Ahh, the mosaic is forming," the captain said, imagining a collection of seemingly scattered facts organizing themselves into an image, the bigger picture. There was the sighting of the India, the encoded music, the appearance of special yachts with titanium bottoms.

Jay said, "Captain, if we get more position information from our encrypted music source, we should go out to the location and see what we see."

"XO, that is a great thought, but we should see what our intelligence sources bring back from observations today, and this Friday. We are getting imaging info from our spot out in the north Atlantic noon today and 1600 local time. I expect a personal 'for my eyes only' tomorrow with the results of the satellite surveillance. Friday at noon and 1600 we will get imaging from the five miles of Iraqi coastline in the Persian Gulf. If we see activity of interest in either of these surveillances, I am sure we can get the admiral to authorize a special operation. For now, we have to focus on our diplomatic mission entering the port of Saint Petersburg tomorrow. Friday is a big reception, that all of us are expected to attend. Lieutenant commanders and above are expected to wear mess dress blues. Lieutenants and below will be in dress blues."

Cassie griped: "Captain, these uniforms are designed for men's bodies. I can't begin to describe how uncomfortable a rack of medals feels like on my, well, on my rack."

Jay said, "Cassie, if you weren't such a highly decorated naval officer, this would not be such a problem."

The captain said, "XO, we have to figure out some sort of way to decorate this boat so we look festive. I want serious, serious festooning out there. Team up with the COB and figure out some way to dress the submarine, and lets get all the off watch sailors and officers topside in peacoats and ballcaps."

Wright said, "XO, what if an officer was to have forgotten their peacoat?"

"Then I see two options: either that officer stands watch in the engine room or finds a coat."

The captain said, "Wright, you can borrow my coat. Slap some electrical tape on the extra 2 gold bars on the shoulder boards."

"Thank you, Captain."

The captain replied, "You did a nice job today on the bridge. I don't want to hear about any other uniform issues. You are going to have to sort it out with the men. Let's all hit the hay. I am calling for an 0600 wakeup so we can get our act together for the port entry. Mark, when are our comrades coming back tomorrow?"

"They said they wanted to be back onboard at 0800."

"Perfect, and the op order says we dock at 1000. We might get a little R&R in mother Russia tomorrow. Between Mark and Jay, who has also visited Saint Petersburg before, we have two very adept tour guides."

That piqued Maximov's interest. "So what brought you to Saint Petersburg before, XO?"

"I am a man of great depth," Jay said with a small laugh, maintaining strong eye contact with Maximov. "I'm not just your usual navy nuke bubblehead, you know."

It took Maximov a moment, Jay could see it in his face, to realize that Jay didn't answer his question and had no intention of answering it.

Cassie spoke to Maximov in Russian. Then, in English, she said to Jay, "I can help with the translation, too, since I speak fluent Russian."

Maximov said, "Captain, your officers are full of surprises."

Jay saw something unhappy in Maximov's eyes when he learned of Cassie's ability. What had been a twinkle in Maximov's eyes now went dull. Was he concerned? Jay couldn't tell.

Perhaps, Jay speculated, Maximov had liked the idea that he was the only Russian-speaking person onboard. It made him necessary. Now, learning of Cassie's abilities, he felt less necessary.

"It takes all kinds of people to run a railroad," said Captain Davis, oblivious to the competitive juices Jay was sensing.

"Or a highly sophisticated submarine intelligence gathering mission like this has turned into," Jay added.

XV

Thursday, September 17th, 1992
Saint Petersburg

0950. It was a picture perfect sunny day, temperature in the low 70s. The sky was beautiful, a high sky with some white fluffy clouds near the horizon. The ocean looked great, showing that graphite color it picked up sometimes at summer's end. But as for beauty, that was as far as it went. Beyond the docks, everything visible was man-made. There were fuel tanks that took up potentially valuable gulf-view property. There were industrial features, power plants and factories. Jay didn't see a tree.

Wait, there was one tree. Some sort of evergreen. It appeared to be coming up out of the center of a concrete parking lot. Jay wondered if the tree had been planted there or if it was just a brave example of nature fighting back.

The crew stood smartly at parade rest on the deck of the *Quincy*, aft of the sail. By submarine standards, the ship was happily festooned (and festooned some more) with pied ceremonial embellishments. Flippety-flapping signal flags were strung from the forward portion of the sail to a forward cleat, and from the after portion of the sail to an after cleat. The captain, Maximov and the three Russian officers from the previous night had a great view of the industrial park from the playpen.

Jay was the officer of the deck. The *Quincy* approached its dock on the north bank of the Nevin River. The dock had a good-and-wide broadside birth between a number of other Russian Navy vessels. The NAV and Cassie were in the control room.

"NAV, I have never seen a submarine with signal flags strung topside for dress ship."

"Nor have I. I hope the men don't trip on them. Fortunately, docking couldn't be easier. The Russian they gave us to do the docking—named Gagarin of all names—can do it with his eyes closed."

"We didn't need a Russian pilot."

"Oh, I know. They're just trying to exert their power."

"That is the nature of the game we are playing," Cassie said. "Russia and the U.S. still playing an expensive game of who's got the bigger dick."

"Not the way I'd've put it, but—"

"True?"

"Absolutely." Jay didn't like pomp and circumstance. Unlike the captain, he'd never met a ceremony he *did* like. Ceremonies never have anything to do with getting the job done. It was just a show, when there was usually real work to do. In this case, since the mission, the overt part of the mission anyway, was diplomatic, Jay figured dressing up the sub really was part of the work, but it didn't feel like it. Besides, Jay was spending more time thinking about the covert portion of the mission.

"You look troubled," Cassie observed.

"There is something intrinsically wrong with dressing up a submarine. They are supposed to be sneaky. Stealthy. Quiet and surreptitious. Colored flags! It makes me think the world is topsy-turvy."

"Russia and the U.S. are friends now, remember?"

"Oh yeah, I can tell by the tone so far," the NAV said.

"Not their fault, really. We were acting pretty suspicious," Cassie concluded.

The submarine was pushed by tugs against the pier. The current was against them slightly so that a little ahead steam to the propulsion turbines kept them stationary.

Cassie got on a periscope and scouted the people on the dock. "Oh good, there's a band."

"What else?"

"Many Russian officers in full dress. Also, a contingent of U.S. and NATO naval officers, of—no!" Cassie's tone changed. "Shit. Shit fuck goddamn. Among them is Captain Royce, the douche bag."

"Pardon?"

"My boss, since the admiral died. Royce. I was hoping I'd left him on the other side of the world."

Admirals Conner and Bennett were there. There were very senior officers from other nations. The scene must've set some sort of record for medals and gold on shoulders. Cassie scanned further and saw a woman that looked like Jay Brown's mother. She figured it must be her imagination. She'd met the woman only a couple of times. Perhaps she was mistaken.

Cody announced, "Conn, radio, I just received a personal for the commanding officer."

This was hardly the time or place to be making an announcement like that.

The NAV wanted to tell Cody to shut the hell up while they had Russians onboard, but instead he said, in an almost lazy drawl, "Radio, this is the navigator. Thank you for getting the captain's personal news and sports scores."

Cody started to reply, "Navigator, radio, the..."

The NAV pulled the fuse for the 27 MC circuit to prevent Cody from further broadcasting details of an eyes-only message for the captain.

The NAV said, "Do you want to go in there and kill him or should I?"

"He's my responsibility. I'll bitch slap him."

"Talk about crazy timing. That must be the surveillance from yesterday."

"I'm not sure when the captain will be able to look at it."

"Go counsel Cody. We will sort out the intel later with the captain."

0956. The view from the bridge was a spectacular array of gray on gray. The band began to play, something brassy with a marching beat. Bumbumbumbum BUMBUMBUMBUM. Bumbumbumbum BUMBUMBUMBUM. The captain recalled the drum-and-bugle corps competitions he saw as a youth—or maybe halftime of a football game. The captain felt like he was in the homecoming parade, with the prettiest submarine of all times. He managed to have these feelings even as he entertained his Russian guests in the sail. The *Quincy* was in place two minutes early, and waited until 1000 on the button to tie up with its own lines. When the time came, Jay signaled the COB topside.

"Send the monkey fist across to the pier." A monkey fist was a heavy knot at the end of the line that made the line easier to heave. Russian line handlers onshore pulled the *Quincy*'s heaving line in, promptly but not too quickly. The Russian line handlers flipped the eye of the line on the shore side cleat/bollard.

The submarine colors were shifted. The U.S. flag was raised on a flagstaff installed on the aft end, while the U.S. flag on the sail was taken down. The shifting of colors brought cheers from ashore. The band started playing Tchaikovsky's 1812 overture. Bombombombom bombom BOM BOM BOM.

A twenty-one-gun salute commenced with the honor guard on the pier of Russian Marines. The first shot fired startled the *Quincy* crew half to death. A couple of the men clearly thought for a moment that they were being fired upon.

When the shooting was through, Jay took his first good look at the people on the pier. He saw his mother talking with Admiral Bennett and a number of senior Russian officials.

"What the—" Jay said aloud. He realized this must be affiliated with something his dad had planned. "Captain, anything you would like me to do?"

"Yes, XO. I am going to head to the pier. If you could check on my news and sports, that would be great. I want to know how my Cowboys made out."

"I'll let you know, Captain."

Jay knew the captain already knew the most recent Cowboys score. He was speaking in code, giving Jay authority to read the captain's eyes-only message.

The captain said to Maximov and the three Russians: "Let's go ashore."

As Jay helped the captain into the hatch, the captain discreetly handed off his safe key so that Jay could decode the message.

As the captain, Maximov and the Russians went ashore, Jay grabbed the on watch radio operator, Second Class Petty Officer Peter Sparks, and took him to the captain's stateroom to help decode.

When the message was decoded, Jay muttered. "You have got to be shitting me." Jay rubbed his temples for a moment and turned to the radio operator. "Please lock this up in radio in case the captain wants to see it for himself. I have to get ashore. But first, please find Lieutenant Commander Voxer for me and send her up here."

"Aye aye, sir."

Jay sat at the captain's desk and stared into space until Cassie arrived.

"Close the door, Cassie," he said. "That personal for the captain says the surveillance and intelligence reports we asked for are held by our buddy Captain Royce. The communication that Royce is carrying is classified as top secret, special compartmented information."

"Sounds like we stumbled upon something of interest to national security."

"I don't like the fact that Captain D.B. Royce is involved."

"No, his initials are…oh, right. I agree. I don't like it either. But I'm not sure there's anything we can or should do about it. Douche Bag is the acting director of naval intelligence. Doesn't make him any less of a creep."

"Something about him is just wrong. We should get ashore. I need to relay this message to the captain and say hello to my mother."

"I *thought* I saw your mother."

"Really, Cassie? I'm surprised you didn't mention that! The message traffic has my mother confirmed as a VIP attendee for the reception. Crazy day all around," Jay said.

Cassie frowned and squinted her eyes for a moment. She couldn't help but think of Jay's mom as a woman of mystery, but they didn't discuss the matter any further as she and Jay made their way off the submarine.

Once ashore, Jay and Cassie saluted every uniform they saw. Sometimes it was hard to discern if the uniforms were of senior officers or not, so when in doubt they saluted.

Jay spotted his mom in a group with the captain, Maximov, the admirals, Royce, and an unidentified Russian naval officer.

"Mom, what the heck are you doing here?" Jay ignored the rest of the dignitaries in the group.

Admiral Connor spoke up to break the awkwardness, "Gentlemen, let me introduce Admiral Brown's son, the XO of the USS *Quincy*, Lieutenant Commander Jay Brown. With all the work that Admiral Brown had performed to make this day a reality we thought it fitting to have his son and widow at this historic event."

Jay replied, "I am surprised my father's widow had not informed her son that she was going to be here."

Jane said, "Last time I checked you were not in my chain of command."

The senior officers and Cassie laughed hardily at Jane's response to her son.

Jay pushed through his confusion and gave his mother a proper greeting. Jay and Cassie snapped to attention and saluted the admirals, who laughed again and returned the salute. Finally, and snapped to attention and saluted the senior officers after the informalities with Mrs. Brown, Jane then gave Cassie a big hug.

The unidentified Russian was introduced as Admiral Oleg Aleksandrovich Erofeyev, the equivalent of the CNO for the Russian Navy. Jay considered himself good at interpreting body language. He could tell the three admirals felt a connection and were comfortable with one another. They looked alike, a little bit. There was definitely a "type" that produced leaders of men, no matter what country you were in.

"This is a historic location," Admiral Erofeyev said. "The *Quincy* is tied up to the dock adjacent to the Mikhail V. Frunze Higher Naval School, which is the oldest of the Russian Navy's naval officer commissioning schools, very similar to your Annapolis."

Jay could see the school off in the distance, an impressive stone structure, looking more at first glance like a fort than a school. Considering its location on the Port of Saint Petersburg, Jay was fairly sure it was both—and had been for hundreds of years.

Admiral Erofeyev added that this school was his *alma mater.* Jay's mom said that they were all staying in the school's VIP quarters.

As the small group chatted, Jay whispered into Captain Davis's ear: "Captain Royce has some information of interest."

The captain acknowledged his understanding with a small nod. The pier began to empty. The band was apparently finished. Admiral Erofeyev suggested that the visitors spend the remainder of the day sightseeing. Tomorrow would be a busy day. Scheduled was the giant reception at the school's main ballroom to celebrate the historic visit.

Captain Davis said, "Before we head out to see the sights, I'd like a quick meeting with my officers."

"May I recommend that your men wear civilian clothes while sightseeing," Admiral Erofeyev said.

Jay kissed his mother. "I'll meet you right here on the pier at 1230. We can grab lunch and then tour."

"You should bring along some of your friends," Mom said, winking at Cassie.

1130. The officers of the *Quincy* and Captain Royce gathered in the wardroom.

"Let's make this quick," Captain Davis said. "We are holding up lunch. I can smell the sliders. First off, welcome Captain Royce. Your officers have done an outstanding job and have represented your command well."

Jay shifted uncomfortably in his seat, unhappy to be in an enclosed space with the man who had his father's job, with the man who gave him the creeps, and of whom he couldn't be more suspicious.

"Thank you, Captain," Royce said. "This was more of a payback to Cassie and Jay for all of their hard work. It was also good timing for them to be out of the office with all of the disturbances and distractions going on in the Pentagon these days."

Captain Davis said, "It has been great having them onboard. We've gotten a couple of hits on the RACTAM that we would like to debrief you on."

Royce said, "Actually, RACTAM was the brain child of my predecessor and that part of the mission is being discontinued."

Jay could not contain himself anymore, "What the fuck?" It was a rhetorical question, and Jay continued without waiting for an answer. "Your predecessor! Last time I checked, director of naval intelligence is an admiral position. You are acting head, not appointed. On what authority do you have to cancel a program?"

Captain Royce stayed very cool and replied to Captain Davis, "Captain, maybe your XO has not had sufficient time to grieve after his awful loss. Have you thought about giving him a leave of absence?"

Jay looked at Royce and he could no longer see a human being. If it was true that dehumanizing the enemy was the key to learning to kill him, then Jay was absolutely justified in his white-hot anger. Because all of the homo sapien had drained from Royce like muddy water into the sewer. Anything of any redeeming value, any soul whatsoever, was long gone. And all that was left, all Jay could see, was a coiled snake, it's forked tongue flicking with menace, coiled and ready to strike, now developing budding horns and revealing itself as some sort of reptile Satan. Jay's thoughts came at light speed. There was no handgrip of civilization in them. They were unadulteratedly wild, based on instinct, and consisted almost exclusively of how he was going to kill this demon without being poisoned by its venom in return.

Cassie grabbed Jay by the hand.

Royce noticed the physical contact and smacked his spoiled thick lips obscenely.

"It looks like you might have some inappropriate relations going on your ship as well," he said.

Captain Davis didn't like this exchange at all. It was obvious that Jay and Royce had a personal animosity, that wasn't the question. The captain trusted Jay a lot more than this nasty spook.

But was Royce's attitude based just on his being a complete asshole, or was he responding—and responding poorly—to suspicions of impropriety being directed at him—as if with a laser beam—by a near-savage Jay Brown?

The captain took his time before he spoke, and began with a little snippiness of his own: "This is a submarine so we call it a boat. A ship is a target to us. You can leave the wellbeing of my crew to me. Thank you for your insights. I am always interested in another officer's perspectives. What seagoing units were in your career, Captain Royce?"

Royce looked like something smelled bad—which it probably did, this being a submarine.

"We are not here to talk about me, Captain. I have some intelligence to deliver to you. The imaging information you asked for at the position specified yesterday came up with nothing. We anticipate the same for your request tomorrow so that order was cancelled."

Captain Davis asked, "Can I see the imaging report?"

"Captain, you don't believe me? The reports are being held by my aide in a locked case. I can bring down the report tomorrow before the reception."

Aide? Jay thought with disgust. How did this captain get an aide? Aides were for an admiral. Royce seemed to feed off the hostility. Jay was thinking of ways to kill him, and the captain was thinking of ways to get him off the *Quincy* before things started to corrode under his atmosphere. Royce looked very settled into his chair at the wardroom table with a cloth napkin on his lap.

The captain nearly spat as he said, "I am sorry you can't join us for lunch, Captain Royce."

Royce was stunned. How rude.

The captain continued, "We need to reserve all these place settings for the watch standers. I am sure you understand. If you want to eat I can set up a second sitting at 1400, but you are likely to be the only one here."

Royce stood. "Thank you, Captain. I understand. I will join Admiral Bennett and the CNO for lunch."

Captain Davis was having lunch with Admiral Bennett ashore and Admiral Conner was having lunch with Admiral Erofeyev. Captain Davis said, "I am sure you know your way off the ship. I look forward to catching up tomorrow. Do you want to plan a follow-up meeting at 1500? I really do want to see the imaging, just for my own piece of mind. You don't see any problem with that, do you, Bob?"

"I will check with the admirals to make sure I am available. My aide will get back to you."

Royce walked out of the forward end of the wardroom, indicating he had no idea how to get off the submarine.

"About face, Bob," the captain said.

With Royce headed in the correct direction, Cody said, "Captain, Royce goes by Robert. He *hates* being called Bob."

"Yes, yes, yes, Cassie told me earlier."

Cody's eyes went momentarily wide. He was impressed by the subterfuge. Cassie laughed lightly.

The captain said, "I was waiting to use that if this guy turned out to be as big of an asshole as you all made him out to be."

Maximov said, "Real wanker, sir. I'm sure he wears skivvies under his kilt, too."

Cody asked, "Is it OK if I eat at two in that second sitting?"

Cassie elbowed Cody.

Jay said, "Cody, you are going to lunch with Cassie, my mom, and me. Mark, do you want to join us? I was going to see if the Weps and Little wanted to join us, too. The NAV and a few like-minded guys are trying to get a tee time and whack it around this afternoon."

Maximov said, "There's a golf outing? Sure, I would love to join you guys, but I love golf. I can already hear the trees screaming."

The captain said, "Cody, go find the good captain and escort him off the boat. I expect him to be around the yeoman's office about now. I would send Jay, but he would show him off via a torpedo tube."

Jay's face hurt. He realized that he was grinding his teeth, gnashing with frustration. He tried to relax a little bit. He was the coil ready to spring, and he needed to dial it back a notch or two. He needed to be professional. He needed to kill Royce and get away with it.

Cody stood. "Aye aye, sir."

There was an announcement over the 1MC.

"*Captain, United States Navy departing.*"

Cody returned. "I really *do not* miss that guy." Everyone laughed.

The captain said, "Comments regarding the departed Captain Royce, and let's try to avoid the obvious. We'll stipulate he is an asshole."

Jay replied, "He is either just a super asshole, a power-mongering control freak, or he is a *traitor.*"

Some of the savagery Jay felt in his heart seeped out—came through loud and clear, in fact—with that last word.

Mark replied, "Given those three options, I would rather be classified as a traitor."

Captain Davis asked his two guests for their expert opinion on Royce: "Has he ever acted in a way that made you think he was a traitor?"

Cassie answered immediately: "I really did not work with him close enough to tell if he is a risk to national security, Captain."

Cody had a note of mischief in his voice. "Why don't we just test him and find out?"

The captain nodded. "OK, Cody. I'm listening."

"The location for the imaging information we asked for is about twenty miles from here. Why don't we head over there and see what we see? Then we compare that with what Captain Royce brings us tomorrow."

Jay placed a strong hand on Cody's shoulder and gave it a firm squeeze. Cody was embarrassed because he could see there were tears in Jay's eyes.

Captain Davis said, "Jay, I know this means a lot to you and it is very, very personal, but I cannot support anything that could be construed as spying on Russian soil. Underwater is another story. The acting director of naval intelligence, asshole or not, has told us to stand down. So just enjoy some time with your mother and shipmates ashore."

Jay, whose every emotion now hit his nervous system hard, felt betrayed by his captain.

"You understand me, XO?"

"Yes, sir."

1230. Jay and his mom Jane, Cassie and Cody met ashore. Jay's mom said she had some Russian cash, so everything was on her. They looked very American in sneakers, blue jeans and ball caps.

Jane asked if they had a game plan.

Jay suggested, "I have an idea. Why don't we grab a bite locally and then take a look around a local marina to admire the yachts of Russia?"

Jane wasn't born yesterday. She had what a writer might call an "ear for dialogue." She knew a lot about people by what they said and how they said it. She was so good at it that she could catch the false notes in conversations she overheard at the grocery store. She could certainly hear a false note in her son's voice.

"Isn't that a tad specific?"

"You'd rather just wander aimlessly?" Jay said.

"When did you take an interest in boats that operate on the surface of the water?"

"Today," Jay admitted.

Cassie said, "I can vouch that his motives are on the side of truth, justice and the Am—uh, and all that that implies." *Ears,* Cassie thought.

They enjoyed a lunch in a nearby corner restaurant.

"Everybody smokes," Cassie said. The war on tobacco hadn't gotten there yet. It looked like Russian addiction was keeping several towns in North Carolina in the chips.

After lunch they tried, without much early luck, to hail a cab. It took twelve minutes of wondering if they were invisible, or perhaps doing it wrong, before finally a yellow taxi stopped for them. To say the car was a compact was like saying the Kremlin was a big building. Everyone got familiar with their own knees, and, in one case, with the knees of another.

Cassie, whose knees may have been involved in that transaction, told the driver to take them to the marina that matched the coordinates of yesterday's imaging information request. They were a little disappointed when they arrived at the location. All they found was a large vacant slip.

Cody said, "Just like Royce said. Zilch."

Jay had a suggestion. "Cody, fire up your little digital scanner. See if you can pick up any amateur radio transmissions."

"I really wish you did not ask me to bring the spectrum analyzer along. I agree there is no harm in looking, but you heard what the captain said. We could get picked up as spies."

"And with good reason," Jane said. "Let me see this gizmo."

Cody reluctantly handed it to Mrs. Brown.

Jane held it up to her ear. "It looks just like one of those new-fangled cellular phones."

Cody said, "Mrs. Brown, you should extend the antenna and keep it as vertical as possible."

Jane said, "Cassie, come over here and operate this thing while I pretend to be talking to it. You can pretend to fix my collar. You boys, go look at the big boats."

Cassie said, "We have a strong amateur radio band transmission on one of our frequencies of interest."

"Direction?" Jane asked.

"Due north."

"OK, Cassie, point me north."

The women strolled without urgency northward on the walkway along the shore. Cassie was impressed with Jane's demeanor under legitimately stressful circumstances. She was cool, and—if Cassie didn't know better—she'd think dear Mrs. Brown was demonstrating excellent tradecraft, an aptitude for intelligence work that couldn't possibly be beginner's luck, but had to be the result of extensive training. But Cassie knew Mrs. Brown's bio. There was nothing about intelligence work in her background, that is, if the background report Cassie read on Jane was real. Perhaps it was all a legend created by the genius minds of United States spookville. Perhaps Jane's cover was deeper than deep, to the point where Cassie wasn't even starting to comprehend it. Or maybe it was all in Cassie's paranoid mind, trained to be suspicious of anything, even a perfectly nice woman who was a recent widow and somewhat inexplicably cool under pressure. That was the problem with spy versus spy as a vocation. It was like spending your entire life in a hall of mirrors. It was a miracle that anyone ever remained sane after doing a stint in the oddly-named field of intelligence. Jane continued to hold the device as if it were a phone. Cody and Jay returned from looking at the big boats and fell in line behind the women. The men intentionally stood between the woman and the direction from which they were most likely to be observed. They walked half a mile and another small marina came into sight. At the far end was parked a large white yacht.

Cassie said, "That looks a lot like the yacht we bumped into a few days ago."

Jay yelled out, "That's it."

They picked up their step as they approached the small marina.

Cody asked, "What are we going to do when we get to the yacht? We are not even supposed to be here."

"Good point," Cassie said.

Jane said, "We're Americans sightseeing. What could be more natural?"

Cody couldn't help himself. He laughed, and then, by way of explanation, said, "I see where the XO gets his firm appreciation for following rules."

Cassie said, "Like mother, like son."

As they approached, a man, also in American garb, with a hooded sweatshirt that zipped up the front, was walking away from the yacht.

Jay asked Cassie, "Should we be concerned about this guy heading toward us?"

Cassie offered Jay a quick body language read, "He is walking fast, looking down, not looking around, seems to be a man heading somewhere, not concerned about us."

"Holy cow! Look who it is."

The man looked up and they recognized him as Mark Maximov.

Jay called out, "Mark, what the hell are you doing here? Golf, my foot! Screaming trees. What the hell are you up to?"

"I could ask you the same thing, but I know what you are doing here," Maximov said.

Jay said, "How did you find this spot?"

Mark replied, "The same way you did."

Cody said, "Do you have…?"

Cassie elbowed Cody. She was getting better at it. Quicker and sharper. She could bruise a rib and no one else even knew she'd struck. This elbow meant ix-nay on any discussion of the spectrum analyzer. Cody received the message and changed his question to: "Do you have the same suspicions we do?"

Maximov replied, "I certainly do. I couldn't let it rest, either. The problem is, I didn't see anything special on the yacht. I checked it out. Feel free to do the same. I am heading back to town before I get caught out here. The captain would not be happy with me. He will be a lot more aggravated with you, XO. We can all head back together, if you like."

Jay said, "I am going to take a look."

Cody said, "I'll go back with you, Lieutenant Commander Maximov. Four people in a Russian cab is painful. Of course, my ride was quite charming, as I was in the middle, between the ladies."

"You never had it so good, Cody," Cassie said, as she, Jane and Jay sauntered down the dock.

Cody and Maximov returned to the street in search of a taxi.

The twenty-five-meter yacht's stern was tied to the dock. The name, *Lavidia 2*, was prominently labeled across the back. There were docks along both sides of the large yacht. As Jay approached, he smelled fuel oil. The hull was wet with sea spray. It looked as if the vessel had recently been underway.

Without hesitation, Jay went onboard, where he saw someone on the bow, a bronzed and oiled woman in her late twenties, early thirties, sunbathing, string bikini, face down on a blanket.

The woman must have had great hearing as she was alerted despite the fact that Jay's footsteps were nearly silent. She turned and spoke.

"*Ya mogu vam pomoch*?"

Jay locked onto her cat-like gaze.

There was a time there which to Jane and Cassie lasted about six and a half seconds, but to Jay and the woman with the cat eyes, lasted much longer. That time, the ticking of each thoroughly ripe second, was elongated and made dense with memories of sights and smells from long ago, of eyes that were then and remained feral, of lips so hot that they burned, and of a hypnotic ability to play the Russian guitar.

Jay removed his hat and tried to speak, but no sound came out. There were just more thoughts of very cold exteriors, very warm interiors, of snow on shoulders, rooms behind black curtains, and a stunning change in game plan that set Jay on his current course in life.

The woman in the string bikini, now aware of her near-nakedness, grabbed for a towel as she said, "You are the American boy that gave me the guitar. I still have it."

"Katarina! Yes, I am Jay."

Cassie and Jane were now on the yacht and approaching this reunion. Both had furrowed brows, as if their conspiracy of the heart were being foiled by a particularly cruel twist of fate. Who was this woman that turned Jay's knees to ginger ale? Why did she have to pop up now? Was getting Jay to this woman part of the plan? Whose plan? The Russians? Was this exercise designed to seduce Jay Brown? Cassie girded her loins against that possibility.

"Of course. You are Jay," Kat said. She had a vague tone, unwilling to admit that she had remembered the boy's name—as if there'd been a day since that long-ago winter night when she hadn't thought of him.

She stood up and wrapped the towel around her. The wind blew just right and Jay smelled her, the scent of heaven. She approached him, and to Jay she seemed a little bit out of focus. Each footstep was directly in front of the other, and she moved in slow motion. Katarina put her hands gently under his chin and kissed him on both cheeks then came very close to his mouth as she whispered, "Yes, I remember you."

Cassie and Jane were even more troubled by this. Not only was this, for Jay, a blast from the past, but a touchy-feely one to boot.

"How have you been, Kat?"

Before the feline beauty could answer, Cassie spoke up with a mouthful of treacle: "Jay, are you going to introduce us?"

Jay was in the most complex social situation of his life. Nothing this complicated ever happened while underwater.

But the complexity doubled when his mom entered the fray: "Jay, what guitar is she talking about?"

"Later, Mom, please, later."

Kat said, "You brought your mother...."

Jane decided the time for letting Jay play master of ceremonies was through. He was clearly in over his head here. She stepped in.

"Jane Brown. And your name?" Jane offered a limp hand and Katarina squeezed it.

"Katarina, Katarina Chernavin," she said. It was so musical that Jay thought she was singing.

"And you?" Katarina faced Cassie.

"I'm Cassie. A friend." Her eyes were blazing with a message that Katarina had no trouble reading.

"Interesting, in Russian, the word Cassie means classified. I would invite you to remain on the yacht for a tour, but it is not mine to show. It is owned by my employer."

Jay said, "Is it OK if we just look around from the outside?"

"That is what you are doing now, of course," Katarina said. She was pleased to see Jay, but not pleased about being walked up on like that. These Americans were bold. And trespassers.

Jane noted that the hull's portholes were completely covered, not with shades but white solid covers. The hull was white above and black below the waterline. It was built to stay steady and rocked less than other boats when a wave came by.

Katarina returned to Jay and whispered in his ear, her mouth so close that he could feel her hot, moist breath working way up into the canal, making him shiver with an unexpected delight. But that delight was short-lived.

"Why did you come here? Why did you find me? You have to go. It is not safe. You must go. You must go now before it is too late."

Jay was still processing what she said, when the sound of boots running up the dock turned everyone's attention. Four men in SWAT attire were running up the dock. As Jay, Jane and Cassie focused on the small incoming army, Kat disappeared inside the yacht. Jane spun with a throwing motion and returned her focus to the incoming.

The men drew their weapons.

Jay, Cassie and Jane raised their hands, assuming this was the correct move.

The SWAT (or SWAT-like, to be more precise) team leader barked in Russian.

Cassie translated. "He wants to know why we are here and what is our business?"

Jay spoke up, "I am visiting an old friend."

Cassie translated.

The Russian spoke angrily. The men ordered the Americans down to the dock. Jay gave the guy a happy lopsided smile and used his palms to push downward at the air, a "simmer down" gesture for the zealous Russian with the big gun.

"He wants to see ID," Cassie said.

Jane started to reach into her handbag, the bag in which Jay saw her put the spectrum analyzer, but one of the Russians grabbed it out of her hand.

"Hey!" Jay said.

"Shhh, Jay," Cassie said.

"That's my mom. Be nice," Jay said.

Cassie translated.

Jay and Cassie had only military ID. They hadn't had the time to provide themselves with a documented cover. (Cassie could have put that together quickly, too, if she'd known she'd be snooping on Russian soil.)

"We were talking to a girl I know. She was just here," Jay said.

The men searched the yacht, but came up empty.

"There is no one here. We are taking you all in for questioning."

XVI
Friday, September 18th, 1992
USS *Quincy*, Saint Petersburg, Russia

0900. The captain, Jay, Cassie, Jane, Cody, Maximov and the NAV collected in the wardroom. Jay, Cassie and Jane looked like the morning after, and were wearing the same clothes as the day before.

The captain was not happy. He was already mid-speech before Jay began to register actual words.

"In some ways I can't fault you for what you did, but on the other hand you disobeyed a direct order from your captain, which I cannot overlook."

"Captain, we were just…"

"Jay, save it. We all know why."

"But we found the yacht, Captain."

"You found a large yacht at a marina. You could not tell that it was the same yacht from looking at it on the periscope. It was not even in the location where we asked for imaging."

"There's more, Captain. It was transmitting amateur radio transmissions on the same frequency we detected before."

Cody said, "We, actually Mrs. Brown, used a spectrum analyzer, a portable radio frequency detector, that I brought along."

Captain Davis was agitated now. "Are you kidding me? And Jane, you are qualified to use this equipment how?"

Jane shrugged.

The captain continued, "We are lucky I am not on the phone with the president explaining why we were conducting espionage without authority. So where is the device?"

Jane said, "I threw it in the water when I saw the storm troopers coming towards us."

Cassie was impressed again with Jane's cool.

Jay said, "Nice job, Mom."

"A mother tries," she replied with a small laugh. She knew she'd done well.

The captain did not like the mood. He was scolding these people, and they were congratulating one another. They should be shaking in their boots, but they were too goddamned excited by their adventure to care that they were getting their asses chewed.

"I am sure that device cost a bit of our tax payers' money. I will be sure to have the cost of the device taken out of your pay, Cody."

Cody said nothing until he received Cassie's sharp elbow and said, "Yes, Captain."

The captain turned to Maximov. "And what the heck were you doing there?"

"Same thing, Captain."

"But the vessel was not in the location we requested. How did you know where to look? Were you carrying espionage equipment too?"

"No, sir. I suppose there was a great deal of luck involved, although I'd prefer to think of it as intuition. I saw the empty marina at the site we requested and took a walk along the coast. I gave it a quick once over, but I am not as sure as the others that this was our close-encounter vessel."

Jay now raised his voice, "Really, that's not what you said at the..."

The captain jumped in. "Jay, you are in no position to be placing moral judgment on anyone, you got that?"

"Yes, Captain."

"Jay, I think you are losing your shit. I have no choice but to have you temporarily relieved as XO after the reception tonight. The navigator will take over for you. Start the turnover process tonight. Cody and Cassie, I am going to turn you back over to Captain Royce. You two are to remove yourselves from my submarine tomorrow morning. All three of you will go back to the U.S. and, after an investigation is conducted, you will be tried via court martial at a time and place to be determined. You are all still members of the United States Navy but are relieved of your duties pending trial."

Cody said, "What about Maximov?"

The captain snapped, "Maximov did not conduct unauthorized espionage on foreign soil like you did, so all he gets is a non-punitive letter from me into his official record for disobeying an order. Because of the letter, Mark is likely to stay a lieutenant commander for at least a year longer than he was planning. Is that punishment OK with you, Cody? You should be worried about your own sorry ass. Last time I checked, spying is punishable by death." The captain decided he'd gone too far. The bad news was devastating enough without hyperbole. "No one's getting the death penalty. But you are still fucked. You could be dishonorably discharged. In the mean time, I do want you to attend the reception tonight. There is to be no mention of what went on. I don't want our Russian hosts to know the severity of what you have done. From outward appearances, you guys were simply sightseeing, and it was a big misunderstanding. If you are not visible tonight it could indicate that something bigger was going on. We do not want to hurt our relations with Russia; this is supposed to be a diplomatic peace-keeping mission. Everybody got that?"

Jay, Cody, Cassie and even Jane sounded mighty gloomy as they said, "Yes, sir."

"You too, Mark."

"Aye aye, sir."

"Your professionalism tonight will help to mitigate the charges of your indiscretions of yesterday. God help each and every one of you if you do anything that could be construed as spying, disrespect or unprofessional by the U.S. Navy or our host nation."

All Jay could hear was blah, blah, blah.

1700. The naval college's grand ballroom was filling with dignitaries. The U.S. Navy officers wore dinner dress blues, the navy equivalent of a tux, with a gold cummerbund. Cassie's came with a skirt. Maximov wore a kilt, Jane a long black gown. Cassie, Jay, Cody, Jane, Mark and Captain Davis entered the grand hall together. The room was spectacular, the size of a football field, all walls and fifty-foot ceiling covered with dark carved wood. Officers looked up with their mouths opened. A small orchestra played in one corner. Jay visually scanned the musicians. Yup. There was a classical guitarist.

Captain Davis said, "It is best for you three that were detained by Russian authorities yesterday to not spend all of your time together."

Jay whispered to Cassie, "What can they do, kick us out of the navy twice?"

The captain overheard and whispered back, "You are lucky you're not in a Russian jail as the bitch of some giant named Boris."

Jay, Cassie and Jane split up and started to wander around the large crowd. The caterers were doing a great job. The waiters kept coming: wine, vodka and cognac; black caviar, crab and salmon.

Then Jay saw her. Kat. In a long gray dress, clingy. Clingy to the point of being magical. They made eye contact and her eyes were unmistakable. Jay saw recognition and then fear in those eyes. Katarina turned her back to Jay and walked away. Her gait was normal at first, and then the swing of her undulating hips betrayed her urgency. Jay would have none of that, and followed her with strides that were impossible for Kat to match because of her garb. He caught her just as she reached a tall man with a grey beard, a Russian admiral—who had a big and familiar grin. Jay was struck by how much they looked alike, that this admiral looked more like he could have been his dad than his actual dad.

Vlad.

Kat looked at Jay with an expression of consternation and spoke in a disturbed tone to her father in Russian.

Vlad waved her off and said, "Hello, Jay. It is a pleasure to see you again after all of these years. I am pleased to see that you took my advice. Kat tells me you paid her a visit yesterday."

"You, sir, I…How is it that you…and Katarina—" Jay couldn't put together a sentence.

"As you know, Jay, I have been retired for a long time." Vlad said, by way of explanation. "But I was a very high-ranking officer in the navy, so they let me come to things like this. I was in charge of the entire submarine fleet at one point—and I did go to school here. It doesn't seem likely, but I learned to be a man and an officer within these walls."

"Do you still have the music shop, Admiral?" asked Jay.

"Yes, I do. And yours is still our finest guitar."

Kat snorted, impatient to cut the niceties. "Didn't yesterday make it obvious to you that you should avoid me? How did you get released?"

"We didn't do anything wrong. We were just asked a few questions then they let us go."

"It's not that easy," Kat said. "They released you so they could watch you. You are in danger talking to us."

At that moment the classical guitarist began to play, Mikhail Visotsky's "Along the River".

Jay, never known for his poker face, turned toward the band and blurted, "Oh my God, are you kidding me?"

Kat snorted again.

Vlad's smile faded. "You know more than I realized."

"I know nothing—except that I am in a lot of trouble."

Vlad said, "But you are so close. I have to believe you are going to fix this."

"I have no idea what you are talking about. Seriously. I am about to get thrown out of the navy."

Kat turned to her father and said angrily, "See? I told you."

"All is not lost," Vlad said calmly. "Jay, you need to keep a close eye on your Captain Royce. He is responsible for the death of your father. You need to avenge your father's death."

Kat said, "Enough, Father."

"How do you know this?"

Kat was frantic: "You are going to get us all killed."

Vlad explained, "By the end of this song, Royce is going to leave this reception for a short time to give his fleet of malcontents instructions with the new frequencies to monitor. He is staying in a special room in the east wing of the school. When you see him leave, you must follow him."

"Vlad, you have no idea how much trouble…"

"Jay, you are going to have to trust me. Kat and I are being forced to do things against our will."

"Father, I am so sorry to have done this to you."

Jay looked puzzled and Vlad said, "This is not the time to talk. It is the time to catch Royce as a deadly criminal. Very, very deadly if he were to get his way, for his goal must certainly be to start a nuclear war and thus the obliteration of mankind."

"Father is astute," Katarina said, and flashed Jay an enchanting flirty face. She remembered.

Vlad continued, "He is making his move now and he is very dangerous. If he sees me or Kat following him he will order to have us killed instantly. He can't just kill you."

"But that's exactly what he did with my father," said Jay.

"You have information on your side, Jay. I can help, but not with Royce. You have to trust me."

Jay looked into Vlad's eyes, then Kat's eyes. He saw nothing but sincerity, and shrugged. "This is either the smartest or stupidest thing I have ever done in my life," he said.

Jay watched as Captain Royce made his way through the crowd, heading for the east exit. Jay followed.

Jane and Cassie had, of course, been monitoring Jay's interactions with the young lady and the large Russian admiral. The crowd was thick now, and it was harder to move from place to place. The speeches were about to start. Jay followed Royce. Cassie and Jane followed Jay.

Royce led the procession out of the ballroom, and into the dank innards of the ancient naval school. Jay felt as if he'd fallen into an endless nightmare, a descent into the pits of hell, each stage being weirder and more painful than the one before, from his dad's death to this creepy place. There was little light, and the stone building was old. He heard the sound of water dripping, from somewhere, from the infrastructure of this monstrosity of a school that looked, with each fraction of a second, more like the ruins of his old life now overcome. The hallways and stairs were windy and narrow. Jay felt he was in a submarine, tailing Victor Three. He needed to keep on the subject's tail without being detected. Staying in Royce's baffles wasn't going to work. No pressure, but a fuck-up would probably prove fatal.

Jay walked on his toes. Behind him, both ladies held their shoes. Only the echoes of Royce's purposeful steps could be heard. Cassie would have no trouble following those steps by sound alone, such was the accelerated nature of her senses. But she wasn't so confident in Jay's hunting ability.

Jay, as it turned out, was doing fine. He picked up the pace of his stealthy steps, and moved so that he had a visual on the subject—and it was a good thing, too, because in that hallway, Royce turned a doorknob and disappeared into a room.

At that moment Jane and Cassie turned the corner and saw the shadowy figure of Jay, and he quietly knelt in the hallway and put his eye to a keyhole.

Jay took in as much information as he could. Royce's room was all dark wood, similar to the giant hall. Royce toyed with a book on a bookshelf and a secret door opened in the panel.

Jay could hardly breathe. On the other side of the secret door was another large room, and Jay caught a quick glimpse of electronic equipment. Jay stood, turned the knob and let himself into the outer room. He tiptoed to the secret panel, which remained open, and he peeked into the other room.

It was a full-fledged communications center. Broadcasting and receiving. Royce sat with a headset on, typing on a keyboard. To the left of the keyboard was a machine that looked as if it had been designed by aliens or men from the future. On top of it was a TV monitor with the numbers 028003 displayed in green.

Jay deduced that Royce was telling his contacts what frequency to monitor for their next instructions.

To spy at such close distance demands breath control, an ability to remain completely silent, and Jay thought he had that down. He could force his body into an even strain even if his life depended on it. Unfortunately Jay discovered that some sounds are uncontrollable. He hadn't eaten in a long time. Just as Royce removed his headset, Jay's stomach made a loud rumble and Royce's head snapped around. Jay snapped his head back, but he was too slow.

"Lieutenant Commander Brown, what the heck are you doing here?" Royce smacked his lips as if lustfully contemplating cannibalism.

"Captain, I was going to ask you the same thing." Jay saw a frequency detector resting on a tabletop, apparently identical to the one his mother had used to find the suspicious yacht.

"I am asking the questions here. You are in a lot of trouble. This is a secure space the Russian government has loaned to me."

"Give me a break. Let's talk to Admiral Bennett, or better yet Admiral Conner, and see if they know about this."

"You are correct, Jay. That is not a question I want asked. Too bad you are never going to have an opportunity to ask it."

"Don't threaten me..." Jay put his head on a swivel once inside the room and saw that only three-quarters of the space was for business. In one corner were a bed, a night table, a couple of easy chairs and a small refrigerator. A fellow could have a party.

"Oh, no threat," Royce said. "Just filling you in on your limited future. You are going to have an accident. You are snooping around again after you were told not to, and now something very bad is going to happen to you. I am calling Russian security right now."

As if on cue, Jane Brown and Cassie strode into the room. Jay's brain spun around inside his skull. He had come to grips with the fact that he was going to die, a son dying in pursuit of his late father's honor. He was OK with that. But now that Mom and Cassie had blundered in, he was going to have to think of a way to get out of this. He was thinking that running might not be the worst option, but his mother didn't run, so that was out. Royce didn't look so tough. Maybe he could just take him, take him out just long enough to get away.

Ha! Who was Jay fooling? Not even himself. If he ever got his hands on Royce he would not be able to stop until Royce was dead. He would put his thumbs on the man's throat and watch his rheumy eyes pop.

Royce's reaction to the women's dramatic entrance was hysterical. He gave a little speech: "Give me a break. You brought your mother and your girlfriend? That's precious. That is special. You three were just picked up as potential spies. You are all going to be charged as spies. You have no business being here. You, my snoopy friends, do not have a need to know."

Cassie noticed Royce glancing nervously as he spoke, in the direction of the bed in the corner. Cassie's eyes focused hard and she saw that the mattress was propped up by something near the foot. Just a couple of inches, but visible. Something dark stuck out between the mattress and the box spring. Royce had to go into the outer room to make the phone call. He stepped through the secret panel and began to dial. Cassie shot across the room in a flash, grabbed the thing that was protruding. As she suspected, it was a gun. A pistol. Cassie returned to Jane's side. She handed Jane the gun behind her back. "Let's take him," Jane said. The three entered the outer room. Royce realized he was in trouble. He waited until they all cleared the inner doorway before he threw the phone down and managed to get past into the inner room. He ran straight for the bed and stuffed his hand under the mattress.

Jane brought the gun from behind her back. She calmly chambered a round in what she could now see was a CZ-75. A nine. Perfect.

"Are you looking for something, Captain Royce?" Jane had both hands on the pistol.

"You aren't going to shoot me. I am calling security on you all."

Royce walked with tellingly small steps and lunged toward Jane. He grabbed the gun in both hands.

Jane pushed instead of pulled with her gun hand, squeezed one off. Bang. She shot him low. Jay and Cassie were surprised at how muffled the shot was. Jane had pushed the barrel deeply into Royce's belly fat. The bullet tore through his stomach and exploded out the left back. Blood and a handful of assorted guts splattered on the wall and the bed. The only sound he made was a gasp followed by a gurgle. Blood began to flow steadily from the corners of his mouth. Royce looked like he was going to fall forward, so Jane used both hands to push him away and he fell on his back instead. Timber!

There was a stunned silence. For a few moments, they stared at Royce, the body that used to be Royce, which was on the floor in a growing pool of blood. The eyes not just open but wide open, as if the last things Royce had seen were the opening gates of hell.

Jay walked over to his mother and gave her a hug. "Are you OK?"

"He killed my husband, and, in the end, he didn't give me a choice. If he'd gotten the gun from me we would've had that accident he was talking about."

Jay used a handkerchief to put the phone's receiver back on the hook. He took the gun from his mother and wiped that clean as well. He placed the gun on Royce's hand and squeezed the dead man's fingers around it to leave prints.

Jay said, "It was self defense. We should tell Captain Davis and Admiral Bennett."

Jane said, "Yeah, that will go over well. We really had no business being in this room."

"Interesting, a Czechoslovakian pistol. Why didn't Royce have a standard navy issue pistol?" Jay asked.

His mother was quick with the answer: "Because Royce is a murdering traitor. We all know that."

Cassie said, "Royce committed suicide. It's been going around. I'll work on staging the body better. Jay, memorize everything in the electronics area."

"I'll keep lookout," Jane said, impressed by the way Cassie took charge.

Cassie took a framed photo of Royce and his wife from the outer office desk and placed it in Royce's free hand.

Jay confirmed Royce's final transmission, and typed on the keyboard:

"I JUST CAN'T LIVE WITH MYSELF ANYMORE"

Jay didn't push enter. The guy at the other end wouldn't get the message, but the guy who found the body would. Royce's safe was open. Jay grabbed the manila envelope that held the imaging information that the *Quincy* had requested. He put the frequency detector in the envelope as well, folded the envelope, and stuck it in his jacket pocket.

The three of them examined the scene and admired their work.

"I'd say he committed suicide," Jane said.

They turned and headed back to the party. Jay strode off on his own. He passed Vlad but didn't stop.

"What's up?" Vlad asked.

"It's all set," Jay said.

Vlad looked perplexed.

Jay needed to see the captain. Vlad spotted Cassie and Jane. They tried to duck him, too, but Vlad reached out and grabbed a handful of Jane's arm.

Jane was alarmed at first.

"Beautiful woman, you are mussed," Vlad said.

He took a handkerchief and wiped at the side of her neck. He then showed her what the "muss" was: blood.

"Thank you, kind sir," Jane said.

Now Vlad understood what Jay meant by "all set."

Jay saw the huddle not far from the entrance. Captain Davis, Admiral Bennett and Cody were chatting with a number of Russian officials, one of whom had the damndest eyebrows Jay had ever seen. Eyebrow. One thick and protruding caterpillar. You could fit a listening device in that eyebrow.

Jay greeted Cody physically, with a friendly embrace. The captain wondered if maybe Jay had been drinking. As he hugged Cody, he slid the folded envelope into the pocket inside Cody's jacket. Cassie came up behind Jay and joined the group.

"Have you two been mingling separately as I directed?"

Cassie and Jay replied, "Yes, Captain."

Mrs. Brown, no longer mussed, joined the group seconds later.

"Yes, I'm sure you have," the captain said, rolling his eyes. "Has anyone seen Captain Royce?"

Cassie, Jay and Jane shook their heads.

The music stopped and there was a commotion as a SWAT team entered, one armed man per exit.

"Them again," Jane said, wearily. She bit her tongue. Luckily, the Russian officials were distracted and hadn't heard her.

The captain said, "What the hell is this about?"

A Russian official said, "I will find out, Captain, and let you know."

The room grew loud with a noise collage of jittery conversation.

The Russian official returned and said, "Captain, we are in lock-down for everyone's protection. One of your comrades was just found dead in his room. We think there may have been foul play. We are looking at the security tapes of the area to figure out what happened."

Jane said, "Don't bother checking. I shot the bastard with his own gun." She opened up her blazer to show the blood on her blouse.

A woman screamed. People shouted in Russian. Armed men charged Jane from all directions. Jane raised her hands and smiled at Jay and Cassie. She had a look of comfort and satisfaction on her face.

Vlad and Kat subtly approached and made eye contact with Jay and Cassie. Vlad made a head gesture for them to follow him. They entered a coatroom that had a large wooden lattice grate on the wall that Vlad lifted open.

"One of the benefits of going to school here is I know where all the secret passageways are," Vlad said, delighted with his own cleverness.

There was a three-by-three-foot opening in the wall.

"It seemed so much larger when I was a boy," Vlad said.

They crawled into the space just inside the exterior stone wall of the ruins. They heard the scuttling noise that rats make when they run across rock.

"Lovely," Cassie said. She considered herself a tough broad, but rodents gave her the willies. Chipmunks were OK. The others creeped her out.

Jay wondered if anyone had been through the secret passageway since Vlad graduated a half-century before. To Jay's amazement, they came upon a spot that was connected to the rest of the world by a vent, and enough light came through to see for a few feet. Hanging on the wall were three battery-powered battle lanterns. Vlad unmounted one, clicked it on, and discovered the battery was dead.

"*Der'mo*," spit out Vlad.

"Try the others," said Cassie.

The remaining two lamps did light, although one was a good deal brighter than the other. Vlad took the brighter lamp and led the way. They stepped tentatively down a single-file flight of stairs, then another, then a hallway and a third down staircase.

"Isn't this where the *Phantom of the Opera* had his clubhouse?" Cassie asked.

"That was in Paris," Vlad said. "This is musty, true, but the phantom was in a sewer."

Vlad was taking them to the bowels of the earth, and Jay could feel the rock surfaces becoming damp and mossy. They went through a door and were inside a huge tunnel, a cavern! Jay could tell by its smooth and rounded surfaces that it was man-made.

Vlad explained, "These are the dark passages of Saint Petersburg's underground transportation system. This tunnel is no longer used, but we can get you to a place from here where no one is looking for you."

They walked along the rusty tracks as if searching for the center of the earth.

Cassie was dripping sweat. There were times when she wished she didn't have near-superhuman senses. She could not only hear the rats now, but she could see them, see them in the dark, and they were huge, running in packs down the tunnel, bounding as if on springs, hurdling one another like lemmings toward the cliff.

Vlad said, "We are approaching the still-active portion of the system. Stay well to the side and do not touch anything or you may get run over or electrocuted."

But no trains came.

After several miles they reached a station and climbed onto the platform. Then, as if on cue, a train came and the pushed air blasted them in the face.

There were a few other people waiting for the train, but no one seemed too surprised that three people in uniform and one woman in a formal long gown had just climbed onto the platform.

Jay said, "Our escape plan is via the subway?"

Vlad said, "I was thinking about taking a cab. I've had enough underground for the moment."

All agreed that being above the earth's surface would be a good thing.

Cassie said, "As I recall, Russian cabs are not very big."

"All four of us won't fit. Kat, you take Jay. I'll take the young lady."

"Admiral, my name is Cassie. Where are we going?"

Vlad replied, "Ahh, yes, Cassie. And you must call me Vlad. Of course, how rude of me. We are going to my guitar shop."

Jay felt a thrill at the thought of revisiting the guitar shop, the warm haven. He didn't want to sound too nostalgic in front of Cassie, and as usual overcompensated.

"Beats a Russian jail, I guess," Jay said. Vlad took no offense because Jay was so transparent.

"A few more days of freedom sounds like just the ticket," Cassie said.

"If things work out," Vlad said, "no one is going to jail and you both are going to be heroes."

Jay said, "Right now, I'd settle for getting my mom out of jail and a dishonorable discharge."

"Me, too," Cassie said.

"This is not the time or the place for this," Vlad said. "We will talk at the shop."

They exited the platform and walked upstairs to the street. They were about to split up when Kat said, "Wait, Father, I have no money."

Vlad handed his daughter a few Russian bills. "I would like the change please," he said.

Kat replied, "*Spasibo,* of course."

"Do not speak in the cab," Vlad said directly to Jay.

Vlad flagged down a Lada, not yellow, and spoke with the driver.

Jay was troubled. "This does not look like a cab."

Vlad waved the car off, turned back to Jay and said, "Was that not clear English? I said do not speak. We will be much safer in a gypsy cab than a yellow cab, believe me. Now please be quiet."

Vlad waved down another car, spoke with the driver, and nodded for Kat and Jay to enter. Kat stayed between Jay and the driver as best she could in a vain attempt to keep the driver from noticing Jay's uniform. Jay was not unhappy about it. When in the cab, Kat draped herself across him and at one point was practically sitting in his lap. He smelled her and he smelled her some more. The door was barely shut behind them when they were roaring toward their destination.

Kat, her breasts against him, whispered, "Put your arms around me, Jay. Put your arms around me and just relax."

Jay did as instructed. He managed to adequately feign relaxation.

"Put your mouth to my mouth," Kat said.

What choice did he have?

The driver said something and stopped the car. Kat had to undrape herself from her smitten escort in order for her to pull out her money. Jay was impressed that the woman had gone through the entire night in a tight evening gown. He ached badly with desire for her.

"We're here," Kat said.

They got out—he with some difficulty. In seconds, the car carrying Vlad and Cassie arrived. Jay looked at the storefront of the guitar shop that he had visited so long ago. His life passed before his eyes like a slide show, a series of still images depicting his biography. When it came to the part where he played guitar, it seemed so foreign to him, so devoted and faithful had he become to his submarine duty. The slide show did not shy away from the horror as well. He saw the look on his mother's face at Dad's funeral, her refusal to take the American flag. He saw her shove a handgun into a traitor's belly and pump him with lead. He saw Cassie, afraid of rats, walking bravely through the subway tunnel. He saw the inner ruinous hallways of the ancient naval school, and recalled how they came to symbolize for him the ruinous turn his life had taken. Vlad, Kat and Cassie were quiet as Jay stood mesmerized.

Cassie couldn't help but wonder if Jay banged this Kat woman during that visit so many years ago. Jay wasn't the type to leap into intimacy like that—but Kat seemed like a bit of a sexpot to Cassie.

The slide show in Jay's head got to a photo of his father still living, quizzing him. The *Turtle*. The *Hunley*. The *Nautilus*. The *Thresher*!

Vlad took out his keys. He unlocked the grate in front of the door, and then the door. They were ready to go in and Jay still stood in his trance. Kat finally put an arm around his shoulders and led him inside.

Cassie thought Kat and Jay seemed pretty doggone comfortable with the touching.

Inside, Jay scanned the walls until he saw his guitar. Kat took it off the wall. They went through the black curtain and sat in the back room. Vlad's memorial to his career, the shadow box and other items, were just as Jay remembered it. Kat started playing Visotsky. "Along the River."

She still played with passion and perfection.

When she finished she said, "I don't get to play much these days."

Jay said, "You are still great. The piece played by you, Katarina, is a spiritual thing. There is something so soothing about the rhythms and tasty little licks throughout the piece that makes me feel like I've died and gone to Heaven! It is startlingly hypnotic. I love Visotsky, and I remember you guys do, too. You have his poster on the wall of your music shop."

"The piece is beautiful," Kat said. "But I cannot forget that—later, in this same work—the composer includes a piece of music called 'Stern Husband.'"

"It's about gypsies, Katarina," Jay said. "It's hard to judge the nomadic world. They aren't like you and me. They don't have time to, to negotiate. They don't have roots."

Vlad heard Jay grow just a bit colder as he said those words, as if they accompanied an inner decision that he wasn't discussing.

"Is that the music you two played together years ago?" Cassie asked.

"No, that was *Tetris Son*," Kat said.

The old man decided it was time for an explanation. "Gypsies have no time for negotiation. No one has much time for anything these days. If you haven't figured it out yet, there are some very bad things going on."

Vlad explained: A rogue Russian submarine with its two mini subs has been used to smuggle nuclear material for bomb-making to Iraq at a very high price.

As he heard the phrase *mini sub,* Jay thought of midget submarines, and his dad was back inside his head, unwelcome this time, a distraction at a time when Jay needed to concentrate. But, as usual, Dad had his way.

"What type of submarine did the Japanese use during the attack on Pearl Harbor?

"Midget submarines, sir."

"Were they effective?"

"No, sir."

"How did they get to Hawaii?"

"They were towed by a larger submarine and released off the waters of Hawaii."

"Not now, Dad," Jay said in a small voice. Truth was, he hadn't intended to say it out loud, but he did, and only Cassie with her feral ears heard him. Cassie gave Jay a quick glance of concern.

Come on, big guy, hold on, Cassie thought. Jay had been through the wringer, once, twice, three times, and he was being held together by bubble gum by this time.

Jay forced the disembodied voice out of his head so he could once again pay attention to the important info Vlad was dishing out.

Vlad explained that rogue elements within Russia were providing and moving the atomic material. Iraq was accepting and paying for the material. And some bad guys in the U.S. were playing middleman under the guise of the nuclear material clean-up operation. Communication, as they had so cleverly found out, was through the music. There was a fleet of three custom-made yachts, each built so that a mini sub could nest underneath. The mini subs had very little range, so they needed to be carried from place to place. They either rode on the India class sub or were nested under a luxury yacht. The mini subs loaded up nuclear material in the Kola peninsula. The India class submarine brought each mini sub to a location in the north Atlantic where it was transferred to a yacht. The yacht transported the nuclear material to an Iraqi port. There was a special underground dock in Iraq. Once there, the mini sub separated from the yacht, unloaded the nuclear material and then loaded up the payment, which came in gold bars. The mini sub nested back under the yacht and the yacht returned to the marina in Russia. After a time, the empty mini subs were towed back to the Kola peninsula to load up with nuclear material again.

"How long does each circuit take?" Jay asked.

Cassie was glad to see that Jay was again in the here and now.

"About a month," Vlad said, "from loading at Kola to returning to Kola empty. Each pound of plutonium is exchanged for a hundred pounds of gold. There are about ten pounds of plutonium on each run. Interestingly, the plutonium is wrapped in so much shielding that it is an even exchange weight wise. Each run is about ten million American dollars.

"Why was Kat on that yacht?"

"Unfortunately, Kat is right in the middle of this…" Vlad said.

"I'll speak for myself," Kat said. "The story is not a happy one and I'm afraid I couldn't come off as more of a loser. I got involved with and subsequently married a man that is deeply involved in this. He's a submariner like all of you."

Cassie, not a submariner, thought about mentioning it, but let it go.

"Where is your husband now?" Jay asked.

Kat replied, "He is assigned to the USS *Quincy*."

XVII

Saturday, September 19th, 1992
Saint Petersburg

1200. It was clear and cool, temp in the 60s. Vlad, Kat, Cassie and Jay pulled into the marina where *Lavidia 2* was docked. Vlad drove a beat-up Russian pickup truck.

"The last time we came here we were arrested," Cassie commented.

"They say that lightning cannot strike in the same place twice," Jay said reassuringly.

"Bullshit," Cassie said. "Well at least we don't look odd," she added facetiously.

Vlad, Cassie and Jay were all in wet suits. There were three dive bags and three scuba tanks in the bed of the pickup truck. Kat was dressed in jeans, sandals and a blouse with a windbreaker, and she carried a canvas bag.

The divers finished suiting up. Kat, not at all certain that their plan was going to work, was armed to the teeth as she led the way toward the yacht. The others followed, thirty feet back.

Kat climbed aboard the yacht and was greeted by a man that helped her aboard. The man grabbed her bag and led her to the cabin below. Once down there, Kat reached behind her back and under her windbreaker. She grabbed one of several tasers that were tucked into the back of her pants. She fired into the back of the man in front of her. He went down with a loud clunk.

The three divers boarded the yacht with swift and quiet steps. They left the scuba bottles on the dock but boarded the vessel with their dive bags.

Cassie had worried that Vlad would be a liability on an action operation because of his age, but it didn't appear she had anything to worry about. Vlad was robust despite his age. One could only imagine what he was like in his prime.

Vlad unzipped his dive bag and put a roll of duct tape around his wrist. He held a fist full of large tie wraps. He went into the cabin and knelt on the back of the downed man.

"Good work, Kat."

"Thank you, Father."

Vlad duct taped the prone man's mouth then tie-wrapped his hands and feet together.

The footsteps of the invaders couldn't have been stealthier, but the loud thump of the falling man attracted the attention of the two remaining crewmembers. They came running. Entering the cabin, the first one reached for his gun, and was immediately incapacitated by a Taser.

Jay tackled the third crewmember. Kat, on a roll, came over to tase the third man as she had the first two. But her luck had run out. She fired at the crewmember, but instead her Taser went into Jay's back. The third guy was now down with Jay twitching on top of him. Vlad pulled the guy out from under Jay, rolled him onto his belly, and put his knee on his back. This allowed Cassie to tape his mouth and tie his hands and feet. Cassie hog-tied the remaining crewmember as well. Kat collected pistols and knives from each man's belt. Kat placed the knives on a table. The guns went into her bag.

Vlad and Cassie tended to Jay.

"Not exactly as planned, but effective nevertheless," Vlad said.

Jay twitched as they lifted him onto a bench seat.

Vlad said to Jay, "You were supposed to tackle him after Kat tasered him, not before."

Jay was drooling with his hands contorted in front of him. He tried to speak but only made a grunt that caused more drool to come out.

Kat grabbed a towel and wiped Jay's face.

She said, "I am sorry I electrocuted you. You will be better in a while."

Kat kissed Jay on the forehead.

Cassie didn't like that. She rather angrily pulled the Taser probes out of Jay and kissed him on the forehead as well. Cassie glared at Kat who returned her gaze with a puzzled expression.

It was difficult and they sweated heavily inside their wetsuits, but Cassie, Vlad and Kat teamed up to move the incapacitated men into separate cabins, where they were further bound to support columns.

Jay managed to sit up. He saw the knives on the table and reached for one.

Vlad said, "Don't touch those. They are a particular kind of Spetsnaz knives. Extremely dangerous."

Jay pulled his hand away slowly.

Vlad grabbed a cutting board that had been tucked in the gunwale of the vessel and picked up one of the knives. He pushed a button on the knife and the blade came firing into the cutting board with serious force.

Vlad said, "A Russian switch blade. Never really used by the Spetsnaz, but very dangerous. Spetsnaz has become the catch-all name for weapons of a type once made to suit the specific needs of special forces."

Toys, Jay thought. Fancy toys for grown-ups in a real-life James Bond world. Damn, Tasers hurt like hell.

Cassie looked at the blade sticking out of the board. "I had heard of these before. I didn't realize they were actually in use."

Vlad replied, "Only by the kind of people Kat is acquainted with." It is a sad moment when a father uses his daughter's name as the dirty word in a sentence.

Kat spoke up, "We are trying to change that, Father."

Cassie didn't like the rapport Kat and Jay shared, or the fact that she had tased him, but she did sympathize with Kat's man problems. Cassie knew about making bad choices with men and put a hand of emotional support on Kat's shoulder. Vlad reloaded the knife into the handle and put the three knives into a sink.

At that moment, there was a working lunch taking place on the USS *Quincy*. In attendance were Captain Davis, Admiral Bennett, Cody, Jane Brown, Mark Maximov and the acting XO, Joe "NAV" Silio. Captain Royce's bagged body was in the freezer. Jane Brown was under house arrest. Cody had already shown the imaging information and the pocket scanner to the admiral and Captain Davis.

The captain asked the admiral, "So what do we do? Leave two officers on foreign soil and just deliver our body and accused murderer back to the United States?"

Admiral Bennett replied, "Those, in fact, are your orders. I'm here to make sure you do just that. The Russian authorities have assured us they will immediately extradite Brown and Voxer as soon as they are captured. Nothing good comes from us staying here any longer. We will continue with our new orders to the letter. But that does not prevent the USS *Quincy* from continuing to train. I think it would be great practice to track a yacht from Saint Petersburg to wherever it is heading."

Cody started to say something. In Cassie's absence, Jane gave him the elbow.

Admiral Bennett turned to Jane. "Ma'am, I am not sure what happened in that room. I am not sure why you were there, and why you did what you did. You are innocent until proven guilty in our country. There cannot be any discussion of that incident. I am assuming the XO's stateroom suits you."

"I am very comfortable, sir. I will not be any trouble to you or the crew of the *Quincy*. I hope your training exercise turns out to be fruitful."

"All right," the captain said. "Let's plan on getting underway at 1500."

1500. Saturday, the 19th of September, underway on the *Lavidia 2*. Cassie, Vlad and Jay were sitting on athwart ships bench seat next to the captain's seat where Kat was calmly driving the yacht.

Vlad, Cassie and Jay had put their wet suits to use. They went underneath the yacht and gave the nested mini sub a thorough once over. If and when they decided to use that mini sub as part of their plan, they first needed to know that it was sound—and it was.

They didn't linger down there, however, as they also had reason to believe the mini sub was radioactive. The *Quincy* had not collided with the yacht, but with the mini sub nested underneath. Vlad gave a thumbs-up to Jay and Cassie, meaning it was time to surface. Up on the yacht, they changed into civvies. And there was a moment for conversation.

Vlad said, "Naming a boat *Lavidia* in Russia is like calling a boat the *Titanic* in the United States."

Kat said, "I would argue this vessel is more a ship than a boat."

Vlad challenged back, "A ship ships, a boat boats."

"Father, if you didn't notice the mini sub nested amidships, the *Lavidia* ships."

"OK, I'll give you that. But naming this little ship *Lavidia* has to be bad luck. For Jay and Cassie, I will explain. The *Lavidia* was built in the 1800s and had pontoons mounted adjacent to its keel for stability. It ended up being flawed engineering, and the vessel almost sunk on its maiden voyage and was never really used again."

"This ship resembles the original *Lavidia*—except for the pontoon, and we have a mini sub nested under us completely submerged," Kat said.

"Lovely company you keep," Vlad said.

"You introduced me to him, Father," Kat said.

"Ah, yes. An inadvertent blunder, I'm afraid."

Jay didn't care to listen to this any longer and asked, "How about we figure out how to work the electronics down there?"

Kat asked, "What do you want to know? We are transmitting our coordinates on 28.003 MHz via Mikhail Visotsky's 'Along the River'."

That was when Jay got it. "Kat, you are the creator of this cipher. It would take someone like you to create such a thing."

"Someone like me? I am not sure how to think of this. Yes, of course. I was a good Soviet girl, daughter of the admiral. I am a musician, but I am also a mathematician, and a cryptographer."

Cassie decided to plant the seed for possible future matchmaking: "Wow, you and Cody have a lot in common."

"Not that much in common," Kat snapped.

Jay asked, "Why did you do it?"

Kat replied, "Do what? Do you think I am a traitor?"

"I am not sure what to think about anything, Kat."

Kat said, "When I started this five years ago, I thought I was doing legitimate work for my country. I'm sure you and Cassie understand how I felt. With time, things stopped making sense. My operations were too secret. By the time I explained what I was doing to my father, I was in too deep and it was too late to get out for a number of reasons. I built the technical infrastructure for the musical cipher. The system is proprietary and I have benefitted monetarily. While everyone else in my homeland is struggling to put food on the table, I have been living very comfortably. I sunbathe on a yacht. I have seen very little of my double agent husband in the past two years. He has done a good job of keeping your NATO forces away, until now."

"He told us he was half Russian and half Scottish. Is that true?" Jay asked.

"No, that is merely part of his cover. His cover story is extensive."

"Is he really Jewish?"

"He is really nothing. He is no longer really anything. Pardon me if even I am vague on all of the details. There are some things for which I am not on a need-to-know basis. He took the Scottish identity two years ago. My husband's transformation was the last op for a mastermind Russian spy, the same guy, code-name Master Cylinder, who turned a Russian agent named Alec Hidell into Lee Harvey Oswald. That case involved a general's daughter. My husband endured plastic surgery, vocal-cord adjustments—crazy, crazy stuff. I'm certain there were drugs involved, too. Mind control juice. They toyed with his mind until the original man I knew was no longer there. He lost his mind. It was replaced by something cunning yet evil. He became obsessed with greed and money. He will sacrifice anything for the gold. Our own child is being held hostage."

"You have a child?"

Her father answered for her. "She told you it was hard to get out of this for a number of reasons. They took my grandson away last year when I tried to get Kat out of this crazy circus operation. We have no choice but to succeed."

"If one hair on my son's head is hurt I will kill them all, or die trying. And yes, if I have to, I will kill my husband. It is a fact."

Jay had an idea. "Kat, we need to alter our signal to let the *Quincy* know that Maximov is a bad guy."

Kat said, "That's complicated. The India class sub is monitoring the carrier signal and has equipment I designed that spits out the rendezvous point coordinates. If the coordinates change, the India is ordered to abort the mission. The time can change, but the coordinates can't."

Jay said, "Let's change the time in a way that we can send a signal to Cody."

Kat said, "We would have to change too much. It might alert the India to the fact that there is an issue. We also don't know if and when either the *Quincy* or the India will copy the signal."

"If I remember correctly," Cassie said, "your cipher works based upon a string being played in a measured bar one time. If the same string is played out of baseline twice it reverts back to baseline. What if we tried to capture a code by playing the same string two or three times out of baseline—then sent it as an ASCII message?"

"That would work," Kat said. "The receiving equipment will still read the same location. It will butcher the song worse than we already have. But how would the *Quincy* know?"

Cassie replied, "Cody will know. He is a constant tinkerer. The minute he sees a change, he'll go to work figuring it out."

"I can do this," Kat said, with a startling burst of enthusiasm. "Can someone take the wheel? I already know the message I am going to send."

1700. Saturday, the 19th of September, periscope depth. Cody was in the radio room. The admiral, Captain Davis and Mark Maximov were in the control room. Joe Silio, acting XO, had the conn. Cody had info for the control room.

"Conn, radio, I have copied a broadcast and have ten minutes of radio twenty-eight zero zero three, playing your favorite and mine, 'Along the Spooky River.'"

"Radio, conn, where's it coming from?"

"Captain, it's coming from the bearing of our radio directional finder that matches our contact sierra 15."

"Silio," the captain said (he didn't like calling him XO), "go deep and continue to track sonar contact sierra 15. Cody, analyze that music. Tell me if you come up with anything."

Cody grabbed the tape and high-tailed it into sonar—his home away from home. He sat down at the music-analyzing computer stack that he and the Weps made.

Sonar operator, Petty Officer MacIntyre Symms, said, "Sir, do you think the XO and Lieutenant Commander Voxer are going to be all right?"

Cody replied, "They have the truth going for them. They aren't traitors. In fact, they are heroes. I don't know how far the truth will get them, though. The former Soviet Union isn't famous for its truth." Cody felt proud of himself. He thought his response showed wisdom, a trait he was not known for. Smart, yes. Wise? Not so much. "As am I, they are only guilty of seeking the truth."

Symms said, "The truth can be made to look like a lot of things. My dad used to say, 'Believe none of what you hear and half of what you see.' I didn't realize how smart my daddy was until I started working in this business."

"I like it," Cody said. "Your dad wasn't Ben Franklin was he?"

"Really? Busting my balls?"

Cody smiled and started running his analysis on the tape.

1800. Saturday, the 19th of September, aboard the *Lavidia 2.* Kat, Vlad and Jay sat on the athwart ships bench seat next to the captain's seat where Cassie was driving the yacht.

"Think we should feed those guys down there?" Jay asked.

Kat hissed with a hunched up back, and then purred, "I have some rat poison I think would be a good option. They are responsible for taking my son away from me."

Vlad spoke up, "If we kill them, we will be no better than they are. Jay, they will be fine. We will give them some water in the morning."

Cassie asked, "Did Maximov try to protect your son from being taken hostage?"

Kat laughed bitterly. "Hardly. He directed the kidnappers. All he wants is gold and power."

Jay asked, "How much danger is the USS *Quincy* in with him on it?"

Vlad said, "Dmitry—that is his real first name—has a submarine and Spetsnaz background. He could kill the entire crew and sleep like a baby before the bodies were cold."

1900. Saturday, the 19th of September, USS *Quincy* submerged, heading westbound out of the Gulf of Finland. Cody began his fourth hour of analyzing tape.

"Holy shit," said Cody, who raced to the control room and asked Silio where the captain was.

Silio replied, "Halfway through the movie."

"I need to talk to him. For his ears only."

"Important?"

"Very."

"All right. I'll call him." Silio talked to the captain and relayed a message to Cody: "It better be important. They were just about to get to his favorite part of *Top Gun* where Tom Cruise makes out with Kelly McGuiness."

The captain arrived in the control room with Maximov right behind him. Cody looked at Maximov and went white as a ghost.

"Cody, what's so goddamn important?"

"Very private, Captain—and personal, sir. Can we talk in your stateroom?"

"All right, Cody, let's go in my stateroom."

In the stateroom, Cody locked both the head door and the main door.

"All right, Cody, what is your problem?" The captain noticed that Cody's hands were shaking.

"Captain, I am just going to cut to the chase. The music has an additional message imbedded in it in addition to the location information. I can explain the cipher to you, or I could just tell you what it says."

"Get on with it, man. What do you think it says?"

"The message says 'Maximov killer spy follow watch wait Brown Voxer."

"How sure are you?"

"They added another signal and started using the ASCII range. You could have the NAV and Weps recreate exactly what I just did by going back up to periscope depth, capture the music then have the Weps decode it like I did. I am certain of it. I believe he was the one who had the *Lavidia 2* moved."

"What is the *Lavidia 2*?"

"The yacht on the imaging and the yacht we are following."

The captain opened his combination safe and removed a Beretta 92FS 9mm service pistol. He loaded it with a fifteen-round clip. He holstered the gun and clipped it to his belt. "I am not sure if I one-hundred percent believe this, but just in case. Maximov is standing out there."

"I'm not sure if I believe it either. Voxer and Brown could be under duress and sending information designed to disrupt our operation."

The captain said, "Let's exit via the XO's stateroom. Maximov knows you were analyzing that tape. He will be suspicious."

The captain and Cody stepped quietly through the shared head of the CO and XO, passed through the XO's stateroom, cracked the door and looked aft toward the control room. The curtain was drawn between the control room and stateroom passage. The captain opened the door further, looked both ways, and stepped into the passageway. He walked with his hand on the pistol and his back facing the sonar equipment space, headed for the control room.

Ah, for a moment there Captain Davis had looked good with the gun, looked like he knew what he was doing, but when crunch time came he looked just like a submariner.

In the blink of an eye, Maximov was upon the captain. Maximov went directly for the gun and slapped the captain's hand away before tugging the weapon from his holster. Maximov looked very comfortable with the Beretta nine in his hand. Relaxed. Kind of nonchalant, he pulled the slide back and chambered a round. Slowly, slowly, Maximov held up the gun and aimed it at the captain's belly.

"Captain, sir, please step aside. I have reason to believe Cody is a spy and was affiliated with Royce's operation. Whatever he told you in there is nonsense and a cover-up."

The captain lowered his hands, but he did not step aside. "Maximov, we can put Cody in custody. No need for the firearm. If you shoot, there is no telling where the bullet will go. It could hit wires or hydraulic lines that could put the USS *Quincy* and her crew in danger. You don't want that to happen, do you?"

"I just want everyone on the *Quincy* safe." Maximov sounded sincere. He wanted to get through this crisis with his cover unblown if possible, but he was skating on a slippery ledge.

"OK, then Mark, there was no need to disarm the captain, was there? Hand me the pistol and we will put Cody under custody."

"Are you going to put him under custody like Jane Brown, who is roaming free on the submarine?"

The captain saw it now. The doubt in Maximov's eyes. It was too late. His cover was blown. This realization brought him in a flash to the icy cold edge of panic.

"Mark," the captain's voice sounded soothing now, "you know Royce was a cowardly traitor."

Maximov said, "*Zatknees, eedee na khuy.*"

"Pardon me, Lieutenant Commander Maximov. That sounded like angry Russian to me."

Cody translated, "He said, 'Shut up and fuck you,' with no sir attached, sir."

Maximov spit savagely at Cody. "You shut the fuck up! Why have you not put him in custody yet, Captain Davis? Or would you just step aside so I can kill him like you allowed my comrade to be killed?"

"You will have to kill me first," the captain said.

"I could do that, Captain, but I need you right now. I am going to take over this submarine from you."

"So, it's a mutiny."

"A change in the old order. There's a new order now, Joe."

"You doing this all by yourself?"

"Me and Comrade Kaboom. I have placed a bomb somewhere special on this submarine." Maximov pulled a small electronic remote out of his pocket. "If I push this button, the bomb goes off. See these wires hanging from the bottom? They are attached to the remainder of the remote hidden on my person where it is monitoring my heartbeat. If these wires get severed or my heart stops, this bomb goes off. So, Captain, you are going to do exactly what I ask."

Maximov put the device back in his pocket. He removed the holster from the captain's belt and clipped it onto his own belt, with the gun in back. He covered it over with his sweater. "So this little meeting is going to result in some change in operations. Cody, you need to tell me what message you relayed to the captain."

Cody said, "It continues to tell us the coordinates and time of the rendezvous point."

Maximov said, "Cody, I really don't need you for anything. You can have an accident right here and now. So how about you spill it?"

"The message said, 'Maximov killer spy.'"

Maximov became extremely agitated. "Cody, I don't have time for this. You need to tell me something I don't know or I am going to put you in a bag in the freezer next to Royce."

"It said, 'Follow watch wait.'"

"And?"

"'Brown Voxer.'"

Maximov said, "*Etoy chertovoy suko*!"

Cody asked, "Who's the fucking bitch?"

Maximov dished out the advice, "Let's keep our wits about us, gentlemen, and go about our day in an orderly manner, as if nothing has occurred. The captain and I will go back and watch the movie. Cody, you will go to bed. I will give you further instructions as I see fit, Captain."

Cody said, "It's kind of early for bed."

"Then play with yourself or read," Maximov said. "I don't want you walking around."

"I guess I'll read."

Cody stepped out of the captain's stateroom first, followed by Captain Davis. Maximov emerged into the passageway last and, just as he was about to close the door behind him, he was injected with a hypodermic needle in the neck by Admiral Bennett.

Beside the admiral stood Jane Brown with tie wraps at the ready.

The captain said, "Nice going, Admiral, sir. I hope you didn't kill him."

"I didn't kill him," the admiral said. "I was listening to the open microphone in your stateroom as you directed. Jane got the corpsman to create a special cocktail for our friend. Morphine mostly, I think, but some other stuff to knock Maximov out for awhile."

The captain emphasized, "We need to make sure that gizmo in his pocket stays attached and doesn't go off."

Cody said, "I think I should be able to disarm it."

Admiral Bennett asked, "What next?"

Captain Davis replied, "Follow watch wait."

XVIII
MONDAY, SEPTEMBER 21ST, 1992
NORTH ATLANTIC

2300. The *Lavidia 2* approached the rendezvous point with the larger India class submarine. The USS *Quincy* was in close proximity. Jay, Cassie, Vlad and Kat discussed their plan.

"So, Jay, you remember and understand everything I told you about the India class submarine?"

"Yes, Vlad," Jay replied, "I know my submarine specifications. The only place I could get fouled up is with the language, but Cassie is fluent."

"The crew of the India will be expecting to see me," Kat said with a small shiver. "So, I will be of no help to you."

"As a diversion, you will be a tremendous help, Kat," Jay said.

"I can operate the *Lavidia 2* in my sleep," Vlad boasted, although no one doubted him. "All of you just be careful. Remember the gas in the scuba bottles is not for breathing."

Kat said, "We have our roles assigned. Let's review the plan one more time from the top."

"Vlad, I am still wondering why you have a cascade of Fentanyl gas in the basement of your guitar shop."

"You never know when you are going to need it, Jay. Honestly, when the iron curtain fell, I was not sure what was happening and I stockpiled as much protection as I could. I was involved in a program to subdue terrorists in a non-deadly fashion. This gas was the result. The first time we used it in a hostage situation, it killed twenty percent of the hostages and the terrorists. This mix we have here hasn't killed anyone. Yet. In low doses it gives you a nice buzz."

Vlad's eyes twinkled, giving Jay the impression that he was not unfamiliar with the world of pleasant intoxicants.

Kat said, "That's why you always come up from the basement so happy."

Vlad replied, "That is just one of the reasons. I have my torture chamber down there, too."

"Not funny, Father."

Cassie, Jay and Kat manned the mini sub, still nested under the *Lavidia 2*. Vlad was at the yacht's helm, in radio communication with the mini sub. Cassie and Jay wore Russian submariner coveralls and ball caps supplied by Vlad.

The mini sub had two seats in the bow facing a busy board of instruments and a small round window in the middle. Kat sat in the pilot seat and buckled up, comfortable with the controls and the operation of the unit.

Jay sat in the copilot seat and said, "A window. Awesome."

Kat said, "Put your seat belt on, Jay. You really can't see much out of it, but it gives you a general idea where you are when you are trying to dock." Kat picked up the microphone. "Father, this is Kat, over."

"Kat, this is your father. I copy, over."

"Stand by for undocking. Father, put your seat belt on. Do you remember where the undock switch is?"

"I have my hand on the switch, awaiting your order."

"Roger that, counting down from five, ready, five, four, three, two, one, undock."

The mini sub dropped rapidly. Kat watched the depth gauge closely. When it read thirty meters, she said, "Blowing out main ballast for a neutral trim." Kat operated a hand switch and steadied the mini sub at thirty meters.

Cassie patted the three scuba bottles. "OK, it's almost show time."

Kat said, "They will want to load this mini sub as quickly as possible with the plutonium-filled lead casks. You two hide in the head. There will be some suspicion when they see I am alone. We usually do this with pilot and copilot. I will tell them I was ordered to go alone. If they call the *Lavidia*, my father will cover. The crew of the India will hand-load the mini sub. Once finished, I will give a look around in the mini sub and let you know when the coast is clear. You drop down into the India with the Fentanyl-filled scuba bottles and our bag of goodies. You are going to have to work fast. You will only have five-to-ten minutes."

Kat operated the mini sub with great expertise, and mounted it onto the hull of the India. The docking was seemingly effortless.

Jay achingly thought of a brilliant analogy involving docking and the feline female. "Put your mouth on my mouth," she had said. The words echoed in the back of his consciousness, tinged with something. Was it shame? Did he feel he was cheating on Cassie, his true love? Jay decided this might not be the best spot to contemplate how slutty he was. In fact, it was go time.

Once the mini sub was locked in, Cassie and Jay locked themselves in the head. They said nothing. They didn't even whisper. They kept their breathing slow and silent, standing face to face for a time. Jay felt terribly conflicted. Cassie became aware of his manly state and they could remain silent no longer.

Jay said, "How about I sit and you can sit on my lap. This could take a while."

"Why not?"

After a few minutes the bottom on the mini sub was opened into the India.

Noiselessly, grinding together, growing less self-conscious as they went, Jay sat and Cassie sat on his lap, squarely on his legs, face forward.

"Better?"

"Sure."

They heard activity outside. The mini sub was being loaded. Men spoke Russian.

"Can you turn sideways? My legs are falling asleep."

"You call me fat?"

Jay said, "Delightfully fleshy. Now, shhhhhh."

The activity in the mini sub stopped. There was silence, then someone was pulling at the locked head door.

Jay and Cassie sat quiet and still, completely unable to breathe. The door continued to be pulled.

"Come on, open the door." It was Kat. Jay unlocked the door and Kat opened it. "I thought I was interrupting you guys joining the fifty-meters down club."

Cassie stood up and walked out, "Yeah, me and my delightfully fleshy ass."

Kat looked at Cassie's ass and said, "Looks perfect to me."

Cassie replied, "Thanks. I guess that's the delightful part."

Kat got down to business. "OK, I am going to go down first. I will make a shush sound, and you will come down behind me. Jay first, then Cassie, you hand the scuba bottle filled with Fentanyl down to Jay. I will be settling up with the men on the India. We are amidships. Cassie, you can connect a scuba bottle to the emergency air-breathing manifold directly beneath this hatch. Jay you need to walk to port and then aft. You pass through the watertight door and connect the Fentanyl bottle just aft of it."

Jay asked, "What if I am seen?"

"This submarine does not operate with a full crew, and they just changed out. There are a total of about forty men, thirty in the forward compartment and ten in the engine room."

"Only men?" Cassie asked.

"Yes, only men," Kat purred. "So don't make any eye contact and keep that cute ass of yours tucked in."

Jay said, "OK, once I hook up the Fentynal, I'll drop two or three smokes. That will signal the general alarm, Cassie's cue to put on her gas mask and drop her smokes."

"I am to hold my breath and run to Cassie to get my gas mask," Kat said. "There will be zero visibility, and remember the gas masks only filter the smoke, not the Fentanyl. We will open up that third scuba bottle before we get back into the mini sub."

Cassie said, "All right, let's do this thing."

Kat dropped silently into the India. Jay and Cassie could look down the escape trunk hatch into the Russian submarine. After a moment, Kat made her "shush" sound. Jay dropped. Cassie lowered the first scuba bottle behind him.

Jay was awestruck by the vessel. He wanted to look at everything at once, and remember it all.

Cassie whispered, "Hey, pay attention."

Jay took the scuba bottle she was handing him and set it aside. The other two bottles were lowered down, then the bag of tricks. Jay donned his gas mask, put three smoke grenades in his pocket and tucked a scuba bottle under his arm. Each scuba bottle was equipped with a two-meter hose fitted to plug into an emergency air manifold. The air supplied to the manifold was forty pounds per square inch (psi), but the first stage of a scuba regulator was 150 psi. If everything worked the way Vlad described, the check valves for the air to the manifolds would be forced shut and anyone that plugged an emergency air-breathing mask into a manifold would inhale the Fentanyl and be quickly knocked out. As on a U.S. submarine, there were emergency air-breathing masks all over the India so crewmembers could breathe even if the submarine's atmosphere became contaminated.

Jay helped Cassie down. She closed the hatch quietly behind her so the gas wouldn't get in their mini sub. It was Cassie's turn to be awestruck by her surroundings.

Jay whispered, "Wish me luck."

"Godspeed, Jay Brown."

He ran toward the engine room.

Cassie stood beneath the amidships pretending to look busy in case someone walked by. She heard footsteps and bent over and started digging through the bag of tricks.

Bending over might have been a great diversion when trying to dump black blankets overboard, but it turned out to be the wrong move when trying to look like one of the guys on a Russian submarine.

The sailor asked her in Russian what she was doing. Cassie grunted and dug through the bag more aggressively.

The Russian slapped Cassie's back so hard it stung and asked, "Why haven't I noticed you before? What are you doing here?"

Cassie responded not with words but with a scuba bottle. She grabbed the hose, opened the valve, and sprayed the Fentanyl in the sailor's face. Cassie almost laughed at the rapid-fire changes in the man's facial expressions as he, first, realized she was a woman, then realized the danger, and then finally felt the blissful effects of the gas. It was: Hey there! Grrrr. Ahhhhh.

The sailor went down, dead weight. Cassie turned the gas off and flapped the gas away so she would not breath it herself. She was too late, la la la la la, and...

She.

Wondered.

Why they didn't pipe smooth jazz into submarines, that a little Miles Davis would do wonders for the stuffy atmosphere. She thought, *I can see why Vlad keeps this stuff in his basement.* Cassie was completely relaxed and calm. She started singing in her head, but it unintentionally came out.

"We all live in a yellow submarine!"

She stopped singing the words but continued to hum as she pushed the sailor against the bulkhead and rolled him so he was facing inward with a lifejacket pillow.

"Awwwww," Cassie said. He looked so peaceful.

The general alarm sounded and Cassie danced toward the scuba bottle, which she plugged into the manifold. She pulled her gas mask from the bag of tricks, and put it on.

Cassie laid out Kat's gas mask, and grabbed three smoke grenades from the bag. She pulled the pin. She decided to dish out the smoke with style, the style of a star of the ladies pro bowlers tour, and rolled the grenade with fine form and a last instant flick of the wrist, so that the grenade didn't just roll, but hooked a little to the left, like a bowling ball that hits the pocket and explodes the pins into a strike.

She took the second grenade and this time emulated a baseball pitcher. She held it on her hip and looked in to the imaginary catcher for the sign.

"Fastball, heh?" she said.

She wound up, gave a surprisingly high leg kick, and delivered the grenade with some mustard on it down another passageway.

For the third and last grenade, Cassie pretended it was a pineapple from WWII. She brought it up to her mouth and pulled the pin with her teeth.

"Down the hatch," she said, and dropped the grenade into a lower level.

Just as the last smoke grenade went off, Kat ran in from the forward compartment and grabbed her gas mask. Jay was right behind her.

Kat said, "Cassie, open the hatch."

Cassie looked at Kat and hugged her. Cassie said, "Kat, that was so nice what you said about my ass."

Kat said, "Oh boy, Cassie is stoned. Jay, open the hatch. We have to get out of here."

Jay allowed himself a fraction of a second to enjoy the comedy of the situation. Cassie looked great when she was relaxed. Her lower lip looked fleshier and even drooped a bit into a sensuous pout.

Jay opened the hatch and climbed up into the mini sub. Kat helped Cassie up then tossed up the bag of tricks. Kat opened the final scuba bottle and rolled it away. She climbed gracefully up into the mini sub and closed the hatches on the submarine and mini sub behind her.

Cassie was on the deck of the mini sub hugging one of the plutonium-filled lead casks with her gas mask still on.

"Does anyone want to play ball with me?" She tried lifting a fifty-pound ball.

Jay saw what he had to do, and removed Cassie's gas mask. He lifted her into one of the passenger seats and strapped her in.

Kat took the pilot seat. "Get your seat belts on. We are sinking and sinking fast."

Jay jumped into the co-pilot seat. "What's going on?"

"The engineers scrammed the reactor plant, so the India has no propulsion. With the added weight of us, they are extremely negative, particularly at this depth. I expected an emergency blow, but the crew must have been gassed before they hit the chicken switches."

"We are at 200 meters and sinking," Jay said. "We have no choice but to undock and see what happens."

Kat said, "I don't want to be responsible for killing all the men on that submarine. Maybe I can deballast while docked."

"I don't think that will work. Undock, trust me, I have an idea."

"Those are Russian souls. I know they have no meaning to you…"

"Please, just trust me."

Kat replied, "Undocking." She flipped a few switches and the mini sub surged free of the sinking India.

Cassie sang, "And the baaaand begins to play: ba ba barump barump barump."

Kat said, "Pumping out to go shallow."

"Don't do it so deep. Get the mini sub under the amidships of the India, then get this thing as light as you can make it."

"You are a genius, Jay. If we can push the India up past the thermal layer it should just pop up."

Kat skillfully navigated under the now slowly sinking India. They could feel the bump of their sail against the India's heavy keel.

Kat positioned them close to the India's center of buoyancy and began deballasting water as fast as possible. Depth: 300 meters.

"What's the max depth for this thing?" Jay asked.

"Five-hundred-plus meters."

"That's great. At least we have some time."

"That's our max depth. The India's is 300 meters."

"Time to drop some steel."

The mini sub's equivalent of an emergency blow was deballasting emergency steel pellets in the fore and after tanks. Once the steel was dropped, the mini sub rose to the surface and could not submerge again until the steel was replaced in dry dock.

"Dumping steel ballast," Kat said. "No turning back now."

The mini sub pushed harder against the India's hull, which made loud creaking and grinding sounds. Kat tried to adjust propulsion to stay tucked under the larger sub, but the mini sub was nonetheless slipping out.

0100. Tuesday, the 22nd of September, USS *Quincy* operating at periscope depth within 500 yards of the *Lavidia 2* and 1,000 yards away from the India. The captain manned the number-one periscope. Admiral Bennett took number two. The Weps was in sonar, and acting XO Joe Silio was officer of the deck. Cody was in radio, monitoring 28003 KHZ. Playing at a low volume was "Along the River."

Cody was feeling good about himself. He had been able to remove the remote control from Maximov. The hardest part was disconnecting the gizmo that was clipped to his left testicle. The booby trap turned out not to be a bomb on the *Quincy*, but was actually connected to the fire control panel, which would have allowed him to shoot a torpedo with the push of his button, presumably to shoot the *Lavidia 2* out of the water. Maximov would have thus destroyed all the evidence against him.

Under interrogation, Maximov explained nervously that he was forced to become a traitor by his evil wife, Kat, and her even more evil father, Vlad. He said the torpedo was aimed at the India, not the *Lavidia 2*. Captain Davis could tell he was lying. One good thing about having Maximov in custody, Captain Davis thought, was that he'd stopped calling him Joe.

"Sonar, conn, we are hearing mechanical screeching and cracking sounds from the bearing of sierra 23."

The captain asked, "Sonar, can you provide a depth estimate for sierra 23?"

"Sonar, conn, approximately 1,000 feet."

Admiral Bennett interjected, "That's beyond test depth for an India."

Captain Davis said, "But less than crush depth."

"Conn, sonar, mechanical sounds are getting louder."

There was silence in the control room except for the soft sound of the music from radio 28003. Every submariner onboard knew the risks. There was always the chance you'd submerge one more time than you surfaced. It was gut-wrenching to think of the India, on the verge of going down but never coming up.

The music stopped and was replaced by a man's voice. It spoke English with a Russian accent. "If anyone is listening, this is *Lavidia 2*. There is a submarine in distress very near my location. It has my daughter on it and two U.S. Navy officers. My coordinates are…" The voice read his precise latitude and longitude, then repeated it.

Captain Davis asked, "What do we do, Admiral?"

"There is no way for us to help them. But it is our responsibility to tell the Russian officials what we have just heard. I will go into radio and establish a secure voice communication with my counterpart in Russia. XO, take the scope from me."

The acting XO took the scope and said, "Holy cow, I see the India popping out of the water. It looks like it might be broken in two."

Captain Davis took the scope back and said, "It is not broken in two. That is two submarines: an India and a mini sub. Diving Officer, emergency surface."

The diving officer sounded the claxton three times then announced on the 1MC microphone: "Emergency surface."

Silio asked, "Captain, what are we doing?"

"Sorry, XO. This is the captain. I have the deck and the conn. We are going to surface and drive over to that submarine in distress and tie the USS *Quincy* to it so it does not sink to its death. XO, get ready to man the sail. Diving Officer, find every line on this submarine and have it ready to be brought topside."

The *Quincy* pulled alongside the India and tied it off on the starboard side. Men with axes stood topside to cut the lines away in the event the India got so negatively buoyant that it threatened to take the *Quincy* down. All sailors topside were armed with M16s, shotguns or pistols. The admiral and captain wore pistols on their belts.

The mini sub and the *Lavidia 2* tied off on the *Quincy* on the port side.

"We have our own flotilla," the captain said.

Vlad called out from the *Lavidia 2*, "Request to come aboard, sirs."

Captain Davis said, "Come aboard, but you will have to be frisked first."

With a twinkle in his eye, Vlad replied, "I love getting frisked."

By the time Vlad passed security, the captain and admiral remembered him as the highly decorated Russian submariner they'd met at the reception.

Vlad said, "I can give you both a history lesson as to why my daughter and I are involved in this, but first I have to tell you: If your Scottish rider is not detained, detain him now. He is very dangerous."

"Vlad, we got your message. He has been detained ever since."

"I love a smart American," Vlad said. "You know about the booby trap?"

"Yes, defused," the captain said. "We're good. Now tell me why I have an India class submarine tied up alongside of me."

"Ahh, finally something you don't know. The India has been gassed with Fentanyl. Not deadly. This is a better mix. The reactor is shut down, but the crew succumbed to the gas before they could conduct an emergency blow."

"How did this thing surface?" the captain asked.

Kat poked her head out of the mini sub and yelled out. "We pushed it up. Look at the top of the sail." She'd had trouble opening the hatch because of the damage.

Kat, Jay and Cassie climbed aboard the *Quincy*. Cassie was still shaky.

"Is Lieutenant Commander Voxer wounded?" Captain Davis asked.

"No, sir. She was in the middle of a heroic assault when she caught a whiff of Russian happy gas," Jay said. "And despite her state of intoxication she continued to do her part to make the operation successful. A few deep breaths of this salt air should do her wonders."

Vlad said, "You pushed it up?"

Kat replied, "Yes, Father, we did. It was Jay's idea."

Jay smiled.

Cassie pointed to Vlad, squinted one eye for better focus, and said, "You have the best gas, man."

Vlad laughed from his belly. "What can I say? It is a gift."

Captain Davis asked, "How long do you think the India crew will be incapacitated?"

"About four hours," Vlad said.

Captain Davis said to Vlad, "Perfect. Just enough time for your comrades to arrive and clean this mess up. Admiral Bennett has already called the Russian officials. I assume there is contraband."

"Yes, Captain," Jay said. "Radioactive material on its way to Iraq."

EPILOGUE
A PROPER NAVAL *DENOUEMENT*

Immediately following the Saint Petersburg intrigue, the navy bought Jane Brown a cruise back to the United States. Admiral Bennett decided it was the least they could do. After her heroics she deserved to return home in style, and planes were not her thing.

On the pier, just before Jane shoved off aboard the luxury liner, she said good-bye to her son, and turned to grab Cassie Voxer gently with one hand on both sides of her face.

"Brave and talented woman," Jane said.

"I could say the same thing about you, lady."

"You remember that you have one more mission to complete?"

"Oh yeah. This one is going to take all of my skills, but I believe I am up to the task."

After the ship sailed, *bon voyage,* Jay wanted to know what that last conversation with his mom was all about.

Cassie said, "Women stuff, you wouldn't get it."

But Jay did get it. And he knew there was something he had to do.

"Jay?"

"Yes, Katarina."

"It was a joy having an adventure with you. I am sorry that we cannot share our hearts."

Jay was silent.

"I am changed. I am not the girl who played for you on that cold winter night. I can still play, of course, and play well, but never again like that, never again like when I still believed in magic."

"Kat, you are the same, you just..."

"No."

"You've had a tough..."

"Hush," she said. "I am a mother and soon, when my son and I are reunited, my days of adventure will be over. But you, Jay, you I feel are different. Your days of adventure are only beginning."

She kissed him on both cheeks. Her lips were so hot Jay expected to hear his skin sizzle.

At the Pentagon, Admiral Conner picked up the phone and called Jane Brown.

"Jane, an official written report is coming out next week, but I want you to be the first to know: Evidence uncovered by naval intelligence conclusively shows that Admiral Brown did not commit suicide, and was not a traitor. He was, in fact, a hero that had gotten too close to uncovering the smuggling operation and was murdered."

"Thank you, Admiral." It wasn't anything she hadn't already felt in her heart all along, but she was pleased nonetheless that the navy was putting its stamp of approval on her late husband's heroics.

Cody returned to Washington, where he was named head cryptographer in the Pentagon. He tackled every code that U.S. intelligence encountered. What a card player he would have been, but instead he used his skills to help keep America free. Cody had an apartment in the Pentagon and rarely left the building. It was great.

The papers had all been filed, and now it was just a waiting game until Cassie Voxer was once again Cassie Jones.

One night while Cassie and Jay enjoyed some well-deserved liberty, she whispered, "So, Jay?"

"Yes, Cassie?"

"You and that Kat woman…?"

"Hmmmmmm."

"You two do it?"

"Nope." He could have confessed to making out in the back of the cab, by why ruin the moment?

"You love her?"

"How could I? I am a one-woman man, and Cassie, you are seriously one woman!"

Cassie pressed herself into him like a heavenly cloud. As her lips found his, Jay thought he heard her humming, "*We all live in a yellow submarine.*"

Mission accomplished.

Jane Brown received two "Hero of the Soviet Union" medals, one on her husband's behalf, and one to her directly.

Katarina got her son back and once again lived with her father above the music shop. Both were exonerated of any wrongdoing. (You haven't seen happy until you've seen Vlad with his grandson.)

Mark Maximov was imprisoned as a spy in a NATO facility, precise location unknown.

Distinguished service medals were given to Captain Davis, Lieutenant Commander Brown, Lieutenant Commander Voxer and Lieutenant Cody. The medals, however, were presented with no citations because of the mission's classified nature.

The extent of the nuclear material smuggled into Iraq was uncertain.

In suburban Washington D.C., in the garage of his mother-in-law's house, Michael O'Brien (Janet's husband) crawled all over Admiral Brown's desk with a flashlight. The rest of the admiral's office stuff has been moved, but the desk remained, heavy and (without a team of marines handy) difficult to budge.

"If Jay is just screwing with me, I'll kill him," he muttered.

Jay told him that the admiral always carved his initials in his furniture, but never in an easy to find spot. Michael had a little time on his hands—it was halftime of the Redskins game, and Jane and Janet were gabbing—so he went initials-hunting.

He was up underneath the desk when he noticed that one of the visible bolts was different from the others. It looked wooden and protruded further than the others. Michael pressed a bold forefinger against that "bolt" and, pop! A little compartment sprung open.

On the side of the compartment was carved "JRB". Inside was an envelope. Where the return address should go, there was a rubber stamp of a submarine.

Written below was: "*If found, please deliver immediately to The President of the United States.*"